The
Thirteenth
Summer

The Thirteenth Summer

A Novel

José Luis Olaizola

Translated from the Spanish
by Susan Ouriou

Red Deer College Press

THE PUBLISHERS
Red Deer College Press
56 Avenue & 32 Street Box 5005
Red Deer Alberta Canada T4N 5H5

CREDITS
Cover Art and Design by Ron Lightburn
Text Design by Dennis Johnson
Printed & Bound in Canada by Best Gagné Printing Ltée for
Red Deer College Press

ACKNOWLEDGEMENTS
Financial support provided by the Alberta Foundation for the Arts, a beneficiary of the Lottery Fund of the Government of Alberta, and by the Canada Council, the Department of Communications and Red Deer College.

CANADIAN CATALOGUING IN PUBLICATION DATA
Olaizola, José Luis.
The thirteenth summer
Translation of: Planicio
ISBN 0-88995-094-6
I. Title
PQ6665.L24P5513   1993   863'.64   C93-091488-0

The translation of this edition was made possible through assistance from the Books and Libraries Branch of the Spanish Ministry of Culture.

AUTHOR'S ACKNOWLEDGEMENTS
The author wishes to express his indebtedness to the work of Fernando Vizcaíno Casas on post-war Spain for helping to bring back to him the period in which his novel is set and remind him of facts and situations lost in the recesses of his mind.

TRANSLATOR'S ACKNOWLEDGEMENTS
The translator would like to express her indebtedness to Imanol Martínez Padrón for his valuable assistance with the nuances of the Spanish language and culture.

To my dear friend
JUAN GUTIÉRREZ PALACIOS
with all my affection and gratitude

Contents

Life Without *Amá* · 15

Life With *Aita* · 145

The
Thirteenth
Summer

Part One

Life Without *Amá*

"PLANICIO!" the Galician's voice rang out in a deep bass. He waited a minute, then called out two more times.

He always used a lower register to call for his son ever since he'd discovered that sound carried farther that way than at a higher pitch. Besides, it didn't really do for the shoemaker from the garret room to be seen yelling for his son who was out playing pelota on the cobblestones of Paseo de Iztueta in back of their building at 10-B Calle de Miracruz, San Sebastian. The street was one of distinction, as was the building itself, but the degree of each resident's distinction was directly proportional to the floor on which he or she lived. The second floor was taken up by a corset shop, the sign on its door advertising the benefits of custom-made corsets for female clients looking to enhance their natural beauty.

Whenever they took the stairs and passed in front of the sign, the Galician complained to his son, "Such deceit, Planicio!"

Planicio wasn't sure he understood what his father meant even when the latter went on to explain.

"Such deceitful creatures, women! You'll learn soon enough."

Although he was a Galician, he spoke Spanish with a Basque accent, his parents having moved away from Galicia in 1909 when he was four years old. However, people still called him the Galician in 1942 because he had spent almost his whole life in the Trincherpe district—the Galician district—of Puerto de Pasajes.

He was not the least bit bothered by being singled out from the others. Even as a boy playing games with his friends, if someone called out the usual "Last one in is a Galician!" it didn't bother him. Since he was never in any danger of coming in last, he would cry out in the middle of the race, "Last one in is a fairy!" and the boys from Pasajes could say nothing as this too was an accepted version.

The Galician got away with a lot because he was such a superb pelota player, a fact that people thereabouts couldn't overlook. He was, for instance, a skeptic and a cynic. When the sons of Trincherpe's Galician fishermen got into stone-throwing fights with the Basques from Pasajes de San Pedro, he saw no reason to join in. Should his fellow playmates confront him afterward, he'd say, "Why fight? Aren't we all God's children?"

And yet, when they played pelota for money, if someone challenged a point he'd made, suddenly he'd forget his divine filiation and fight his challenger tooth and nail no matter what part of the country he came from.

In 1930 Pasajes de San Pedro decided to enter a boat in the September regatta, the Concha regatta, for which they had to enlist the Galician's services, seeing that he measured 5'11", weighed 195 lbs and was so strong he could break an oar in two trying to avoid the sandbar. He agreed to be on the crew because of the one-month training period, which meant he wouldn't have to go out with the other fishermen but would still be paid his wages by the shipowner. In those days, special exercises hadn't been invented for rowers yet; all they had to do was row two hours every afternoon, regardless of the conditions at sea, and eat a healthy diet. In practice this meant a daily ration of one kilo's worth of steak, which they washed down easily with some *chacolí* wine. They also had to forgo female companionship in order to conserve all their energy for the day of the regatta.

The Galician's name was Francisco Lourido, and the coxswain of the rowing team gave him the nickname Pachi. The regatta was held on the first Sunday in September. The sea outside the cape was wild, but the fishermen from Pasajes de San Pedro placed well. They made it to the finish line despite the fact that their vessel was half full of water. They placed well but not well enough to win, which is what Pachi the Galician had thought would happen so he had bet all his money on Orio's yellow team, coxswained by none other than Sarasúa himself.

"Loyalty's all well and good, but a peseta's a peseta," Pachi said.

Times were different then. There were fishermen from Pasajes who had sold the very beds they slept in so they could bet on the home team. The Galician's philosophy did not go over well at all. One night in the tavern, he was beaten up, and he, being a practical and far from vindictive man, gathered together his wife and little boy, Planicio, two years old at the time, and moved to Fuenterrabía.

After the civil war, he left the sea, which was bad for his lumbago, and set up shop as a shoemaker in the garret room at 10-B Calle de Miracruz in San Sebastian. Many things were bad for his lumbago. Others weren't. For instance, the Atocha public pelota court—the fronton—was located back of their building. Every afternoon the Galician strolled over to see what there was to see, it being a well-known fact that a shoemaker's work was singularly lacking in appeal. On the other hand, playing a game of hand pelota was very good for his lumbago, provided of course that a tidy sum of money was at stake. Playing out of love for the game was something the Basques did. The Basques, according to the explanation he was given by the court assistant—a learned man—were a pure European race, direct descendants of Cro-Magnon man. Since he was not a Basque, he played only to win, being a widower with a thirteen-year-old son to support and the countess to contend with.

The countess owned the Miracruz building and would have been only too happy to throw him out into the street because of his carryings on. On the whole, the neighbors were only slightly bothered by Francisco the shoemaker's habit of hollering for his son from the garret room, but Francisca the concierge dreaded it because afterward the countess would say, "Please, Francisca, tell that man not to yell so."

"I've already told him, countess, but . . . "

"I understand, I understand, but do insist because otherwise I will have to . . . "

It was a well-known fact that the only reason the countess didn't evict him was her respect for his dearly departed wife who, before she married Pachi, had been the countess's maid and a good one too.

"That she was a maiden, I can vouch for," the Galician used to say. "Whether or not she was a good maid is another matter." But he only made this type of remark when he had had a bit too much to drink, usually after winning a bet.

The countess lived on the third floor where the marble staircase ended. Whenever Pachi and his son took the stairs and passed in front of her door, the father, as a mark of respect, doffed his beret. They often did pass in front of her door because in 1941 frequent blackouts left them no choice but to take the stairs. Sometimes, even if the electricity was on, Francisca the concierge wouldn't let them use the elevator because she was expecting the countess any minute, and the very thought that the countess might come home and find the elevator occupied filled her with terror—one more reason why the neighbors shouldn't resent his calling for his son from the garret room when one considered how difficult it was, for practical and protocolary reasons, to use the elevator.

The fourth floor was unoccupied, and a nondescript middle-class family lived on the fifth floor; from the third floor up, the windows along the staircase got narrower, and the stairs were made out of a mixture of gravel and cement. The sixth floor was the attic, set far back from the other floors and with an extremely narrow stairway. It was occupied by a seamstress and her two lodgers. She was slightly overweight but still young enough for Pachi. Physically nothing could be said against her, and she couldn't have been more conveniently located. But she more than all the others attached the most importance to living in an attic that could still be reached by the elevator, no matter how recessed it was, as opposed to a garret room, which had no social status whatsoever.

All signs of civilization ended at the seamstress's attic. From there rose a small winding staircase that one had to crawl up in order to reach the flat roof where the chimneys stood, along with a series of abandoned back rooms, one of which had been converted into the Galician's home. Their home, if one could call it that, offered no real shelter from the cold or from the heat. On windy days, the tar used to weatherproof the roof melted. On rainy days, water seeped in from the projecting side roof, but the furniture was strategically placed so as not to get wet. The Galician simply accepted all the inconveniences as facts of life, and in this regard the countess couldn't complain about her tenant who never asked for repairs or improvements to be made.

On warm starlit summer nights, Planicio and his father had the whole roof to themselves. It was a quiet time, no noisy traffic, just the rattle of the tramways along Calle de Miracruz, a noise that had a pleasant, very distant ring to it. On particularly calm nights, they could even hear the whistling of trains at the North Station on Paseo de Francia.

Planicio lay down on the ground, looking up at the sky, and his father sat in a rickety old chair that used to belong to the count.

The Galician smoked a cigarette and said, "To hell with them all."

He was referring to the neighbors in general, not because he felt any anger but simply because he felt so well-off or at least because he assumed he was better off than all the others, even with their elevator. It was a time for family intimacy, a time he used to give advice to his son, recently turned thirteen.

"Don't ever let your pride get the better of you, Planicio. Always look to your future. Anchón came to me one day and said, 'Pachi, that fellow from Logroño over there wants to play a game with someone from his draft group. How old are you?' I didn't even answer. Then he said, 'You're not afraid of someone from Logroño, are you?'"

His father kept silent, pensive, and then asked Planicio, "What do you think?"

His son didn't answer. He knew he wasn't there to voice his opinion but to learn. And especially to be with his father, who hadn't slept at home for the last few nights. Even though his father told him that was normal, Planicio was very unhappy whenever it happened.

Pachi kept dispensing this kind of advice to his son but without great conviction because he had noticed something peculiar about the boy ever since he was little, something that was only confirmed by the famous race between the bridges. As a father, he wanted his son to learn certain lessons that life had taught him too late. Lessons like:

– nobody ever got rich working;

– playing pelota for money was not a pastime but a life's work, and therefore, whether a challenger was from Logroño or Usurbil was irrelevant. What counted was what his hands looked like: broad, slightly concave hands with deformed fingers were the sign of a genuine player. Why agree to play a game for money if you'd never seen the challenger in action before? Elementary knowledge even for beginners;

– there will always be rich and poor—Jesus Christ himself

said so—and therefore if you're part of the second group, make sure you get on the good side of the first group. For example, whenever Pachi reached the third-floor landing, the countess's landing, he took his beret off as a sign of respect even if Francisca the concierge said he was doing it to mock her. In any case, any mockery he kept to himself; from the outside, God himself would see his gesture as a tribute to the countess;

— once over the age of thirty, you must never ever agree to play a singles game of hand pelota because, sure as can be, your breath won't hold out. Always play in pairs, if possible as the back player so the forward has to do all the running and serving too, because if you don't cradle the ball just right, you can maim your hand;

— above all, never get roped into something that's none of your concern, like in '36 when they got all fired up in Trincherpe, saying that the time had come to bring an end to the system of rich versus poor, and when the soldiers joined up with the Fishermen's Brotherhood and the workers' union, the UGT. He, Pachi the Galician, had only worked as a coastline fisherman, but he wasted no time signing up on a codfish boat leaving for Newfoundland since it seemed likely they wouldn't touch his wife or child, but they might very well make him join up with one side or the other. He left Puerto de Pasajes on a boat flying the Republican flag and came back under the red and gold flag. It was really nothing but a question of colors; any way you looked at it, he'd have ended up working under one or the other, working as little as possible of course because, to be perfectly honest, he didn't like work. The priest himself said that work was a curse placed on man by God;

— and where priests were concerned, you had to listen but not necessarily all the time because sometimes they got carried away. Christ spoke of being good but not stupid. Privation would always be a fact of life, but as much as possible you had to avoid privation in matters of the stomach. You could live in an attic room, freezing in winter, stifling in summer, with no better furniture than the late count's rickety chair, and these would be reasonable privations, but you always had to watch what went into your stomach. During the year he spent off of Newfoundland, he managed to get out of working on the nets as much as possible and ended up being the cook, showing the whole crew that fish-based stews did not have to be boring as long as they were made with a bit of finesse and a sprinkling of paprika à la Galician;

– and of course it went without saying that a shoemaker's life was completely devoid of interest. He himself had only agreed to become one to please his wife, Bea, and then she had only had one short year to enjoy her status as a tradesman's wife and benefit, in spite of the floors separating the two, from the aura surrounding the countess for whom she had worked while still a maiden until, as Pachi himself explained, he arrived on the scene.

The countess was extremely sad to see her go because she'd never been so well looked after as in the seven years Beatriz attended to her needs. She consented to the marriage because Pachi was good at putting on a show of being courteous, respectful and very much in love. He succeeded so well that the countess even wondered whether she shouldn't hire the two of them but decided against it because of the children she was sure they would have, being so young and in love. As well, it was highly unlikely that Jacinto, who had been the count's valet de chambre when the count was still a bachelor, would agree to having another man around the house.

Jacinto was an effeminate man, a quiet and exceptionally tidy man who knew exactly how to run a household and who gave manicures to the countess's three daughters. Before the war, he used to drive the count and countess to Biarritz every day in their Hispano-Swiss car with its yellow body, black roof and radial tires. At that time, Calle de Miracruz was a two-way street, and the car drove down the middle of the road because

of the tramway lines on either side. It was the most beautiful
vehicle on the street, and sometimes curious bystanders would
crowd around to get a better look at it. At night they kept it in
a garage on Calle Tomás Gros, but Jacinto didn't trust the people there to keep it clean, and always before the count and
countess embarked, he dusted its surface with a real ostrich
feather duster. He had a certain way about him while wagging
the duster, which passersby remarked on and joked about, but
Jacinto didn't mind because he was from Andalucía and always
had a witty comeback. Besides which, his inclination was not
something unheard of. Look at Socrates, who took the hem-
lock like a man and yet was of the same bent. People in the
neighborhood sometimes called him Socrates.

"Socrates, you've forgotten a speck of dust on the mudguards."

"Thank you, my dear," he replied. "You know if I transferred this spot to your nose, you'd look simply adorable."

If it weren't for his attachment to the count's household, he
would have set up shop as a lady's hairdresser, but he would
have used the French word *coiffeur*. The French *coiffeurs* of
Biarritz and St. Jean de Lux (he never called it San Juan de
Luz) who'd done away with the white button-down smocks the
others wore, which were so like public nurses' gowns, and
replaced them with multicolored models sporting mandarin
collars, short wide sleeves and even a yoke at the shoulder
blades (Why should only women be able to wear yoked blous-
es?) seemed to him to have added another dimension to their
lives quite different from those of their Spanish counterparts,
who stuck to giving permanents by mechanical means.

In any case, life in the count's household presented its own
advantages—especially since the count's death—in that Jacinto's status as a man, in spite of a few hormonal inconsisten-
cies, meant that the administration of the household fell to
him and that he could steal money from under their noses, not
out of greed but simply because old age couldn't have many

pleasant surprises in store for a man such as himself, and it was easier to suffer on a full stomach.

Jacinto was a naturally intelligent man who could appreciate the Galician's talents, but at the same time, he dreaded the Galician's sudden mood changes, which sometimes made him say terrible things to Jacinto in public.

To his son, the Galician said, "Stay away from that one."

This truly hurt Jacinto, who would never take advantage of a young boy and especially not this boy whose mother had been Beatriz, the countess's maid for seven years and such a beautiful woman.

"Listen," said Pachi, "I'm not against your robbing the countess because as long as you go about it the right way, I see nothing wrong with it. In your position, I'd do the same. But don't you go near my son."

Jacinto said nothing. What could he say? He held no grudges and kept turning up at the pelota games the Galician played every afternoon on the Atocha public fronton. He showed extreme caution when placing his bets, preferring a small but sure win. His only weakness occurred when the Galician was playing.

"Pachi, mind that I'm putting my money on you. Don't let me down."

Francisco made no reply. Before a game he thought of nothing other than choosing the best ball from the assistant's box—one with a lot of bounce because the soft balls that were slow on the rebound meant you had to keep bending over (those were the times he felt that perhaps it was true he suffered from lumbago)—and somehow gaining an advantage over his opponents. On the Atocha fronton in those days, the games played were of an extremely high caliber, and in the summer when the days were long, one game followed another until darkness fell and the players couldn't see the ball anymore. Some players had been professionals, others hoped to become professionals and still others were simply town boys who, ever since they were old enough to think for themselves, had walked around with a ball in their hands. These weren't standard games but strange variations on the usual game to make the betting more interesting. Or more impassioned.

"I'll play you left-handed and serve from third."

The challenged, and offended, player—there being no justification for the put-down—retorted, "Twenty duros."

Twenty duros were easily a week's wages, and so some bartering had to occur.

"In that case I'll serve right-handed," specified the challenger.

"You said left."

"I said I'd play left-handed but not that I'd have to serve left-handed too."

There was a minute's silence. Pachi the expert—thirty-six years old—looked first at one, then the other, weighing the odds before placing his bet.

"You can do it man; go on," the crowd egged the challenged player on.

These scenes disturbed Planicio. Silence measured in duros.

All right. He'd serve with his right hand, but in that case, the serve had to be made from square number four and the bet would be for only fifteen duros. The other player agreed, giving a small smirk of superiority designed to enrage his opponent, which it sometimes did.

"Okay. Tomorrow at seven."

If the players were young, they asked the Galician for advice.

"Play over the whole court, and use a ball with a good bounce to it," he'd tell one of them. And to the other, "Play close to the left wall, and use a soft ball."

Jacinto went up to Pachi to ask whom he should place his bet on. Jacinto always wore, even on Sundays, the green vest with yellow stripes that character actors wore in theater productions when they played a servant's role. All the fronton crowd knew he was the countess's servant, but at Atocha it looked more like he was Pachi's valet.

"Have you seen Pachi, the old devil? He's even got his own valet along."

Jacinto was on the fat side, bald and middle-aged—fifty-ish—and his reply was, "Don Francisco is good enough to have a valet and more." And he clapped the Galician on the back.

"Hands off, pretty boy," the Galician said. "We don't want them getting the wrong idea."

Pachi looked younger than his years, and although he was a Galician, his build and speech were Basque. He always wore a dress shirt—tieless—with the sleeves rolled halfway up his fore-arms. His arms were equally thick, which meant that it was just as easy for him to hit the ball with his right or his left hand. He had broad shoulders and a sturdy gait. In spite of his liking for cider, he didn't have too much of a paunch because he evacuated his fluids well. He too was balding, but it was hard to see because he only took off his beret when passing in front of the countess's door. In his view, the head was a very delicate organ that needed protection from almost everything, especially the sun. When he played pelota, he pulled his beret down so that it couldn't fall off when he ran, and only if it was very hot out, in the break between one point and another, did he lift his cap a bit, holding on to the middle with two fingers, to let some air on his scalp.

Since he wasn't Basque, although he'd been living there since 1909, he didn't get too involved. If he won he didn't start bragging the way the Basques did, and if he lost he pre-tended it didn't matter, saying the strangest things to the win-ner.

"You're too good a player for me. It's criminal. You've got a left-hand swing that God himself would kill for."

Generally they fell for it. In other games, the losers could spend hours explaining why they lost and why they shouldn't have lost: because the forward had returned a ball without letting it bounce when he should have and then screwed up the return; because the ball had been in bounds, although everyone else swore by the Virgin Mary that it wasn't so; because he'd twisted his ankle on the third point and so was useless afterward; because the game should have been stopped when it started raining. . . . Later on in the tavern, they continued trying to find excuses for their loss. All of which explains why, generally speaking, they fell for the Galician's line when he told them they were much better players than he was. Besides, Pachi was already getting old and was crazy about pelota.

"Anyway I'd like to play you again."

"Just say when."

"But you'll give me a bit of an advantage won't you?"

That's when the bargaining started. A three-point lead to start off with? Or only left-handed serves? (Pachi's left hand was almost stronger than his right.) Or from such and such a square, etcetera.

It wasn't an easy way to earn one's living, but what choice did he have? A shoemaker's life was not for him. The trade had never been anything but a source of annoyance to him, and he'd only agreed to it to please his wife; and after all that, the poor woman hardly got to enjoy it since she died only a year after they moved to Miracruz. He'd agreed to become a shoemaker not because he knew anything about the trade or because he already had some experience in the field but simply because he was good with the awl he used to repair the leather pelota balls. As well, while he was at sea, he'd been very handy at patching and repairing the fishing nets. He'd also taken into consideration that it was a trade one practiced sitting down, which never killed anyone. Even while Bea was still alive, the neighbors had begun to complain that his work left a lot to be desired because his stitching was too visible.

"What's wrong with that?" exclaimed Pachi the shoemaker.

A lot actually, and so Bea, desperately wanting to stay where they were and keep spending every afternoon chatting with

Francisca and the other concierges from 10-A and C Miracruz while receiving frequent invitations to the sanctum sanctorum on the third floor, urged her husband, "Make your stitches smaller, please."

It was impossible to make them any smaller; his eyes weren't that good (he was no longer a spring chicken), and furthermore (something he never thought to see happen) spending so much time seated was a killer for his lumbago. It was even worse than pulling on the fishing nets. At least the Atocha fronton was just back of the house, and he could be there in five minutes.

"Don't take the boy with you!" Bea yelled.

He always obeyed his wife in this respect and never took Planicio with him, but it was never long before Planicio appeared—at his half-trot soon to make him famous during the race between the bridges—his toes turned out, and started playing with the other children his age in the back corner of the fronton. When the games started in earnest, the children were shooed away. They went off and played their own game against the Urbistondos factory wall in the same street. Their games were a science unto themselves for several reasons.

To begin with, the boys had to be ready to run off at a moment's notice because of conflicting views about whether they should be playing pelota against the factory wall. It was mostly the factory supervisor who said they dirtied the wall, a surprising complaint considering that the last time the wall had been plastered must have been before World War I, and in fact one of the attractions or challenges of playing on the Urbistondos fronton was precisely that one never knew exactly where the ball would bounce once it struck the wall's eroded surface. The police were against the practice as well because of the sign expressly prohibiting pelota games and passing water, not only in that spot but all along Atocha.

When the policeman came upon them by surprise, he confiscated the homemade ball, consisting of tightly wound rags covered with sheepskin, and solemnly walked over to the closest sewer hole to throw it in. From there, through the water conduit, in amongst all the city's waste, the ball began its journey to the Urumea River and the sea.

"It floats," someone said. "That kind of ball floats in the sea because the sheepskin fills with air and it floats."

"Until the rags get wet," said someone else, "and then it sinks to the bottom."

No one spoke as they thought about what would happen to the ball, and they barely heard the policeman's threats. "I warn you, next time . . ."

But there wouldn't be a next time because they decided to post lookouts so as not to be taken unawares. A pelota ball was something of great value, requiring many hours of work and much experimentation to ensure that the rags stayed tightly wound after so many wettings and dryings in the sun. Someone discovered that saliva worked best, and so they all dedicated themselves to chewing cloth until it turned into a pulp that they then pressed firmly together. Sometimes, due to all the experimentation, the ball ended up in a sort of concave shape, but it didn't matter because its shape affected the rebound and thus added a new dimension to their games.

Secondly, playing at Urbistondos required special skill at hitting the ball because, as well as the effect erosion had on the game, the upper middle part of the factory wall housed a small window with bars in it. The window had a grating but no windowpane and led to unknown parts. In any case, if the ball flew through its bars, the effect was the same as when it glided down the water conduit to the Urumea River. The ball was lost to them. And yet, although it was risky, a ball that hit a bar and fell to the ground, even if it didn't bounce, was judged to be in bounds.

Thirdly, the ground they played on was a paved driveway, or had been at one time, but no longer since the driveway ended in the wall. There were a lot of uneven patches, but once again these didn't matter because the soft ball—which it was no matter how much they chewed the rags in advance—bounced well on the rough patches. What did pose a problem was the gravel base on the left side that stopped the ball dead. In spite of this the boys could tell when the ball was headed that way and brushed the gravel away with their left hand to ensure the ball kept bouncing.

The children's games were so exciting, strange and lightning quick that sometimes they even drew some of the spectators away from the real fronton to see how they were managing at Urbistondos. However, the Galician did not approve.

"You're just learning a lot of bad habits. You'll end up like church players."

Pachi was referring to the players in the small Basque towns who learned to play in church porticoes where the game depended on one's skill at finding the edges and angles that would make the ball rebound wildly. Such players attained a certain amount of local fame, but then, when the hour of truth was upon them, when they had to play for money on a fronton such as God had meant them to play on, where what counted was the force with which one struck the ball to get the rebound or to make it bounce off two walls, they made fools of themselves.

The Galician never taught his son how to play because the game—it was never called a sport—wasn't a game one could learn. Instead, one had to watch and practice. During difficult matches, Planicio was his assistant. When his hand began to swell halfway through a match, he'd yell, "Planicio!"

The boy arrived at his half-trot, already knowing what was expected of him.

"Step on it," his father said.

Pachi put his hand on the ground, palm down, and his son stepped on it with one of his flat (plano) feet—the reason for his nickname Planicio—and began to rock gently back and forth.

"A bit harder," said the Galician, and the boy brought more weight to bear.

During particularly difficult matches—increasingly frequent since the years were taking their toll—Planicio had to throw all the weight of his thirteen years onto his right foot to increase the pressure. At first the Galician's hand went numb, its circulation having been cut off, but right afterward he began to move his fingers carefully, and his hand, now back to a more reasonable size, could be used once more.

The whole procedure fascinated Jacinto, and when he saw how hard the boy had to work to exert pressure on the swollen hand, he, with the best intentions in the world, offered his services.

"Would you like me to help you?"

"Help what?" replied the Galician very slowly. "Give me a manicure?"

Everyone within hearing distance got a good laugh out of that. Jacinto wasn't sure whether it was something he'd said that made them laugh, but he didn't care. Besides which, it seemed to him that Francisco clearly could use a manicure; no one should walk around with fingernails as black as his.

"To give you a manicure, Pachi, I'd need a liter of turpentine."

"I'll give you turpentine, right where it counts."

Everyone must have guessed where the turpentine would go, and they all broke into laughter a second time.

And yet a day came to bring the happy times on the Atocha fronton to an end. During the long, calm, summer days, the boys made their games last into the night by the light of a street lamp—a gas lamp still—at Urbistondos. There being no more risks to run—the policeman and plant supervisor were both off duty by then—all they had to do was make sure not to send the ball too close to the window grating. The men in the bar across from the fronton were going over the decisive moments in the game, discussing in great detail the reasons why they had lost or won. Often Planicio's father came to the door and said, "Planicio, off home with you. I'll be there in a little while."

Which wasn't true. Many hours would pass before he'd get home. Sometimes he didn't come back at all during the night, but his father had already told Planicio that that's the way things were. At other times, the two of them walked back to 10-B Miracruz together. Sometimes his father even put his arm around Planicio's shoulder, content, his speech somewhat slurred. It used to be, a long time ago now (two years could seem like an awfully long time to a thirteen-year-old) that his mother would be standing on the doorstep, passing the time talking to Francisca, waiting for them.

"Hey, *Amachu!*" he said.

"There you are, Pachicu," his mother replied. She never called him Planicio, mainly because she said that all the talk about him having flat feet was nothing but nonsense. Then, turning to her husband, she asked, "What are you up to?"

It was partly a question, partly a statement of fact because her husband was always up to something, especially after nine o'clock at night. Planicio's mother was very young. She always wore dark colors and her hair up in a bun. She didn't kiss him much because it wasn't something one did around those parts, but she'd take his head in her hands and hold him up against her. If anyone else was around, he'd feel a bit embarrassed; after all, he was already eleven, and such displays of affection were more for small children. But he liked them all the same.

"So Pachicu, are you hungry?"

"Yes, *Amá.*"

Even if he wasn't hungry, he said, "Yes, *Amá,*" because he knew how important it was for his mother to see that he had an appetite and was a big eater.

"You need lots of food to grow up big and strong like *Aita.*"

If his father was there, she usually added in an aside, "Although let's hope you put it to better use than he has."

Calle de Miracruz in the summer was something to be seen.
It was the continuation of Avenida de España and of Paseo de
la Concha. Everybody who was anybody used the street, and if
Bea didn't know who someone was, Francisca could fill her in.
There were so few cars that they could easily identify every one
of them. Around ten o'clock every night, Francisca started to
worry because the countess might appear at any minute with
one of her daughters, coming back from the theater or a stroll
along Paseo Nuevo. She opened the elevator doors and shooed
everyone else away.

"Out, out with you."

She made them leave because she didn't like the countess to
see her chatting in the vestibule. Only Bea could stay because
she had once been in the countess's service. The Galician will-
ingly complied and headed off to Raimundo's bar just around
the corner.

"Now don't you come back late," his wife said.

"So what is it? Do I stay or do I go?" asked the Galician,
knowing full well what her answer would be.

They sent Planicio upstairs, saying they'd be up shortly.

The countess, a widow who still wore mourning, arrived and
greeted them as a countess should.

"Good evening, Francisca. Hello, Beatriz. What a nice surprise! How are you?"

"Just fine, Countess."

With Francisca and Bea on each side of her, the countess
walked up to the elevator where the two women closed the
doors in unison. Sometimes the countess said to Beatriz,
"Drop by tomorrow. I have something for you."

Generally it was to give her some used but barely worn
clothing. This invariably made Francisca feel a sudden twinge
of jealousy. It never lasted long though; after all, Bea had a
tough enough time as it was with that husband of hers.

Those days, happy days because *Amá* was always waiting for
him in the doorway, were soon over. When she died it seemed

like no one would ever stop crying, but within a week the only person who still cried for her was Planicio, and even he didn't cry too much because his father had already told him that crying wouldn't help matters any and that his mother was a saint and in Heaven. Not having an exact notion of time, since he was only eleven, he knew only that it took him what seemed like forever to stop feeling a tightness in his chest every time he drew near the front door in the evening. The countess took special pains with him. She too said that his mother was in Heaven and that every day and every minute of every day she was watching over him. She made it sound even better than before.

Planicio liked the idea, especially considering that he lived above the attic, so it must make it even easier for her to see him. On starlit nights when the two of them sat gazing up at the sky, Planicio liked to think that his father too was trying to see whether he could see her. Of course, the countess had said that it was his mother who could see them and not the other way round, but you never knew. Whenever he felt like crying he went into one of the abandoned back rooms, where even the locks were broken, and tried to cry softly. Between sobs he'd whisper, "*Amá, Amachu* . . . I'm here," so his mother, who didn't know the whereabouts of the back room, could still find him.

SINCE *AMA'S* DEATH, his father hadn't taken up the awl again.

"I just don't feel up to it," he said.

Somehow he only felt up to going to the Atocha fronton to while the time away with his cronies and perhaps play a short game—after all, he and his son had to eat. And eat a lot at that because they were both sturdy and needed the calories. Their only sit-down meal was at lunch, but it was a real meal because *Aita* had learned how to cook when he was working on the boat off of Newfoundland. Mornings, the Galician couldn't eat a thing, and Planicio had a bowl of milk with leftover bread from the day before. At night he often ate the same thing.

A farmwife brought the milk by every morning in a cart pulled behind a small horse. Francisca picked theirs up at the same time she got her own. The few times the Galician tasted the milk, he always said the same thing.

"They just keep watering it down more and more."

He spoke deliberately, looking at the concierge all the while, insinuating somehow that she was perhaps the one diluting the milk. Francisca ignored him, it being beneath her to pay him any mind. But he insisted that "some people can make one liter stretch into two."

Finally she'd had enough. "You know what *I* think? I think you can just get your own milk tomorrow!"

"The devil you do!" he muttered under his breath, rather amused by the confrontation. He had a curious liking for picking fights with the concierge over a matter—such as milk—that really was of no interest to him in the least. Now if they'd been talking wine, then he would have had his reasons since he could see nothing more sacrilegious than watering down wine.

Sometimes the Galician went too far so the concierge had no other choice but to take offense—in spite of his dearly departed wife and the affection she had for the boy—and stop picking up the milk for him. Then Planicio had to be ready early in the morning. As soon as he heard the bells on the milk lady's horse's collar, he threw on his pants—he kept his shirt on to sleep in—and raced down the five flights of stairs. Mornings were quiet in those days, so quiet that the horse's bells could be heard in the garret even before it turned on to Calle de Miracruz, while it was still on its way down the Ategorrieta hill. In those days San Sebastian was the most beautiful city in the world—everyone knew that—especially in the summer, and if the Galician said otherwise it was just to create a stir. Planicio never doubted it for a minute. Later, when he had to leave, he cried.

The milk lady always wore black with an apron that reached down to her feet. Her face was very red with a surprising white mustache. She didn't climb off her seat to serve her customers. Instead, she pulled up to the sidewalk and straddled the tramway rails. Sometimes the tram arrived while she was still in the way, but she wouldn't budge no matter how much the driver blew his horn, not until she'd finished serving her customers.

"One day you'll be sorry, you old hag," cried out the driver.

But when it suited her, the old hag didn't understand Spanish, and she just ignored him. Planicio kept thinking that someday, to get even, the driver would run over the horse and cart with his tram, and the very idea petrified him. Which was what was wrong with the boy, as his father had already noticed and as was confirmed by the race between the bridges. Planicio was entirely without malice.

To the milk lady, Planicio said, "Half a liter of milk, please, but not milk that's gone bad; otherwise *Aita* will be angry."

Under her breath she said something like, *Aita esne txarreco gizona*, meaning perhaps that his father was the one who'd gone bad, but she might just as well have said it out loud because Planicio hardly understood any Basque. The little he had learned in Fuenterrabía he was quickly losing in San Sebastian.

Usually, however, the tram wasn't there, and Francisca and the milk lady chatted away in Basque while Planicio waited patiently since he was in no hurry. As well as the jugs of milk, the cart was full of vegetables and eggs, everything smelling quite delicious. The tiny new potatoes still had fresh earth stuck to them, and while the two women talked he scraped away at it with his fingernail. The horse was small—they called it a farm horse—but had a shiny coat, a fat body and short legs, and it pulled the cart easily. Planicio reached out to touch its forehead, but the animal drew its head away as though uninterested in his caress.

The milk was kept in two large metal jugs fitted with a lid. The price depended on which jug the milk came from. The Galician told his son, "Take the cheapest one; it's just as good."

Before lifting the lid, the milk lady waved her hands in the air a few times to frighten away any flies. Then she took a ladle that doubled as a measuring cup. Two ladlefuls equaled half a liter.

"Don't forget to boil the milk first," she warned the boy.

He always did, but even then, on days when the south wind blew, the milk curdled. When that happened, Planicio's father told him to complain, but Planicio was afraid to.

"No *Aita*, please. We'll make curd."

His son's reaction worried the Galician. The boy was simply hopeless at bargaining or arguing. Even so, to please his father, Planicio, depending on the milk lady's mood, might say, "The milk curdled yesterday."

"Did you boil it?" asked the white-mustached hag.

"Yes."

"Where is it now?"

In other words, she wanted proof.

"We made curd."

The old woman shrugged her shoulders to show it was no longer any concern of hers. But then she usually gave him an extra pint. On those days, Planicio ran up the stairs to tell his father joyfully, *"Aita, Aita!* She gave me extra."

To him it seemed like a great victory. At other times, the old woman refused to compromise. Instead, she'd give him some advice.

"On really hot days, throw in a pinch of baking soda."

The Galician was by no means one of her preferred customers, and if the milk lady did make a small effort, it was only because of the boy and his big eyes still full of sleep in the early morning light.

SUCH WONDERFULLY happy days they'd been when *Amá* stood with Francisca in the doorway, waiting for her men to come home. Even when she scolded him and said, "I've told you before not to spend all day playing pelota."

Her words were addressed to her son, but she looked at his father. While *Amá* was alive, everyone on Calle de Miracruz held them in the highest regard, and when speaking of Planicio they said, "He's the Garmendía girl's boy."

His mother was born in Alza, next to Pasajes, into the Garmendía family, and her older brother had inherited the family farm. For a while, he couldn't remember if it was for one year or two, he went to the municipal school behind San Ignacio Church, and the teacher called him Pachi Garmendía even though his surname was Lourido.

The countess always called him Paco. He, of course, preferred Planicio even though *Amá* objected, saying, "Don't call the boy that. *Ené,* such an awful name!"

The saddest days were the ones following *Amá*'s departure. Her watching over the garret night and day just wasn't the same. Then a new life began. It was summertime again—calm long days that were good too because even though he stopped being the Garmendía boy and wasn't seen with the same regard on Calle de Miracruz, around Atocha's public fronton he was the expert's boy. When the two of them appeared after having a light snack on the way, people in the fronton would say, "Here comes the expert."

Nobody called Pachi the Galician anymore, not because it mattered to him but because it didn't make sense to keep calling him that when he'd been living in the region since 1909. On the other hand, they called him the expert because he was the one to consult when it came time to organize a game since he knew better than anyone what combination of pairs would make for the most exciting game. What's more, in spite of his thirty-six years, he was the partner of choice since he won more games than he lost. Not that he had much choice.

If he didn't they wouldn't have any food to put on the table.

"Planicio!" he called.

The boy came running at his farm horse's half-trot from Urbistondos.

"Step on it."

And Planicio trod as hard as he could on his father's swollen hand. If someone else offered to do it, his father said, "Leave be. He knows how."

He, Planicio—and not Francisquito as Jacinto called him—knew how to rock gently back and forth and then with all his might so that his father's hand could continue earning their daily bread.

Any way Pachi looked at it, he just didn't understand the boy. Even though Planicio had what it took to play pelota, he often wouldn't press his advantage. Once in a while, Pachi glanced over at his son playing at Urbistondos only to be surprised to see him lose a game he'd been winning handily.

"How in hell did you lose?" his father asked reproachfully.

"It doesn't matter, *Aita;* we were only playing for fun."

Playing for fun. Meaningless words to the Galician for whom certain principles had to be learned from the time one was very young. Sometimes he thought that perhaps it was true, that the best thing for the boy would be to continue his studies.

Every August 15, the Day of Assumption, even when they lived in Fuenterrabía, Pachi Lourido would put on a new shirt and an almost-new beret that he kept for special occasions and head off to the bullfights carrying a big cigar.

"Life's been treating you all right, Pachi!" his wife would say, happy to see him looking so successful.

"Have to keep up the tradition," he'd reply.

The tradition he'd started was even more noticeable since they'd moved to Calle de Miracruz because anyone going to the bullfight had to pass in front of 10-B, five minutes away from the plaza. It was a show in itself, and the whole neighborhood was out on their balconies to take it all in. All the concierges gathered on the doorstep to comment on the passersby. Even Jacinto came down. Pachi stayed slightly apart from the others and greeted his friends with his arms crossed on his chest and his unlit cigar in his mouth. He lit the cigar only when the first bull appeared. If someone asked, "Hey, Pachi, aren't you going to the fight?" he'd reply, "In a minute, in a minute."

He was in no hurry because he already had a reserved seat in the grandstand on the lower level in the sun, and he needed only to get there ten minutes before the fight began. Moreover, by waiting longer, he arrived when the plaza was at its most crowded, and in the midst of all the confusion, he could sneak the boy in with him. But, and this is what concerned him, he had to force his son to come along. In vain Pachi would explain on their way over that he'd go in with Planicio and that nobody was going to ask him anything.

"No *Aita*. I'm too embarrassed."

That was precisely what he wanted to rid his son of. Life was complicated enough without having an exaggerated sense of propriety.

THEN THE LONG calm days of summer, during which they continued to play pelota as night fell by the light of a gaslit street lamp, fine-tuning the skills needed to play on the uneven surface of Urbistondos, came to an abrupt end.

The previous night, like so many others before it, his father had said to him, "Run along home now. I'll be up shortly."

The night was cold and humid, and Planicio tumbled into bed where he waited for a while. On the wall in front of him were shelves full of dishes, an untidy jumble since *Amá*'s death. The shelves were still covered in the same newspapers, now all yellow, that his mother had used to try to protect them. With very little light—there was only one light bulb in this room— Planicio kept himself amused by reading the papers upside down and from a distance. He had no trouble reading whether it was right side up or upside down. One was as easy as the other. The same held true for the light; however little there was, he could adapt. He didn't read much, not having much opportunity or any encouragement. His father always said, "Shoemaker, to your shoes."

Maybe his father wanted him to be a shoemaker, but it didn't make sense because he himself said it was a trade of no interest, which is why the leather—all dried out by now—the awl, and the workbench sat forgotten in a corner.

After a while, he realized that his father wouldn't be coming right up, and he ate a bit of striped tunnyfish in tomato sauce left over from lunch. He ate it cold, not bothering to heat it up because these things didn't matter to him the way they did to *Aita*. On the other hand, he swallowed a mouthful of wine directly out of the bottle because his father had already told him that after tunnyfish or tuna one should never drink water. Of course, according to his father, there were a number of occasions on which one should not drink water. But in this case it did seem clear that water after tunny or tuna gave a bad case of colic. Sometimes Planicio asked his father for specific advice.

"*Aita,* can you drink water after eating sardines?"

His father reflected on this for a minute and then stated, "Go ahead and drink. I don't think it'll do you any good, but it won't do you any harm either. On top of that you're young."

In other words, a young boy could do things with water that might be harmful to an old codger like himself.

Before falling asleep Planicio, as always, said three Hail Mary's just as his mother had recommended he do for purity's sake. He used to say them with her, and it was one of the hardest things for him to learn to do alone. First he said his three, then three more for his mother in case she needed them.

When father and son went to bed at the same time, his father would ask, "Have you said your prayers?"

"Yes *Aita.*"

That night though, they didn't go to bed together, and Planicio didn't even hear him come home, but the next morning *Aita* didn't wake up until late. One side of his face was swollen and his eyes were red. Planicio asked him whether he'd hurt himself, and at first his father didn't answer, but then he said yes. At noon he added that they wouldn't be going to Atocha. He seemed depressed all day, but Planicio thought it was because of the south wind coming from the Maqueto region, which melted the tar on the terrasse and even made the drains smell, especially at low tide; and the Urumea River, which was really an estuary, was left dry.

The next day his father said, "We won't be going back there, understood?"

Planicio went to Urbistondos anyway, not because he was trying to be disobedient—one didn't disobey *Aita*—but because he hadn't understood that he wasn't to go to Urbistondos either, it being a place his father had no interest in, where one learned only the bad habits of church players.

He noticed something strange about the other boys. When he arrived they were in the middle of a game, and he waited for them to finish before joining in, but they didn't want to play anymore. As his father had so often said, Planicio didn't understand malice. Still it was strange that all of a sudden no one wanted to play. It also felt strange not to see the expert seated on the small wall right next to the Atocha fronton directing operations.

He sat down with the other boys on the curb of the former driveway and no one spoke, but that was nothing out of the ordinary, especially when the south wind blew and the air was so heavy that even the children felt depressed. Suddenly one of them got up, looked at him, drew back a little, said, "You Galician *tranposua**,*" and ran away.

He didn't have to because Planicio had been called a Galician before, and it didn't bother him, they knew, because it was

*Translator's Note: Cheater in Basque

true that his father was born in Galicia and had lived as a boy in the Trincherpe district where there were a lot of other Galicians. But this time, the others started to look at him and laugh. They all got up, one after the other, and left him alone. Then he too got up and at his light half-trot, toes pointed out and body pumping, made his way home. Near the Iztueta hill he heard someone running behind him, but just in case, he didn't want to look. It was Ramoncho, a boy slightly younger than he with whom he got along well. When the other boy drew closer, he said, "Listen, I'm not on their side."

"Good," replied Planicio without slowing down.

"If you want," said the other boy, panting slightly, "we can go play at the station." When demand was high and not everyone could fit into Urbistondos or when there was a risk that the police officer might walk by, they usually repaired to a fence by the station, which wasn't all that great but which served the purpose.

Planicio didn't answer because even though he was without malice, a lump had begun to form in his throat and he didn't trust himself to speak. But his companion insisted, presenting a very convincing argument.

"I've got a ball. Look." And so that Planicio wouldn't doubt his word, he showed him a ball covered in worn-out sheepskin, the way they liked it, even though it was slightly concave.

They kept on running. By now they were on the cobblestones of Paseo de Iztueta, and Planicio said, "I don't feel like it. Some other day."

His running mate stopped, caught his breath and because Planicio was going so fast, he had to shout after him, "I'll come get you tomorrow!"

Planicio already understood that, "I'll come get you tomorrow," meant he shouldn't go to Atocha, that Ramoncho would come to him. He greeted Francisca as he ran through the vestibule and began, without breaking his stride, to climb the stairs. Past ASUN'S CORSET SHOP: ENHANCE YOUR BEAUTY on the second floor; then the third floor, the countess's floor, where the marble staircase with its sharp angles that made climbing easier came to an end. Then the next two floors, of no interest whatsoever, and then from the fifth floor up, closer to the large central skylight where there was much more light, even though the stairway and the windows got narrower. It was also much hotter today with the south wind blowing. As for the steep and narrow flight of stairs leading to the garret, he now—the first time had been just a month ago—was able to take it in three bounds, which had even impressed *Aita*.

It was a strange feeling to see the expert just sitting there at this hour, seven o'clock on a summer's evening, in the count's old chair.

"Where have you been?" he asked frowning.

"At Urbistondos," said the boy panting.

His father stood up and, to Planicio's great relief because finally he could start to cry, slapped him—Whack!—across the face. There was nothing unusual about the slap because parents often hit their children in those days.

"Didn't I tell you not to go there!" yelled his father.

"I didn't know that's what you meant, *Aita!*"

"Well next time you *will* know!"

They ate leftovers for dinner without speaking, and before lying down, Planicio said through swollen lips, *"Aita,* I need money to pay for the milk tomorrow."

"You'll pay some other day."

THEY LIVED from day to day, meaning that when night fell, the Galician often went to bed without a single peseta in his pocket.

Those were bad times, really bad. They didn't even have enough for wine. On the third day after the milk lady had voiced her displeasure, Planicio didn't dare go for the milk.

"Why aren't you going?" asked his father.

"I'm too embarrassed, *Aita."*

Not again. But Pachi Lourido felt so depressed he didn't
even feel like arguing. He rarely went outside anymore, and if
he did, generally it was to go to some bar that would still give
him credit. He must have borrowed money too sometimes
because on some days they had a decent meal again. But they
ate without enjoyment because it was a year of much hardship.
No rain had fallen since spring, and all the farmers were
gloomy because there wouldn't even be a harvest to reap.

Francisca the concierge felt quite smug. Hadn't she predicted what would happen to the garret tenants? One day she
called Planicio into her apartment in the half-basement and
gave him a glass of milk and some bread, all the while saying,
"Poor boy!"

He was grateful for the food, but from then on he tried to
avoid going through the vestibule when the old woman was
there. Plus, Francisca's house smelled like cat pee.

Things got so bad that Pachi Lourido made signs of looking
for work. From time to time he walked down to the port, Puerto de Pasajes, to see if anything had turned up. But times were
bad for fishermen too. Because of fuel problems, boats rarely
went out, and there was an overabundance of crews. Still Pachi
must have had a friend or two in Trincherpe because he usually
came back with part of a catch they gave to him, although it
was always the scraps—small codling, small sardines . . . fish
that would normally have been thrown back into the sea. The
worst part was that cooking oil was just not to be had anywhere—according to *Aita,* Franco must need it all to fatten up
the Axis—and it took a lot of willpower to eat the boiled fish
with nothing but salt and a bit of vinegar.

For his part, Planicio climbed the hills of Mount Ulía at his
obstinate half-trot, looking for apples. Robbing apples didn't
make him feel embarrassed because he'd always done it, and he
assumed that the farmers expected it, especially where apple
trees stood close to the road. He was extremely good at it—
lessons learned when very young are never forgotten. It was

easy to know where the farmer was and to come at the trees from the opposite direction. Even if he was spotted, it didn't matter because, despite the fact that he ran with his toes pointing out and that people said he had flat feet, he ran fast enough to flee any danger. In any case, times were tough, and one had to take that into account. Often he simply picked up the apples that had fallen in the field. They were no worse than the others really.

When he saw them, his father said contemptuously, "No better than pig's food."

But they ate them. What else could they do?

Another problem, a serious one, was tobacco for *Aita*. When he couldn't smoke, it was even worse than when he had to eat fish boiled in water. Planicio learned from the other boys how to ask for cigarettes from the German soldiers who by now had reached Hendaye and who, at the end of the summer, often crossed the border with their cameras. They were blond with red faces, content, not bothering anyone, happy to please the children who drew near asking, "Zigarettes, zigarettes! . . . "

They took out their packages and gave them a couple of cigarettes. Sometimes they shook their heads no, but gave them a piece of chocolate instead. Since Planicio would rather have the cigarettes, he learned to say *father* in German *(vater)*, which worked better:

"Zigarettes, *vater!* . . . " And then he thanked them. *"Danken."*

The first time, his father looked at the short white cigarettes suspiciously. He lit one up and consumed almost half of it in one drag.

"Ené! Will you look at that?"

Then he began to experiment with the cigar butts Planicio brought back for him as well. The Galician chopped them up very fine with a razor blade and mixed them in with the German tobacco. Whenever he managed to get hold of a little bit of honey, he mixed it with a lot of water and moistened the blend to wipe out the cigar butt smell. His system made the cigarette last longer and meant that he could roll his own, which is what smoking was all about. He was very careful to put the honey-moistened blend out to dry in the sun on the terrasse, in a spot sheltered from the wind so it wouldn't be blown away.

Jacinto the countess's manservant, more of a busybody than ever, watched the situation closely. In the countess's household, once the horror of the civil war—which of course was won by those who should have won—was over, things had gone back to normal, and the countess had asked him, Jacinto the household administrator, to purchase another car. Secondhand, of course, because there were no new cars in those days. Jacinto was thrilled at the thought of bringing out his ostrich feather duster once again to keep the vehicle shining like a medal and looking like new. As well, the purchase afforded him a wonderful opportunity to skim off a commission for himself, and with a purchase as large as this one, it would be handsome. He needed every last peseta for the old age that was lying in wait for him.

In spite of the titles he'd accumulated—valet de chambre, manicurist, household administrator and chauffeur (once again)—he didn't forget his friends in need. In spite of the indubitable prestige he'd earned in the household, he kept on wearing his green vest with yellow stripes, and whenever the opportunity arose, he went up to the garret.

"Pachi, Pachi . . . " He was very respectful of others' privacy and would never think to cross over to their room without first being invited to do so.

"I've brought you a casserole that should be just to your liking."

The Galician had always been a man free of prejudice who knew how to accept a gift graciously. He heated up the casserole because it always came in times of dire need and couldn't wait, and invited Jacinto to have a seat.

Pachi was a man who knew how to be gracious but who also told things the way they were.

"The ingredients are good," he opined while chewing the hake, "but don't let yourself be fooled into thinking the cuisine they serve you is worth much. You call this hake *à la sauce verte?* I call it hake in flour paste and parsley."

Jacinto assumed a remorseful expression, but deep down he was delighted; the cook was the one person he couldn't abide in the countess's household, yet he had little hope of ever seeing the last of her because she had worked as a kitchen maid in the Madrid palace when the count's parents were still alive. In other words, she'd been cooking for three generations of the count's family. It was hopeless. All he could do was suffer in silence and hope that God would welcome her into His fold as soon as possible.

"She's never been a good cook. The countess says it's because of her age, but let me tell you, Pachi, and you can swear by it, that woman never knew how to cook. How she makes me suffer when there are guests! You never know what you'll have to take out to the table. And of course I'm the one serving the slop, and they may think I'm to blame. I tell you, Pachi, it's a nightmare."

The Galician kept on eating voraciously, ignoring the personal issue, which was of no interest to him, to concentrate on the real issue.

"See here, Jacinto. To make hake *à la sauce verte*, you have to use less flour and stir the sauce more. Understand? The sauce has to be thickened, of course, but by stirring it over the heat, not by adding flour. Do you see what I mean?"

How could Jacinto not see? Of course he did, but what could one do?

"To make matters worse," continued Jacinto, his face contorted in a grimace, "she's dirty. And then to top it all off, the countess says I must be charitable toward her and her years."

"Now just a minute," said Pachi Lourido. "What does charity have to do with hake *à la sauce verte?*"

But he kept on chewing and sponging the parsley concoction up with his bread, if he had any, because times were tough, truly tough.

"As for her cleanliness," philosophized the Galician, "let me tell you. When I was in Canada, I knew a Portuguese cook whose kitchen was so filthy you couldn't even walk into it. But his cooking was out of this world."

"Oh, how revolting! In that case, I'd rather go without food!"

Jacinto didn't go to Atocha anymore either because without Pachi it wasn't the same, and besides, it was risky placing a bet when you didn't have good advice to go on.

The way things stood, the Galician was grateful for Jacinto's company. He'd quit worrying about the boy too; Jacinto was obviously inoffensive. At the end of September—the month the elegant set spent in San Sebastian—the count's household would move back to Madrid. Pachi and Planicio would miss Jacinto.

Before winter set in, Jacinto did them a teensy favor—he loved using that adjective—and found a job for Francisquito as an errand boy for ASUN'S CORSET SHOP: ENHANCE YOUR BEAUTY. He got along famously with the corset shop owner, a woman after his own heart who welcomed his comments on the pectoral enhancement of the women from the count's household who were customers of hers, thanks to his intervention.

There wasn't that much work because there weren't always deliveries to be made every day, and there'd be even less once winter set in. Asun warned both father and son, "No guarantees."

By that she meant that his salary consisted of his tips to which she'd add a little something as common sense dictated. For example, if a delivery had to be made to some far-off place, she gave him money for the tramway; no ride cost more than two five-centimo copper coins. Planicio kept the money and made the delivery on foot at his famous farm horse's half-trot, by now his usual way of getting round. Splat, splat! he ran, covering a lot of ground in spite of the way his toes pointed out. Rain was a problem, especially if he had to cross the Santa Catalina Bridge. If he came back soaking wet, Señora Asun might suspect he'd kept the tramway money for himself, which would really embarrass him. There weren't any clothes at home he could use to protect himself from the rain—not a raincoat, a windbreaker or an umbrella—so he got by with a piece of tarred canvas from the days when his father was still a sailor. The tar was old though and didn't work very well.

His father said, "If we give it a bit of linseed oil, maybe it won't get as wet. Let me see what I can do." But Pachi didn't do anything because he was still depressed. In any case, there was nothing wrong with getting wet; as any fisherman knew, getting wet was just a part of life.

Planicio didn't know how old Señora Asun was, but he had a fairly good idea of how old the girls he liked to watch were— some were younger, some were older than he was. But then there were others, older, much older than he, but on another level, who the school priest had already said he shouldn't be looking at. And finally there was a category of women—Francisca, the countess, the seamstress from the fifth floor—who were divorced from all time. Señora Asun was one of the latter. Two of her nieces worked with her in the corset shop and belonged to the second category, but he could look at them without danger because they were singularly ugly. There was also an apprentice his age, but she was the same. His father always said, "*Ené,* what a bunch! They should start by enhancing their own beauty. Of course I don't know what they have that could be enhanced. They don't even have a good foundation to start with."

When the Galician talked about a woman's foundation, he was mostly referring to her hips.

After every delivery, Señora Asun asked him what his tip had been. When there'd been no tip, she insisted, "Did you wait around?"

In other words, he wasn't supposed to deliver the package and run off. Instead, he was to stay, standing with an expression on his face that said, "Look at me, I'm still here."

"Yes," replied Planicio, "I stood there and didn't move till she said, 'Do I have to sign something?' I said, 'No,' and then she said, 'Good-bye,' and closed the door."

Then Señora Asun asked him what the woman who had opened the door looked like, whether she was short or tall, this way or that way, and once she figured out who it was, she always had a few choice words to say. When Planicio first started working for her and said there was no tip, Señora Asun's eyes bored into him, trying to see if he was telling the truth. The boy realized what she was doing and felt trapped. He said in a strangled voice, "I swear she didn't give me a thing!"

"Don't swear; it's not polite," replied the corset shop owner, who kept her eye on him all the same.

But it didn't take long for her to realize that Planicio was as unlike his father as could be. From then on, she only asked him in order to see what amount common sense dictated, in other words, enough to see that the boy got an average of a duro a day. At first Planicio sat waiting in the vestibule to be sent on an errand. Sometimes he spent all morning or even all day there. They finally agreed he could wait in his garret room instead and that they'd call him when there was an errand to run. They called up from a narrow enclosed patio that was capped by a skylight and had air vents leading onto the flat roof.

"Planicio!" the apprentice or one of the saleswomen cried out softly. And he, ever on the alert, ran at his own special trot over to the skylight and replied, "I'm coming."

One day when they met up in the vestibule, the corset shop owner said to his father, "You have a well-behaved boy, truly well behaved."

"I can't complain," sighed the Galician, "and he's a great help during this bad streak of luck we're having."

According to information Señora Asun had, the shoemaker from the garret earned his living playing pelota for money on the Atocha fronton, and his bad luck came from cheating. But she was a woman of principle and so asked the man whether he didn't have any prospects. Job prospects, she meant.

He said regretfully, "It's not easy at my age."

"At your age? But you're still a young man!"

"Not where work is concerned." He himself realized that his answer was somewhat lacking in reason and changed tack in midsentence. "I mean that in times of scarcity, it's harder for a man my age to find work."

She was a woman of principle in that she liked to take an interest in others and dispense advice, and sin didn't frighten her. She belonged to the San Ignacio Church women's group and said to him, "In any case, I can speak to the priest to see if he knows of any work for you."

The Galician didn't know what to say since experience had shown him that the type of work priests usually found was completely devoid of interest for men such as he. But he knew what his response should be and said, "I'd appreciate that, Señora."

In the meantime, he managed to get a Christmas Eve dinner out of the church women's group but tried to avoid meeting up with the corset shop owner in the stairway again because she always said, "I haven't forgotten my promise to you."

"Thank you, Señora," he replied, frightened by her tenaciousness.

In January his fears were confirmed as Señora Asun joyfully announced that the priest himself was waiting to speak to him.

San Ignacio Church was located on the small square of the same name, across from some wine and vinegar shops that smelled so foul he suspected they trafficked their product, and so never bought anything there and warned Planicio not to either. The square was only about 500 meters from his house, yet he rarely went there. It was only of relative interest because it held the church, which took up a great deal of space, the municipal schools on one side and behind it all, the sea, which, ever since he'd left his profession, he'd avoided because the humidity was very bad for his lumbago or his rheumatism, whichever. At his age, given the hardships he'd endured in his lifetime, it was only natural to be suffering from one or the other, especially during this long rainy winter when the big house at 10-B Miracruz was so humid.

"The Lord be praised!" He practiced saying "The Lord be praised" in preparation for his interview with the parish priest since he supposed he'd have to say something along that line at some point or another.

The sexton knew him and was surprised to see him there.

"You here, Pachi?" When he heard that Pachi had come to see the priest, he said, "You must really be in a bad way."

Pachi saw no reason to provide him with an explanation. It wasn't as though they were friends or anything. They only knew each other from having met bar hopping and during a card game or two.

The priest commented first that he'd never seen Pachi before. It looked bad for Pachi, not that he was overly concerned, seeing that the important thing was to keep on that damned corset shop owner's good side and by the same token hold on to the six duros Planicio brought home every week. That the priest had never seen him was interpreted by the Galician as a reproach for his not attending church. He decided to pretend he didn't understand since the priest, to begin with, spoke to him in Basque.

"Have a seat, have a seat," said the priest in Spanish, taking out a tobacco pouch that he offered to his parishioner. It was an obvious sign of goodwill and clearly showed that the priest was not going to make a scene about his absence from church.

Pachi thought he should perhaps give some kind of excuse for not attending mass, but he couldn't think of a reasonable one right off the bat so he just rolled himself a cigarette as fat as the tobacco paper would allow. It was a standard cut tobacco, uncured and full of cuttings that had to be discarded—only the big pieces, of course, because otherwise nothing would be left. The priest was busy doing the same and said, "It just keeps getting worse" (referring to the tobacco) and added, "They have no shame" (referring to the government).

This was an opinion easily agreed to, and Pachi nodded his head.

The priest continued. "These cuttings burn like coal, live coal. Just look at what they've done to my soutane."

He showed Pachi a burn hole, and Pachi once again nodded his head in agreement.

"Well now," pronounced the parish priest, "to the business at hand. I've been told you are a sailor. . . ."

"Was a sailor," Pachi quickly broke in. "I'm retired because of my rheumatism."

"So what is it then?" asked the priest. "You would rather have a less active job?"

To Pachi the priest's question seemed quite a devious one, but he too had a role to play, and he knew what his answer should be.

"Aside from my rheumatism, I have a thirteen-year-old boy I can't leave all alone either," and he added sorrowfully, "His mother died almost three years ago."

"Oh, yes. I understand. I knew your wife. She was a Garmendía girl from Alza, isn't that it?"

That was it. The reason why he couldn't go back to the sea—aside from his rheumatism—was that he couldn't leave his son on his own.

And so the priest's question about whether or not he was a sailor had only been to feel him out because what he had to offer was an actual job—taking a gentleman, an invalid confined to a wheelchair, out for walks. The gentleman in question had been a civil servant for the Revenue Delegation, a senior civil servant, but for the past year, he hadn't been able to go into his office. A case of progressive general paralysis. The man was a Christian gentleman who accepted his misfortune with admirable fortitude. A saint, a genuine saint.

At this point, Pachi was able to say what he'd prepared on the way.

"The Lord be praised."

He spoke with a sigh as planned but without letting down his guard because, among other reasons, the priest was now saying to him, "I tell you anything done for this man is a true act of charity."

The Galician quite agreed with everything that had been said up to this point, but he waited before assenting because the priest must already realize that he was not in a position to carry out acts of charity.

"Fortunately this man has been left with a sizable pension, almost 100% of his salary, and can pay for the service."

Once again Pachi repeated, "The Lord be praised," but under his breath to himself because it seemed to him that the job—considering it was a job offered by a priest—was not all that bad.

"So," concluded the priest, "we'll see how you two get along." And he stood up to signal the interview was over. In saying their good-byes, he said to Pachi, "Perhaps I'll see you in church one of these days."

"Yes, Father," replied the parishioner humbly, his beret still in his hands.

As things went, he did go to church often because every Sunday and holy day, he took Don Román Aldaiz to noon mass. Don Román lived on Calle de Ramón y Cajal, almost on the corner of Avenida del Kursaal, and from his house one could see the sea. He was fifty-two years old but would have looked younger if it weren't that he was obese, a result of his forced immobility. He was constantly fighting to stay on a diet and stop gaining weight, but it was often a losing battle, as Pachi Lourido would soon learn and share.

The first day they met, the question of payment was not broached at all. Instead, Don Román inquired into the Galician's life. He was very particular about everything he did. For instance, he wanted to know what name Pachi would like to be called by.

"Your name is Francisco, isn't that right?"

"Yes, sir."

"But what do people call you?"

"Pachi or Pachi the Galician or just the Galician."

"Ah! You're Galician, are you? But looking at you, I would have sworn you were Basque."

Pachi explained that he'd been living in the region since 1909, which was why he had the look and the tastes of a Basque.

"What tastes?" inquired Don Román.

"Pelota. I play pelota, but," he added quickly, "only when my lumbago isn't bad."

"Hand pelota?"

"Yes, sir."

"A great sport. What other tastes?"

The Galician shrugged his shoulders because the other tastes he had might not please a man as Christian and resigned as the parish priest said this one was.

They both agreed to give it a try, and starting the next day, Pachi took Don Román out for a walk every afternoon. Don Román waited for him around four o'clock every day, seated in his invalid's chair and placed in front of a mirador from which a good part of Paseo del Kursaal could be seen, the sea in the background. An unmarried sister—he himself was a bachelor—looked after him. They had a maid but never the same one because his sister could be difficult, and the girls didn't always stand for her fits of anger. His sister, Señorita Menchu, was good looking, even, in the Galician's opinion, blessed with a good foundation, but in spite of her youth—just over thirty—she had the look of a spinster. There were four brothers and sisters in all, but the other two were married and lived outside of San Sebastian.

When Pachi arrived, Don Román said, "I feel so lazy." Lazy because he was so comfortable in his chair, either half asleep, or looking at the sea or at the people going by on Kursaal.

If Pachi arrived before four o'clock, he said, "Let's wait until this program is over. Have a seat, do."

In those days, EAJ-2 Radio San Sebastian was only on the air for a short period, and the daily program finished at four o'clock in the afternoon. Once it was over, Don Román had run out of excuses. He'd say, "Fine, let's go."

Señorita Menchu brought his wheelchair over, placing it next to his chair. It was an ordinary chair except that the right armrest could be removed, making it easier to transfer Don Román to the wheelchair. The first few times, Pachi tried to use his own strength for the maneuver—after all, he measured 5'11" and weighed 195 lbs, in spite of the scarcity of food during the winter—to show off a bit in front of the don's sister, the one with the good foundation.

But Don Román refused. "Careful, Pachi, careful! It isn't the amount of strength you use that matters. It's a question of skill."

The skill lay in having him, Don Román, move over to the edge of the seat, then, with such concentration and effort that his face turned purple, manage to stand up and in this position, erect with both hands on the edge of the chair to keep his balance, wait until he felt the seat of the wheelchair just behind his knees and then let himself fall back into it.

At first Pachi, in spite of being a skeptic and a man not easily moved, regarded the operation with something akin to terror and worried that if Don Román misjudged when to let himself fall back, he'd end up splattered on the floor. For this reason, he tried to help the invalid and stop him from having to exert himself, particularly the violent effort it took to hike himself to a standing position, which turned his face purple, but Don Román would hear none of it.

"You watch," he said, "what Señorita Menchu does, and then you'll see."

Señorita Menchu carried out the operation with consummate ease. She brought the wheelchair close, waited for her brother to stand up, pulled his chair back slightly, pushed the wheelchair up to behind his knees, gave him her arm to use for balance, waited for him to sit down and helped him get comfortable in his new seat. The wheelchair had only one armrest, on which the invalid leaned.

Sometimes he whispered to his sister, "Careful, I've got a crease." Then Señorita Menchu adjusted his trousers until all the creases that were bothering him were gone.

"You can call for the elevator now," his sister said to Pachi. They lived on the second floor, and one summoned the elevator by calling out to the doorman down the stairwell.

Every afternoon brother and sister kissed each other goodbye, an unheard of practice in the Basque region, but the difference in their ages was considerable. Don Román was the eldest of the four siblings and Señorita Menchu the youngest. And then their circumstances were special, both of them being unmarried because of his progressive paralysis. Her brother said the same thing every afternoon.

"You get out now too. It's a beautiful afternoon to be out and about. Isn't that right, Pachi?"

Pachi nodded.

"Call your friends to go out with you, all right? We won't be back before seven o'clock at the earliest. Right, Pachi?"

Once again he nodded.

"And if you want, go to a movie afterward. After all, the maid is always here, and I won't need a thing."

But more often than not, when they got back, Señorita

Menchu, contrary to her promises, would not have gone out. This always distressed her brother, who complained, "That girl!"

Although Señorita Menchu had the bitter air of a spinster and spoke sharply to the maid, she was pleasant with Pachi and explained things to him quite agreeably. She even had a few private conversations with him to explain how it was best to help her brother as little as possible during the transfer because the exercise was good for him.

"Yes, Señorita."

"Of course, it won't stop the disease, but it will take a little longer."

She didn't say what would take longer, but her meaning was unmistakable. Pachi heard her out with some dismay and wondered whether he hadn't made a mistake accepting the job, thinking that, just as he had feared, it was turning into the kind of job a priest would find. But down in the street, things were different. As they learned to trust each other and as time went by, Don Román and Pachi had a few mini-adventures of their own. Gastronomical and otherwise.

AFTER THE FIRST week, Don Román gave Pachi twelve duros.

"Will that do?" he asked.

It would since one couldn't expect much more just for taking the man out on a walk for two or three hours every day. Besides, Pachi's sixth sense as a man in constant need told him that other opportunities were to be had in this household. It took him only a week to realize that Don Román was a well-known man in the city. By the time his paralysis had progressed to the point where he could no longer go into the office and had to retire, he was the province's Revenue delegate. A silver plaque in his house dated June, 1941, read: FROM THE OFFICIALS, EMPLOYEES AND SUBORDINATES OF THE GUIPÚZCOA REVENUE DELEGATION IN TRIBUTE TO

THEIR DELEGATE, DON ROMAN ALDAIZ, AND IN GRATITUDE
FOR HIS CONCERN FOR THEM. When he retired, they put on
a banquet that was even reported in the newspapers (Pachi
didn't read the paper, or anything else for that matter, because
he didn't know how to read) at which time they presented him
with the plaque. Don Román started out teaching business
and then took the liquidators exam. Once he became a liq-
uidator—he was living in Madrid at the time—he began to
study law.

"A man of great virtue," they said.

"And what was he to do?" he replied.

The symptoms of the progressive paralysis had begun to
appear when he was still very young, and although its progress
had been very slow at first, he realized his life wouldn't be like
everyone else's, which is why he dedicated himself to his studies
and to his administrative career, and why it was of great satisfaction to him to finish his career as the Revenue delegate in
San Sebastian. His father was from Vitoria, but his mother
hailed from Donosti, and he too felt as though he were Donos-
tian, although he was born in Salvatierra in the province of
Alava.

Since retiring, he worked helping students prepare for Revenue job competitions. He let on that it helped keep him busy,
which was undoubtedly true, but he was also a bit obsessed
with money, knowing that the day he died, his sister would be
left penniless since she would no longer be entitled to his pension. For many years he'd invested all his savings in certificates
and shares in his sister's name. He kept up the practice, which
is why he welcomed the additional income tutoring brought.
At any rate he still thought of his sister as a young girl who
would marry some day and be able to use the savings as her
dowry. This explained why he was always trying to talk her into
getting out and going to the movies. He thought that she
might meet somebody there who would be suitable for her. He
didn't want people to see her out in the street with him because

he was afraid that the idea of her having a paralyzed brother might frighten away potential suitors.

In February the rain stopped, the weather grew milder and the days sunnier; meals were more substantial in the garret at 10-B Miracruz, and life in general seemed to be worth living again. In the back of his mind, Pachi still harbored the hope—and why not?—that come summer he would be able to go back to the Atocha fronton; a long winter could erase many insults. Not to mention Señorita Menchu who was blessed with a good foundation, although he, Pachi Lourido, had no special designs on her, but you never knew. . . .

Times had been tough, truly tough, and so the few duros—the father's and the son's—that came in with surprising regularity every week were a godsend. Of course, it wasn't enough to allow them to afford to eat meat, but they'd never aspired to that in the first place. There was a happy medium, however, between the rotten apples—pig's food—that Planicio brought back from Mount Ulía and meat, especially when you knew how to cook the way Pachi did. They didn't spend money on clothes, and they didn't pay rent for the garret room either because Jacinto told them before leaving, "Don't worry about it, I'll talk to the countess. We'll work it out in the summer." A fairy he might be, but to them he'd been a savior.

Planicio desperately wanted to meet Don Román because of everything *Aita* had told him about the man. He first saw him from a distance, one Sunday at noon mass, in the wheelchair his father pushed. The San Ignacio usher who carried a pad-locked brass money box and charged ten centimos for the use of the church chairs—straw-seated priedieus from the begin-ning of the century for kneeling or sitting during the ser-mon—was notorious for the unusual fierceness with which she carried out her task. If some poor soul neglected to pay her, she'd shake the box in front of his nose, making an infernal racket, and if, in spite of her blandishments, the person in question played dumb, she invited him to give up his seat. If he refused, she insulted him in a loud voice. Don Román was different because he had his own chair and so didn't have to pay, but even then he usually threw fifty centimos into the box and gave another fifty centimos to the usher. Although Pachi tried to avoid being too familiar with the don, he did say, "You need charity and then some to give fifty centimos to that witch."

Don Román smiled. He enjoyed Pachi's comments, and no doubt about it, the Galician had added a new dimension to his life. Before, the doorman was the one who took him out on walks when he could fit them in. When he didn't have time, Don Román was taken down to the sidewalk by the side of the road, and either his sister or the maid would go for a walk with him. They never went any farther than an esplanade to the right of the Kursaal building where the circus set up in the summertime. There his sister or the maid positioned him, facing the sea. In any case, they never took him on the bridge over the Urumea. He sat there watching the fishermen rod fishing for eels and grey mullet. And that's all he'd do until it was time to go home. He wasn't all that interested in getting out, but the doctor insisted he get some fresh air and not grow too lazy. When he was feeling depressed, he tended to think that the only reason for the doctor's advice was that he couldn't think of anything better to say; after all, Don Román was suffering from generalized progressive paralysis. That was a known fact, and sooner or later, whether he got fresh air or not, the paralysis would attack his vital organs.

"Yes, yes," admitted the doctor, "but don't forget that it is progressive and that the rate of progression depends on you."

He didn't believe this either, but no one could say he didn't try. And so he hired Pachi to take him out every day, even in the pouring rain. At least until Menchu married. Once she was settled, perhaps he'd let the progressive paralysis take over.

The Galician added a new dimension to his life because, in spite of Pachi's lumbago or rheumatism—it wasn't clear which of the two he was suffering from—he had no trouble pushing the wheelchair. This meant they could venture out on excursions to places that would have been impossible for Señorita Menchu to reach, given her limited strength. As he was being pushed down Paseo Nuevo, which ran along the seashore until it ended in the Fisherman's Wharf, Don Román thought that life from a wheelchair had much to offer: the blue sky, the flight of the seagulls, the white foam of waves splashing against the rocks, the odor of seaweed, the sea breeze, the music of rippling water, the images evoked by a sailboat on the horizon, the green slopes of Mount Urgull, the children playing pelota on the last esplanade next to the Wharf, and a mother calling out, "Careful, don't drop the ball into the sea." Life had just as much to offer whether one walked on his own two feet or was pushed in a wheelchair. Pachi remarked on it at home to his son.

"Don Román is sure easy to please."

One sunny afternoon—February had been beautiful—Planicio had to make a delivery to Calle Aldama, close to Paseo Nuevo, and he said to himself, Maybe I'll meet up with them. At his light half-trot, he calmly started up Paseo Nuevo—splat! splat!—until he saw them past the breakwater.

Aita was pushing the wheelchair effortlessly, and Don Román turned around every once in a while to say something to him. *Aita* answered and they both laughed. In the winter, *Aita* wore more or less the same thing as in the summer, the main difference being that he added a jacket. Planicio remembered him having only one—dark grey, almost black, with white stripes that with time had faded almost completely away. The other difference was that when Pachi took Don Román out, he put on his new beret, not that it was new but just not anywhere near as old as his other one, which still had fish scales on it from when he'd been a fisherman. From the back, *Aita* looked like a giant; it was only normal that he should push the wheelchair with so little effort. Planicio already knew that his father was a man of colossal strength who'd been in a regatta in the Concha Bay once with the crew for Pasajes de

San Pedro, and another time—how could he forget?—with the Fuenterrabía crew. And if it weren't for Pachi's lumbago—or rheumatism, whichever—that came from spending so many years at sea, the number of his exploits would have continued to grow. Planicio stopped running and followed them, walking at a safe distance because, all of a sudden, he felt embarrassed again. It was a workday and the Paseo was almost deserted. It must have been about five o'clock, and the sun was still hot as it dropped to the horizon and outlined the contrasting silhouettes of *Aita* and Don Román. He followed them a bit farther and was about to turn back because, there were no two ways about it, he was too embarrassed to approach them, when his father turned and looked back. The light was in his favor, and so in spite of the distance, he glimpsed Planicio. Pachi stopped the wheelchair and said something to Don Román. Then he turned the chair toward Planicio and gestured to him. The boy began his half-trot, blushing bright red because of the situation he found himself in.

Aita asked him, "Don't you know how to say hello?"

But Don Román spoke first.

"Good afternoon. How are you?"

Planicio answered, "Fine," and laughed nervously.

He noticed that *Aita* didn't seem to mind that he'd been spying on them. In fact, he even seemed pleased to have Don Román meet him, in spite of which, Pachi said, "How messy can you get? Just look at your shirt!"

He meant that Planicio's shirt tails were hanging out, but he couldn't do much about it; it was a shirt he'd had for two years that was too short and couldn't be made to stay in his pants no matter how tight he cinched his belt. That sort of thing usually didn't bother *Aita*, but Planicio understood that in front of such an elegant gentleman, his father had to say something. He undid his belt and held his pants up with one hand while he used the other to tuck his shirt in, although he already knew it would come out again as soon as he started running.

"What brings you out this way?" asked *Aita*.

"I'm coming back from a delivery."

"What an industrious boy," said Don Román. "How old are you?"

"Thirteen."

"He's going to be a strapping young fellow like yourself. Are you in a hurry?"

Planicio said no because he knew that at this time of day he wouldn't have to make any more deliveries.

"Well then, why don't you walk along with us for a bit?"

They resumed their walk, Planicio holding back slightly because he didn't know what to say. Don Román, as usual, wanted to know everything about his new companion. Why was he called Planicio? Pachi explained that it was because of his flat feet. The don broke into laughter.

"But do you think they really are? I don't think so. He's a very good-looking boy."

The subject of their conversation, Planicio, thought he was past the age when people should be commenting on his looks, but of course he said nothing.

The don asked him, "Do you like being called Planicio?"

Planicio shrugged his shoulders, and his father asked him whether the cat had got his tongue. "It doesn't matter to me. That's what they always call me."

His father added, "That's what we've always called him."

"It's a nice name," said the don. "Planicio. I like the sound of it."

Then he got on to the subject of school, and somewhat reluctantly Pachi pointed out that his son hadn't been to school for two years.

"Oh, no!" cried the don mournfully. "That's not right. Do you like to read?"

"Him?" broke in his father. "He can read any which way. Right side up or upside down—even sideways."

"Is that true?" asked Don Román, turning to face Planicio.

Planicio would have just shrugged his shoulders to show that it really wasn't important, but he didn't because *Aita* had already asked him whether the cat had got his tongue.

"Yes, Señor."

Aita motioned for him to come up alongside Don Román so the don wouldn't have to keep turning around to speak to him.

"Let's see then."

Don Román moved to take out the day's paper he always brought along in case he felt like reading, although generally he didn't, especially now that he was with Pachi and there was always something new to do. The newspaper was between him and the only arm of the wheelchair, the right one, and it was quite an effort for him to get it out with his opposite hand, his forearm being the only part of his arm he could easily move. At first Pachi had tried to help him in similar situations, but the don always said, somewhat curtly, "Leave be."

Finally he managed to take out the paper and show it to Planicio upside down. The surprising thing, even for someone as learned as Don Román, was the speed at which the boy could read in this strange position, without hesitation, rattling off the headlines and the small print with equal ease.

"Marvelous," he said in admiration. "Now we'll try sideways."

Planicio read just as well sideways.

The don said, "I think it's easier sideways, isn't it?"

This time Planicio did have to shrug his shoulders to show it didn't matter one way or another.

"Let me try," said Don Román.

He could read upside down and sideways too but only by changing positions so as to see better. It took him a lot longer than the boy. When he finished, he said, "Here, take this. You've earned it."

And he gave him a duro. He took it out of one of his vest pockets, a vest he wore all the time, winter or summer. It was a comfortable vest with somewhat larger pockets than usual that could hold just about anything—pens, pencils, agenda, billfold, coin pouch, handkerchief. . . . He used it because it was relatively easy for him to lift his hands to his chest.

It was a silver duro, and Planicio stretched out his hand timidly to take it, even though *Aita* was already saying, "No, in God's name, don't worry about it, Señor," because he knew that these were just things you had to say. But *Aita* had also taught Planicio that you mustn't offend anyone.

"Go on now and play with your little friends," said the don.

"Thank you very much." And Planicio left them at a half-trot.

The don said, "Come back sometime."

"Yes, Señor."

"We still haven't seen if you know how to read right side up." And *Aita* and he started to laugh.

Between the Paseo Nuevo breakwater and 10-B Miracruz was a whole world of possibilities for someone who had a silver duro, so different from the greyish bills Señora Asun gave him. Planicio wanted to save it, but at the same time he wanted to spend it, even if only part of it (spending it all at once would be a big mistake) just because of the way the don had given it to him. He would spend it but in good company. That's why, without a second thought, he went looking for Ramoncho, the boy who was younger than he—in fact he was a year younger—who'd become his best friend when the other kids from Urbistondos called him a Galician *tranposua*. Actually only one of them called him that, but the others had laughed. Not that he cared, the proof being that he was still their friend. The reason he didn't go to Atocha anymore was so he wouldn't displease *Aita*. But his real friend was Ramoncho, and together they played pelota against the fence at the station, although ever since *Aita* had quit playing, Planicio wasn't very interested in it anymore either.

He went to wait for Ramoncho outside the school yard, off

to the side a little so that he wouldn't meet up with a teacher who might ask him why he wasn't in school. When he saw his friend appear, he whistled their signal. Ramoncho lifted his head, alert, and Planicio whistled a second time to help give him his bearings. As soon as Ramoncho spotted Planicio, he left the others, came over and stood in front of him without greeting him because they never did; he just stood there as though asking what he wanted. Planicio opened his right hand and showed him the silver duro.

"Wow!" Ramoncho said with great satisfaction because by showing him the money, Planicio was implying there'd be fun to come. And just as he'd suspected, Planicio said, "Let's go."

His friend started up at the mandatory half-trot because he knew that with Planicio there was no other way to go.

"Where are we going?"

"To Berridi," answered Planicio.

Of course. In the summer, they could choose between it and the ice cream shop on Paseo de Colón, but in the winter, it was a foregone conclusion: Berridi's pastry shop. And once they were inside the shop, there wasn't much hesitation either because the Berlin cream puffs, fried on the outside with cream on the inside, were unrivaled as to price and quantity. They each took one, and Planicio ordered two more, wrapped to go. They stopped off at Ramoncho's house so his mother wouldn't wonder why he hadn't shown up for his after-school snack of bread and chocolate, and then went to the Trueba movie house, to the entrance to the peanut gallery, which cost fifty centimos. The theater was divided into orchestra seats, mezzanine seats and the upper gallery. The latter was outfitted with backless wooden benches on an incline; tickets for it weren't sold in the main lobby of the theater, but in a side alley from which one entered as well. Usually pandemonium reigned at show time, and it wasn't hard to sneak in, although Planicio of course never tried. On the rate card, it was listed as the upper gallery, but everyone called it the peanut gallery.

They saw the *Hyena of Fifth Avenue,* which was about an old lady who wore a hairnet and a cameo on a ribbon around her neck, and had to walk using a cane. For reasons that were never fully explained, she had to kill quite a number of people, generally by putting poison in their tea, but once, when the poison didn't work, she finished off a man with her cane. All of them were relatives of hers, an inheritance was involved somehow and the main heiress was a niece, very pretty, with whom Planicio fell immediately in love. It was hard to take because the whole plot revolved around the aunt pretending she loved her niece dearly when in truth she was just waiting for the right moment to kill her. The house on Fifth Avenue was equipped with many secret doors, and every time one of them opened close to the beautiful niece, the whole peanut gallery of the Trueba cinema roared out a warning. Fortunately a reporter who suspected something was up fell in love with the young girl, which was only natural (any other man would have done the same) and at the last minute saved her from her aunt—the hyena of the title—who offered her some of her special tea and was preparing to finish her off with a knife, just in case. But the reporter had substituted a light tranquilizer for the poison and arrived in the nick of time with a small brigade of policemen, thus preventing her from dealing the final blow, but just barely.

Ramoncho left hugely relieved that all had ended well, but Planicio was less so because he couldn't rid himself of the picture of the room they had discovered full of all the dead bodies she'd murdered.

Ramoncho went on his way. "Bye and thanks." Then he added, "You know."

"You know," meant, "When I can I'll treat you too."

Planicio crossed the road and was home already because the Trueba movie theater was just across the street. Francisca the concierge told him that his father hadn't come back yet, and he stood there telling her about the movie. The concierge kept exclaiming, *"Ené,* how awful," but it didn't stop her from asking for more details about the murders. Afterward, in exchange, she told him about a crime in the village of Rentería that also involved an inheritance. She knew all the gory details because when it happened she was still living there.

With his head full of crimes and his father still away, Planicio climbed up to the garret and fell asleep feeling somewhat frightened but not too much because he started to think about the girl in the movie and imagined he was the reporter.

ONE AFTERNOON in March when it threatened to rain, Don Román and Pachi began their journey down Paseo Nuevo but not without certain misgivings. Just in case, they had brought along an umbrella, and Señorita Menchu had covered Don Román's legs with a gabardine. The don didn't like having it on because it made him look even more like an invalid, and when they were out of sight of the house, he asked Pachi to take it off. Pachi did so and put it on the back of the chair where the umbrella hung. Before reaching the breakwater, Pachi remarked to the don, "Don Román, it looks like rain."

"Don't tell me a sailor such as yourself is afraid of a bit of rain?"

"I only mention it because I used to be. I'm not talking about a bit of rain; I'm talking about a real storm. We'd better go this way."

The preceding days had been much too hot for March, which usually meant they were in for a stormy northwest wind. Just then, a huge gust of wind blew up, accompanied by large drops of rain. Pachi stepped up his pace. With this wind blowing, it wouldn't be easy to open the umbrella, and he was afraid what a drenching would do to his charge. On days when the weather was poor, Señorita Menchu always warned Pachi before he set out, "Please, Pachi, make sure he doesn't get wet."

Whenever she spoke to him, Señorita Menchu spoke in a gentle tone, quite different from the one she used with the

maid or even with Don Román. He in turn showed due respect
to the don's sister, a genuine lady with a good foundation—not
for him of course—and long slim legs, always clothed in silk
stockings, and such an austere dress that it was difficult to
fully appreciate the beauty Señora Asun referred to in her sign.
Señorita Menchu's face was that of a timid girl, although her
youth was behind her now, but this, in Pachi's eyes, gave her a
certain air of a woman needing comforting. If it's comforting
you want, it's comforting you'll get, said the Galician to himself, examining her foundation. He had a very crude idea of
the type of comfort a woman needed and didn't really distin-
guish between one woman and another. Women are all the
same, he philosophized, but Señorita Menchu was slightly different, and he liked that such a refined woman treated him
with regard, which is why he didn't want to have to go back
with Don Román drenched to the skin. He thought he'd have
enough time to distance themselves from the sea and make it
to the Boulevard to take shelter under the arcades, but it
wasn't meant to be because the storm broke earlier than
planned.

It was a strange afternoon. They had barely enough time to
find shelter under the eaves along Calle de San Vicente, close
to the old quarter and San Telmo Museum Square. It was
incredible the way the rain fell, and as for Don Román, he was
quite entertained by their adventure. Pachi put the don's raincoat on as though he were a child and without Don Román
raising any objections. Taking advantage of the fact that there
was very little wind in their shelter, Pachi opened the umbrella
for further protection from the elements. As for Pachi, he
could do little. He had to get wet because there wasn't enough
umbrella or eaves to shelter them both.

The don remarked, "But you're getting wet."

"It doesn't matter."

"Some fisherman you are," joked Don Román. "You don't
even know when a storm's going to break."

"No, but I warned you."

"You warned me too late."

The elaborate display of lightning and thunder increased in intensity, and the rain fell so hard they couldn't even see San Telmo Square anymore. But they could see the sign for the Aita Juan bar and restaurant right in front of them, under the eaves of their refuge.

"Should we go in?" asked Pachi loudly because the sound of the rain was deafening. Without waiting for an answer because there could be only one answer, he began maneuvering the wheelchair, no easy task if he were to stay under the sheltering eaves. With his right hand, he opened the door to Aita Juan, and with his left hand, he lifted the wheelchair over the step in the entranceway, first the front wheels, then the back ones. In order to maneuver properly, he had no choice but to drop the umbrella. It was immediately picked up by the wind and carried off down the street. Pachi stepped out, and in one sprint caught the umbrella. Turning to face the wind, he managed to close it.

As he entered the bar, he said to the don, "It's none the worse for wear." He was referring to the umbrella, which was dripping large quantities of water while Pachi checked the ribs and smoothed down the fabric. Afterward, he turned to the woman behind the counter, a wholesome lass with a bit of a mustache, and said "We're going to have to leave you with this mess."

The girl gave an understanding nod—in a bar such things happened—and said, "Bring it on over. I'll put it up to dry." Pachi gave her the umbrella and the girl added, "Your jacket too if you want. It's soaking!"

Pachi hesitated since he wasn't sure he should take off his jacket no matter how wet it was, but he finally gave in.

Don Román, protected as he'd been by the raincoat and the umbrella, wasn't the least bit wet, which was a source of some satisfaction to his assistant. Although Don Román wasn't in the habit of going to bars, he was a man of the world and so said to Pachi, "We'll have to buy something, don't you think?"

Yes, yes, he did think so. What's more, Pachi usually had no trouble making his choice: a bit of wine always went down well. A glass of *chacolí* or cider would do in certain circumstances, but red wine, a Rioja red from a wine skin, was good anytime. He ordered two small glasses without asking Don Román for his opinion. The latter just smiled in surprise.

"Wine at this time of day?"

Yes, why not? Although this wasn't his district, Pachi had, as it turned out, been in this bar before and knew they had a truly fine wine. As it turned out, there were very few bars Pachi didn't know and very few wines that didn't seem fine, truly fine to him.

The bar wasn't busy at that time of day—six o'clock in the evening. Some people were playing dominoes at two tables, and at another table two fishermen were smoking in silence. At first the players eyed the new arrivals since they weren't a usual pair, but they did so discreetly. People around here didn't make it their business to pry. As soon as Pachi saw Don Román pick up his glass and taste it with pleasure, he said to himself, He likes it.

"Yes, indeed," admitted the don. "You were right; it is a fine wine."

Pachi ascertained that Don Román liked wine in general and not just the Aita Juan's. He ordered two more small glasses with little reluctance on the don's part, and they began trading confidences. Don Román told him, "At home, they add water to my wine."

Pachi made him repeat what he'd just said, certain that he must have heard wrong.

"I'm not supposed to drink much because I put on weight, obviously. Since I don't exercise . . . So with my lunch I have a glass of water, that's all, but mixed with a bit of wine to add some taste. And another one at suppertime."

Pachi spoke with great conviction, "In my books, mixing the two of them together only serves to ruin them both."

Don Román laughed because his two small glasses had left him feeling quite happy.

From time to time, Pachi went to the door and said, "It's still raining."

They had to wait until eight o'clock until the shower turned into a more tolerable drizzle. At seven—the time they usually got back—they did two things. They called Señorita Menchu so she wouldn't worry about them being late, and they ordered a light meal. As to the first, it was a good thing they did telephone because the storm had the señorita worried, although she'd already assumed that he, Pachi, would have managed to find a place of refuge for them. As to the second, it was an even better idea because Don Román hadn't had a meal of cod sounds for years since it was well known that gelatin from the cod sounds was extremely fattening.

"That's ridiculous," argued Pachi the *Cimarrón*. "They're very easy to digest, and something that easy to digest just can't be fattening."

He spoke with such authority that Don Román felt comforted since he'd forgotten what a wonderful thing cod sounds in sauce could be. While they ate and drank—they had ordered their third and last small glass—Pachi related in minute detail the foods that were good for one, the ones that weren't and the circumstances that made a food fattening because they created empty fat instead of pure muscle. He went on to tell about the food they'd eaten while preparing for the Concha regattas without gaining any weight at all.

"Pachi," interrupted Don Román, "I'm afraid you can't compare my case to the oarsmen. I get fat just drinking a small glass of bottled water."

He spoke without bitterness, even with a touch of humor, although it was the kind of joke Pachi couldn't fathom or didn't want to because he'd been struck by the realization that the storm and the refuge they'd had to seek in Aita Juan had opened up new vistas on his condition as an assistant. Life wasn't just walking down Paseo Nuevo always facing a sea, which at times as he well knew could be inhospitable. Life had other things to offer that were within Don Román's grasp as well. The latter, after his cod sounds and wine, was beaming his satisfaction.

"Now all you have to do," comforted Pachi, "is to turn down supper when you go home and that's that."

Don Román concurred but had one objection. "Yes, but when Señorita Menchu finds out what I had to eat . . . "

"Who says she needs to know?" advised Pachi the *Cimarrón*.

When he was sailing off Newfoundland, the others used to call him the *Cimarrón*. Used by seafarers, the term usually meant a lazy sailor, but in Latin America—and many of the Basque sailors had worked routes in the Southern Hemisphere—it was also used to mean an animal or even a man who was untamed . . . and cunning. Pachi once sailed with a skipper who soon had his number and used to say to him, "You've turned into a real *cimarrón*." Actually he was referring to the cunning Pachi showed in always doing less than his share, and the way he'd only do something if there was something in it for him.

By the time they left, the drizzle was almost imperceptible, and above the sea, the clouds raced across the sky, opening onto empty spaces and star clusters lit by a lunar clarity because it was the March full moon.

"Tomorrow the tide will change," remarked Pachi. "Let's walk along the seashore so the sea breeze can blow away the color the wine's left in your cheeks."

Don Román laughed with obvious complicity because he had decided not to say a word to his sister. Not a word on specifics. He'd simply state that they'd eaten a little something—grilled hake, for instance—and that he wouldn't be having any supper. He wouldn't say that he didn't feel like having supper because his sister knew he was always hungry; even right after a meal, he was still hungry.

On the bridge over the estuary, it had stopped raining. The clouds were racing even faster across the sky, and the moon shone on the water. The tide was low and the estuary smelled strongly of sea verdigris. In those days, there were no terrible industrial smells.

"Stop here for a minute, please," asked Don Román. "Look over there. You can see the lights on Ulía."

Of course they could, but to Pachi's way of thinking, there was no special reason for commenting on it, although he understood this to be a reflection of the don's state of mind. Pachi had had occasion to be taken aback by other declarations Don Román made from time to time, like, "I owe a vote of thanks to God."

To Pachi this seemed to be the type of declaration one could expect from a Christian gentleman, which is what the don was known as in the parish of San Ignacio, but all the same it was not quite fair, considering the poor don had gotten the raw end of the deal. The man could barely move, and on top of that, eating a half-dozen cod sounds in sauce was a once in a lifetime occurrence, although he, Pachi, would soon change that.

PLANICIO LIKED his father's job with Señor Aldaiz, and in his budding adolescence he thought it only fitting to see *Aita* pushing Don Román's wheelchair and talking about what he supposed were important matters because the don was an important person. As well as a saint. Señora Asun kept reminding him of that fact.

"Your father is so lucky to work for Don Román. The poor man is a saint, a true saint." Then she'd add, "His sister is another matter." Señora Asun only knew the don slightly from having seen him in church, but she was categorical. "Your father is an extremely lucky man. And he certainly needed it."

This last bit she slipped in for another reason, to point out

to the boy that his father was not exactly a model of good con-
duct and that consequently the company of a saint would help
him change his ways. But Planicio thought she was referring
to the fifteen duros the don gave them every week.

In the budding adolescence of that year in which he was to
turn fourteen, Planicio was glad *Aita* had quarreled with the
Atocha pelota players and had become an assistant for the man
who had been, as his father put it, the Director of Revenue.
One day he went to look at the building behind Fisherman's
Wharf that housed the Provincial Revenue Delegation in San
Sebastian, a huge building made of sandstone with two guards
at the door, and was truly impressed to think that Don Román
had been at the head of all this.

"I," announced *Aita* in the surrounding taverns, "am now
the aide-de-camp for the man who used to be Director of Revenue."

He used the term aide-de-camp because he thought the title
sounded much more impressive in French. From the first
afternoon Don Román and Planicio met and from the day
Don Román and Pachi conspired together in order to savor
various gastronomical delights, the ties linking them had
strengthened.

"I'd like to see the boy again sometime," said Don Román
to his assistant who conveyed his words to the boy in question
who in turn endeavored to see the don as soon as he could.

"Señora Asun, do you think there will be any more deliveries this afternoon? I'd like to go and see Don Román."

Doña Asun always let him go since she felt she'd played an
important role in this friendship brought about through her
good graces—not directly but because she was active in the
parish—which could only be of great benefit to a wayward
father and an abandoned son.

Pachi—aide-de-camp—was quite pleased to have a second
assistant—his son—because it meant they could have even
greater adventures and between the two of them could push the

wheelchair uphill, sometimes as far as the top of Mount Urgull. Don Román was reluctant at first and protested.

"But I hate to think of you pushing me when I'm so heavy and the slopes are so steep."

"Nonsense, Don Román. The boy could even do it alone."

Pachi the *Cimarrón* quit pushing, and Planicio redoubled his efforts and pushed the wheelchair with great gratification. If the slope happened to be gentle at that spot, he'd start up his farm horse half-trot.

"God Almighty!" said Don Román.

"Leave him be!" encouraged Pachi. "He enjoys it."

Pushing the don uphill was in fact a source of great enjoyment to Planicio. When they arrived at a short steep incline or a pronounced curve, his father put out his hand to help.

"No, don't *Aita*. I can do it myself!" protested Planicio, who wanted to go as far as the flat stretch where the old cannons were without anyone helping him. Mount Urgull—backed by the old quarter, facing the sea and bordered by Paseo Nuevo—had always been a place of fascination and adventure for Planicio. Lately the adventures his friends were interested in left him puzzled. They said, "Let's go to Urgull and watch the couples."

Rumor had it that couples went up to Mount Urgull to embrace in spite of the zeal with which the local authorities, who in those days were very concerned with questions of public morality, tried to prevent such behavior.

"See that?" And they'd show him the sign saying NO TRESPASSING AFTER SUNDOWN. "That's there because once the sun goes down, all the guys and broads come up here to neck. Once I saw a girl with her skirt up around her waist."

The idea of seeing a lady with her skirt up around her waist did not excite Planicio in the least, but he went along with them sometimes anyway. They peered down every pathway, looking for couples in action, but usually they never saw a single soul. If they did happen to chance upon a couple, the latter would be in an uncompromising position, walking down the paved road, their fingers intertwined as was the custom at the time.

"It's because they're hiding," one boy complained.

"It's 'cause we have to come at night. I told you so," said another.

They kept talking and swapping stories, and finally decided to call out something rude at a safe distance to one couple or another, no matter how uncompromising their behavior.

But during the April afternoons, days of wonderful displays of light and color, they had Mount Urgull to themselves, and the two guards on duty greeted Don Román and his assistants with respect. His father lifted his hand to his beret in response. When they passed in front of the British cemetery, Don Román told Planicio the story of the Englishmen who came to lend a hand in the battles against the Carlistas or the Liberals, he wasn't quite sure which. The cemetery was in a state of utter abandon in the years during which Spain was no longer on friendly terms with the English, and blackberries grew everywhere between the tombs. They stopped and Pachi remarked, "Those bushes have great berries. Do you like black-berries, Don Román?"

Don Román nodded his head. Generally speaking he liked everything.

"In June then," continued Pachi, "we'll have to come back." He thought for a minute and then added, "It would be better in late June when they're ripe." But then after further thought, he pronounced, "This year mid-June might be best. Our spring has been so exceptionally warm."

"Aita," interrupted Planicio, "if you come picking too late, there'll be nothing left."

"I know where a few bushes are that not even God himself could find."

"Pachi, please," said Don Román reproachfully; he didn't like his assistant's habit of taking the Lord's name in vain.

The *Cimarrón* excused himself because he understood the don's position, although he'd already explained that he didn't do it on purpose.

"Blackberries," he continued. "When they're ripe, I like eating a few off the bush, but to be delicious, truly delicious, they need a bit of wine and sugar. And," he paused because he had something important to say, "against all logic they're better with white wine than with red wine."

He spoke these words humbly because it was well known that he preferred red wine and held white wine in contempt. But where blackberries were concerned, he'd had to bow to the evidence.

"But they'd be so fattening prepared that way," said Don Román.

To each his own obsession.

"What on earth can be fattening about them? Nothing at all! How on earth can a few blackberries in a bit of wine be fattening? They just make it easier to digest."

Leaving the British cemetery behind them, they continued uphill toward the esplanade where the old cannons stood. As they climbed, the noise of the waves slapping against the rocks along the shore dimmed; the sea seemed to stop moving, but its scent was still carried by the breeze as well as the scent of the mountain: wet earth, green ferns, wild mimosas, hydrangea here and there. . . . Don Román breathed in deeply, as deeply as possible because he knew that death would be his once the paralysis—which was progressive, one mustn't forget—reached his intercostal muscles and his lungs could no longer work as they should. Inhale, exhale, inhale, exhale . . . The air entered and exited his lungs fluidly, showing that his pectorals were still working properly. That's when he said, "I owe a vote of thanks to God."

Pachi the *Cimarrón* said to himself, Now I wonder if *that* isn't taking God's name in vain. But he didn't say a thing. Instead, he steered the conversation back to his pet subject.

"The sea breeze burns off fat, all of it."

"You think so?" said Don Román astonished. He didn't think so, but he reveled in the air of confidence Pachi took on when making such an assertion.

"And why not? I've got proof of it. The iodine in the breeze burns fat. Just like alcohol. If you throw some fat into alcohol, does it or does it not dissolve?"

"Yes, but . . ."

There were no buts about it. The same thing happened with iodine except that naturally the fat didn't dissolve immediately. Instead, it dissolved gradually as the iodine from the sea did its job.

The world of Pachi Lourido, who had at one time dispensed homemade medical remedies in Pasajes de San Pedro, was an attractive and primitive world, one that suited Don Román, who had spent too many years as a semi-invalid and was now becoming increasingly immobile, a precursor to the final immobility. Sometimes he felt that the people who surrounded him—Señorita Menchu, his other brother and sister when they visited him, and even the parish priest who had the best intentions in the world—were preparing him to accept the lot that must fall to him. As if it weren't going to happen to them, perhaps even before him. Meanwhile, they'd assigned him the role of a Christian gentleman. He didn't care if they charged him with being a gentleman and even less so a Christian as long as the charges were separate; the two together sounded ridiculous. Pachi not only encouraged him to drink wine without water, he convinced him—no more, no less—of its effectiveness in dissolving fat. And Pachi took liberties with him that the don had to nip in the bud, not without feeling secretly pleased however.

"Did you get a look at that woman, Don Román?"

Naturally he'd "gotten a look" at her, but it was better not to look too long because she was truly gorgeous, and his general paralysis wasn't as generalized as all that since it didn't affect his genitals in the least, and he had his problems in that regard just like everybody else. When he was sorely tempted, he sometimes felt that the wonderful gift of procreation was a mixed blessing, especially in his case, but as time went on he decided he'd rather have to put up a fight and be a whole man than be forced to be a eunuch. It seemed to him that most people saw him as the latter, which is why he was pleased whenever the *Cimarrón* said, "Did you get a look at that woman, Don Román?"

"Yes, Pachi, I have eyes in my head."

As long as his pectoral muscles were in good working order—inhaling and exhaling the sea breeze, the smell of fern, of moss, of earth, of fir trees, of grass, of wet wood—he owed a vote of thanks to God. Likewise if the other worked well because it was a sign of life, and life was something wonderful, especially when Planicio, all excited, said, "We're there, Don Román!"

They arrived at the walled-in ancient cannons where they parked his wheelchair like one more cannon in an empty embrasure.

"Let me do it, *Aita*. I can do it," and the boy maneuvered the wheelchair by himself to a safe vantage point from which Don Román could see forever.

Feelings, perceptions, love. The shameless Galician perceived that he, Don Román Aldaiz, also felt the pull of that good-looking woman they'd passed on the Kursaal Bridge, and he looked at him, the invalid, with curiosity, sympathy. It was a malediction but God be praised because many were worse off than he, and they didn't have Pachi or Planicio to take them along on extraordinary adventures. He felt a tremendous surge of love for the boy who was so happy he'd managed to place the don's wheelchair just right in the embrasure, giving him a panoramic view of their surroundings. The whole world stretched out in front of him, Mount Igueldo to the left, rising up from the bottom of the sea against an azure sky, topped by a watchtower, and to the right Mount Ulía. Was there anything else in the world to see? The three of them stayed there without speaking, and Pachi rolled a cigarette, one not made out of butts.

Tobacco ration cards were used in those days, and Pachi had Don Román's card as well as his own since the don didn't smoke but had agreed to take out a card, somewhat against his principles, for his assistant. As well, his old friends from the Revenue Delegation gave him confiscated tobacco to hand out. One of the people he handed it out to was Pachi, who thanked him, drew on the cigarette like a true connoisseur and said to his benefactor, "Your friends smoke good tobacco."

Don Román enjoyed seeing his pleasure. He told his friends about the Galician. "That man is like a child. It doesn't take much to make him happy."

Don Román thought San Sebastian was the most beautiful city in the world and Planicio agreed. Pachi, for his part, remained skeptical.

"Why do you think this pinhead," referring to his son, "says it's the most beautiful city in the world? Could it be he's seen all the other cities?"

Don Román, who obviously didn't know every other city in the world, felt the remark was being directed at him.

"Pachi, dear fellow, it's just a saying. I don't know many other cities either, but of those I've seen, San Sebastian is the most beautiful."

"So you can say it's the most beautiful city you've seen, and it would be true, but this pinhead who's never been any further than Fuenterrabía, how can he say it's the most beautiful city in the world?"

Planicio kept quiet because Don Román was there to defend the principle, but the don didn't want to insist too much and settled for a compromise: that Concha Bay was exceptional, only to be compared with the bay in Río de Janeiro, which none of them had seen personally, only on postcards, but which those who had seen all agreed on.

Planicio started climbing the rocks. He gained altitude quickly because they were so steep. In a matter of minutes, his father and the don were outlined against the sea in miniature. Having gone as far as he could—a rock peak that went nowhere—he called down, "Don Román!"

He called out to the don because he knew he'd be amazed by his feat. In effect, he saw the don move his head in the direction from which the call had come, with difficulty because his neck had already been affected, and then *Aita* turned the chair around so he could see better. The don gave a slight wave of his forearm, and Planicio responded, waving his two arms like the blades of a windmill over his head. He started down again, looking for footholds in the rock, happy in the knowledge he was being watched. For the last part of the descent—still rocky but no longer steep—he jumped nimbly from boulder to boulder, nimbly and bravely, such that when he arrived, the don said to him, "It gave me a scare seeing you up that high."

"Someday he'll break his neck," added his father but with a touch of pride in his voice. Sometimes Pachi grabbed his son's head and said, "Knucklehead."

Planicio had noticed that *Aita* was more affectionate with him in front of the don. When Don Román insisted that the boy had to go back to school, his father sighed as though crushed by the weight of fatherhood in such bad, such difficult times, especially for a widower suffering from health problems—lumbago or rheumatism, whichever.

They noticed the sun beginning to set—a sign that it would soon be the forbidden hour on Mount Urgull, the witching hour for lustful couples—and began their descent. In the steep bends, Pachi said to himself, Easy does it, trying not to think what would happen if they let go of the wheelchair; but Planicio held on tightly, and just in case, Pachi kept his hand on the handle. At the end of the Paseo where the lights of the city—actually of the old quarter—started to twinkle, the two conspirators bade farewell to the boy.

"Off home with you," his father said.

Most days Don Román insisted on giving him a peseta, and Planicio took it so as not to be disrespectful, but often he would rather not have it.

"Don't bother, Don Román. I don't need it."

"You'll come tomorrow?" asked Don Román.

"Yes, if I can, Señor," and he set off at his half-trot.

The two conspirators penetrated the old quarter.

"Someone told me about a place. I've never been," warned the *Cimarrón* prudently, "but they say it's got the best pea stew around. It's called Zandi's. I don't know exactly where it is, but we'll find it."

They found it of course without even having to ask directions. They were conspirators because Don Román had told Señorita Menchu it was better if he didn't eat a late meal since he slept poorly afterward and had nightmares. Instead, he had a light, very light, meal at seven, which was enough. Whether or not it was light depended on the Galician, who struck up conversations with the waitresses, half in Spanish, half in Basque, to see what that evening's offerings were. Don Román could understand some of what they said, but he let the Galician translate for him.

"She says they have a codfish in tomato sauce that's out of this world."

Before a decision was made, Pachi would debate the point of whether codfish could be cooked in tomato sauce or whether it had to be in a coriander sauce. Also, for Don Román's benefit, they discussed its digestive properties, although there was proof enough it was hard to have an upset stomach if one ate with relish.

"No, I didn't say it upsets my stomach," Don Román defended himself, with little conviction however, "but that it's fattening."

Pachi pondered the situation, then grasped the dish with his hand, his broad pelota player's hand, and concluded, "Don

Román, don't be silly. How could this dish be fattening?"

The former medical charlatan and gourmand from Pasajes de San Pedro might very well be right because Don Román hadn't gained much weight over the preceding month and his tests had come out fine. In other words, they showed a moderate amount of fats and cholesterol but not much more than before. Of course, he was quite careful about how much he ate, although he encouraged Pachi to have more.

"You'll have seconds, won't you?"

After some display of resistance, Pachi did have seconds, and Don Román, seeing his enjoyment, had to call on all his willpower. His appetite was huge, but he had an obligation to live as long as possible under the best possible conditions. For Señorita Menchu's sake and for the students he was tutoring for the liquidators exam. And what else? For Planicio too, up high on the rock, calling out to him in excitement, Don Román! And for this little wine he had to make last so as not to have more than two glasses. It made it all worthwhile. Life itself made living worthwhile, although many mornings he would rather not wake up so as not to have to go through the enormous effort of doing what had to be done to be seen living out his life—getting up, washing himself, shaving, getting dressed—with the feeling that just knotting his tie every day required that extra little effort and was that much more difficult.

"Pachi, tell me about the time you rowed on the Fuenterrabía crew."

HIS AIDE-DE-CAMP wouldn't allow routine to set in. Around four o'clock he appeared at the apartment on Calle de Ramón y Cajal, and by the way he rang the bell, they knew who it was. The first ring was long and could have been anyone, but it was followed by a rash of short rings in groups of three.

"He's here now," Señorita Menchu said.

She said "he" instead of Pachi but not out of contempt

because Pachi was very refined and educated around ladies. In fact, she felt a bit envious seeing how much her brother loved his afternoon walks. She was happy for him obviously, but there was almost too much of a contrast with the way he used to act when the doorman was responsible for taking him out and he had to be forced to go.

"Where will you go today?" Señorita Menchu asked.

"I don't know. It depends on what he feels like doing."

Don Román referred to Pachi as "he" as well, following his sister's lead, but he started getting nervous if the maid took too long letting him in or if Pachi was late because "around four o'clock" could just as well mean four-thirty or a quarter to five. Among other reasons, his aide-de-camp didn't have a watch and saw no need for one since "the Man upstairs"—he touched his cap respectfully whenever he said this—was doing all the counting, and no matter how often you looked at the time, the hours had already been measured out in advance.

"We're late today," Don Román said reproachfully.

"Don't worry. We've got lots of time."

Pachi didn't need help anymore getting the don ready for the outing, and the whole procedure of transferring his charge from the armchair to the wheelchair was carried out with admirable precision. There was not one superfluous movement on his part, and he made sure that Don Román did as much work as possible. Watching the don get out of his chair was still a wrenching experience when first he'd concentrate then throw his huge fat-laden body upwards. It reminded Pachi of the effort involved in the first stroke of the oar, an abrupt pushing of the oar against the water with all his might because the start that his team got off to could be a decisive factor in its final placing in the regatta. Similarly, if Don Román couldn't manage to give himself enough impetus initially, he stayed bent over, his face livid, suspended an instant in space before plummeting back into his armchair. There was no point reaching out to him because he invariably said quite curtly, "Leave be."

The important thing was for him to make the effort alone because the day he could no longer stand up on his own, he'd know that the progressive part of his disease was getting too close to his vital centers. That spring he managed every time, however; generally after the first try and always after the second. When he did have to try again, he usually said, "I'm getting so lazy!"

In other words, the reason he hadn't made it on the first try was that he hadn't tried hard enough and not because his condition was worsening. In any case, every time he began the whole procedure, Señorita Menchu said, "Be careful."

That was all. "Be careful," without being specific. Just like a woman, thought Pachi while he examined Señorita Menchu's foundation on the sly. He sometimes thought her face looked too flaccid, unmade-up as it was, but from her neck down, she was perfect. No matter how little attention she paid to enhancing the beauty Señora Asun touted, she could in no way hide the firmness of the flesh around her foundation. When she helped him push the wheelchair over, he, with a careless hip movement, could verify that fact to his satisfaction with no protest from her.

During the transfer they usually kept silent. Once Don Román was standing—he had to be standing just right with his back positioned so as not to lose his balance—the tension dissipated because the rest was just a question of skill. Once seated in the wheelchair, Don Román wore the look of a contented child. Señorita Menchu accompanied them to the door and said more or less the same thing every time.

"Take care of him for me."

She spoke in a motherly tone and the Galician replied, "Don't worry."

She usually added, "Don't come home too late."

And the Galician nodded his head. That her brother had a light meal instead of dinner suited her fine, not for dietary reasons but because it meant she could go for tea with friends to

Garibay, and then they didn't have to prepare dinner. If the maid wanted to eat, she could fry herself an egg, although eggs were scarce these days. The price of farm eggs was out of this world, and storebought eggs tasted stale. Sometimes they were inedible. But her brother, at night, when he saw she hadn't eaten either, asked her, "Has the girl eaten?" Yes, of course. What a thing to worry about. A saint he was but a foolish one because these freeloaders ate better than they did; no beans or chick peas for them.

Once in the street, the aide-de-camp turned into a field marshal and began giving orders.

"Don Román, today since the sea's rough and high tide's at six o'clock, we can go watch the waves breaking. How does that sound?"

It sounded fine and on the way, Pachi told stories about his trips at sea with waves crashing over the boat. That was why the *Cimarrón* knew what a real wave was and what it would do in any given circumstance, and so he knew where to put Don Román's wheelchair so he could watch the waves breaking against the Paseo as though he were in the first row of the theater, without getting a drop on him.

The sea rose up about half a mile from the coast, taking on a threatening air. It looked like the wave taking form would be so huge it would wash away half the esplanade in its wake, like the February tides had done, but Pachi said, "It won't reach us. It'll stop at the breakwater."

Pachi didn't explain why, but his prediction was borne out. Don Román didn't ask either, fascinated by the mystery of not knowing the reasons for its behavior.

"That's where the next wave will be," said the Galician crossly, and he yelled at some children playing next to the breakwater to watch out, they were going to get wet. But the children ignored him; they wanted to get wet.

Close to the coast, at no more than a quarter mile, the sea suctioned up all the water foaming noisily over the rocks, leaving them bared, shining with mussels, goose barnacles and lichen. Out of this mass rose a headlong wave that curled up, fine as a whip, then exploded against the edge of the breakwater, sending a bubbling flood weeping over the esplanade, and drenching the children and any unsuspecting passersby. It never touched Don Román—why else did he have an aide-de-camp who had spent twenty-two years at sea? Sometimes, depending on the sun's position in the sky, its rays hit the fan created by the water on the esplanade, and for an instant a rainbow appeared. This was what Don Román liked best, which Pachi could understand, although Pachi himself had seen more than his share. But he encouraged his charge.

"You'll see, Don Román, when it's time for September's strong tides. . . ."

Neither man spoke because the September tides were legendary and on more than one occasion had leveled beach houses; even the breakwater had had to be rebuilt.

"Then those numskulls," referring to the children who were laughing happily at their sodden state, "will have to be careful if they don't want to be swept out to sea by a wave."

Life with Pachi was an explosion of promises: when summer came, or even slightly earlier, they'd go up the mount to pick ripe blackberries in a place so hidden that only he, Pachi, and the Supreme Creator knew of its whereabouts, although the *Cimarrón* couldn't even be sure about the latter. Then they'd prepare the berries in wine and sugar, given—as an exceptional exception—that in this case white wine was better than red. Ever since Pachi had mentioned the possibility a month ago, Don Román could feel the exciting taste of the wild secret blackberries on his palate. In September Pachi would take him to see the strong tides with waves so high they cleared bridges like race horses but with no danger to him because he, the clever *Cimarrón,* knew of a place so protected that not even a drop would reach his charge. To the don who spent his mornings drilling Rate III into his students, it seemed that Pachi was a pact he had with hope, a pact that the summer solstice would be there for him too and that his pectoral muscles—in and out—would continue functioning reasonably well.

To Pachi it seemed that when they turned their backs on the building on Ramón y Cajal, his charge became another man. In the apartment, in the elevator on the way down, even on the stairs at the entrance, the don seemed worried, upset at all the maneuvering his departure required, its complexity adding a contrasting movement to the sonata of hope for a summer sol-stice. On the street he let himself be led—let's go here or there—quite naturally. In the apartment, the don fought too hard for something that obviously couldn't be. If they would let him, Pachi could easily transfer the don from his armchair into the wheelchair and thus spare him the anguish-filled effort of standing up on his own. Once, when he first began working as the don's assistant, the experience was particularly trying because the don failed on his first attempt and a fairly loud noise escaped from him. Too loud to be ignored.

Pachi said, "To your health!"

It was a custom at sea, as long as one didn't go too far either burping or farting, to show some solicitude to the person responsible. Not of course when they had eaten pork and beans, and were having farting contests. Youth would have out, and then there was the boredom of being on the seas. In any case, they held the contests on deck so there was no problem with odors, although some went farther than they wanted to.

And so when the don broke wind, Pachi found it only natur-al under the circumstances to say, "To your health!"

Don Román, however, who because of the effort he was making should have been purple, turned red to the very roots of his hair and didn't even thank him for his expression of concern. Pachi also noticed Señorita Menchu's expression undergo a sudden change, and he remembered that his late wife, Bea, who was from a refined household and had taken needlework with the nuns when she was little, used to say to him, "When someone breaks wind, don't say a word, not one word." But he hadn't said anything. He'd just expressed his good wishes and nothing more.

In any case, they were better off out in the street where that kind of situation didn't arise. He also thought there might be a few problems with the excessive fondness with which Señorita Menchu asked him, "Look after him for me." It would be natural to think the fondness was for her brother, but it wasn't all that clear. The señorita might have designs on him, not in the usual sense, but more like hoping he'd be a better father and attend church more often since she too was part of the church women's group. She did always refer to Planicio as "That poor boy." It wouldn't have surprised him either to find out she had other designs because Pachi had always been a lady-killer, and that's why he'd married a Garmendía girl from the Alza family farm when he was nothing but a fisherman from the Galician quarter of Trincherpe in Pasajes. The eldest brother, who was an asshole, was the legal heir and refused to even let his sister into the family home under the pretext that she'd married against her parents' wishes. After the war, in spite of the tough time they'd had, her brother never even sent them a lousy bean.

Don Román was a special kind of man who inspired confidences, and even his aide-de-camp had confided in him somewhat. Pachi thought it a waste of time and quite impractical to hate one's kin, very impractical, but if he could he would stab his brother-in-law with a knife, the kind used to chop off tuna fish heads.

"In the stomach," he specified to Don Román. "I'd stab him in the stomach, so I could see his face when he realized it's me."

Don Román, although it could be expected of him, did not point out how un-Christian something like that would be. He just listened.

"When Bea died he came to the funeral so there wouldn't be talk in the village. He tried to talk to me, but I said in front of everyone, 'Now that I don't have to hold back for her, some-day I'm going to kick your balls so hard, they'll pop out through your teeth.'"

Although this act was horrible to imagine and the language crude, Don Román knew enough to give an understanding nod.

"He acted as though he took it all out of respect for the deceased, but I wouldn't even let him in to see her. He should have shown more concern for her while she was still alive; he couldn't even send us a lousy bean after the war when we didn't have a thing to eat."

Don Román agreed with him but told him his brother-in-law had suffered enough for being who he was and what he needed more than anything was compassion.

"Compassion? The same compassion he showed *them* then. When *the others* arrived in town, he was so afraid of having his house taken away from him that he made quick to denounce all the Reds. Because of him more than one person was ruined in Trincherpe." Pachi, when he mentioned the war of '36, which was very rare, referred to "they" and "the others," and everyone knew who he meant, but he also made it clear that he didn't belong to either camp, which is why he'd gone fishing off Canada for two years. He didn't tell Don Román that because it was better not to mention such things. But he did say, "The old fart struts around now wearing a red beret, saying he's always been a traditionalist, and do you know why?"

No, no, of course Don Román didn't know why, but Pachi explained it to him. "Because they had a grandfather they say was in the first Carlist war. Do you know what he really did?"

No, no, Don Román didn't know that either.

"He smuggled in mules from France, which he sold to the Carlist army. That's the money they used to buy their house with."

Don Román was a perfect person to confide in because he was a good listener and was genuinely interested in other people's lives.

"Today the Garmendías think they're really something, but everyone in Fuenterrabía knows the grandfather was a smuggler and that my father-in-law, before he inherited the house, was one too."

But as far as he was concerned, they could all screw themselves; he'd taken Bea away, the only one in that whole family with any sense. Pachi was cold and skeptical, but in spite of everything, he couldn't rid himself of the idea of the knife in the stomach—not for his sake but to repay them for making his wife suffer.

Don Román, as well as being a good listener, also knew how to adapt to the mental process of the person he was speaking to.

"Look, Pachi," he argued, "do you really think your late wife cares one way or another whether you have it out with her brother? Or that your son, Planicio, cares?"

"No," Pachi assured him. "I wouldn't go through with it."

"Sometimes it's worse to think about doing something than doing it. If you did end up stabbing him, the deed would be done once and for all, but . . . spending a whole lifetime thinking about doing it can't be healthy in the long run. You're not on the right path, the right religious path, Pachi."

"No, I'm not. That's true," admitted the culprit.

"If you keep piling sins of hatred onto each other, you'll end up worse off than if you had carried through with it. Take, for example, the thought you had on the day of your wife's burial, the one about kicking your brother-in-law in a certain place so hard that a certain something would come out of his teeth."

Pachi was shrewd. He knew what the don was getting at, and he thought it a show of great confidence for the don to joke with him this way.

LIFE WITH PACHI was an explosion of possibilities that only grew when Planicio appeared. The boy never erred in his instinct about where to find them. On nice days—and that spring the weather was almost always nice—he looked for them down by the sea; the sea held a magnetic attraction for Don Román.

"At a distance and under sunny skies, I don't mind it either," conceded his aide-de-camp. "But it was another story being out on it."

In 1932, while training with Fuenterrabía, their boat capsized outside of the headland. The sea was rough, and it took two hours before they were rescued because not even the fishing boats could come looking for them. He'd already told the coxswain that it wasn't a day to be out rowing, but the latter had retorted, in front of the others, "Shithead Galician. What do you want? A row on the town pond?"

"Me, a chickenhead?" said Pachi infuriated, having misunderstood.

"No," replied the other in Spanish. "Shithead, with *sh* for shit."

"Oh, all right then."

In those days coxswains had a great deal of prestige and authority, and they treated their oarsmen poorly, insulting them with many references to their testicular deficiencies. They pestered Pachi too about his being a Galician, something that didn't bother him in the least. He might be a Galician, but when the chips were down, when they needed the person with the most guts and the most of a certain something else, they'd end up putting him in the bow.

Pachi told these stories while pushing the wheelchair along paths bordering the sea, either toward Mount Ulía or along Paseo Nuevo. Don Román listened with interest, asking for details. Not too often because sometimes he had trouble speaking—a facial rigidity that made him stutter. There were good and bad days, which made him think that the problem was more related to nerves than anything else.

Sometimes Planicio went the wrong way. He'd start up Paseo Nuevo and halfway up realize they weren't there. Without batting an eyelash, he'd do an about-face and begin to run toward the other end of the city, to the outskirts, in the direction of Mount Ulía. His easy stride is what eventually brought him fame as a runner, the prelude to the bridge challenge. When he glimpsed the unmistakable pair off in the distance, he accelerated his half-trot. On quiet solitary days when the sea was calm, Don Román heard the footsteps—splat! splat! (Planicio ran flatfooted, which made the flapping noise)—and said to his aide-de-camp, "Planicio's here."

At other times it was the boy who called out from a distance, "Don Román!"

The don had Pachi stop and, despite the effort it cost him, turned his head slightly and waved his forearm in welcome. His smile wasn't pretty because his face was so fat, and sometimes the tip of his tongue stuck out between his lips, but his eyes were big and dark, and they were laughing when Planicio drew closer. The two looked at each other without saying a word, and the Galician, so as not to be left out, grasped his son by the shoulder.

He did things like that around Don Román, although it was out of character for him and his kind, so Señorita Menchu would stop saying, "That poor boy." It was obvious Señorita Menchu wasn't interested in the boy, whom she'd only seen a couple of times, nor was the kindness in her expression the usual one for her relations with her brother, nor needless to say, with the maid. Frequently Pachi thought that the brother and sister were concerned for his soul; Don Román had insinuated as much. But Señorita Menchu's concern could be of another sort, especially seeing that his attempts at ascertaining the width of her foundation had not met with any resistance. Although he knew he was a lady-killer, he was not in the least bit interested; he was quite content with his role as aide-de-camp. He saw a future there and had no intention of complicating matters. Aside from that, her seeming compliance with his attempts at brushing up against her might not mean anything, especially in a social class he knew absolutely nothing about. He kept his thoughts to himself, but then, stubbornly he said to himself, Maybe. But all women are the same. He was referring to their anatomical similarity and to their reactions.

The two looked at each other, and Planicio said, "Did you bring it, Don Román?"

"What was I supposed to bring?"

It was like a child's game, and Pachi contemplated them benevolently.

"The book you promised me, Don Román."

Robinson Crusoe, Buffalo Bill, Dick Turpin, Twenty Thousand Leagues Under the Sea, Voyage to the Centre of the Earth, Around the World in Eighty Days, The Black Pirate, Sandokán, and *Raffles, the Gentleman Burglar.* Books with yellowed pages, the same ones Don Román had read forty years ago and that he kept carefully on the bookshelf in a spare room, together with the ones he'd used to prepare for the liquidators exam, these last books carefully underlined in red and blue.

"But Don Román, what book was it you gave him yesterday that had him sniveling all night long like an idiot?" said Pachi reproachfully.

"Which one was it, Planicio?" inquired the don.

The boy kept quiet since he was ashamed to admit he'd cried with Uncle Tom who'd saved, at great risk to his own life and without a second thought, the girl Evangeline from the turbulent waters of the Mississippi. Evangeline, the daughter of the rich landowner Augustine St. Clare who, in spite of his promise, did not free this exemplary Negro. And *Aita* didn't know it, but when Evangeline, before she died of tuberculosis, gave a lock of her blond hair to the Negro Tom, he, Planicio, had broken into such sobs he had had to go out on the terrasse to cry openly. "Oh, *Amá!*" he'd said because it reminded him of his mother. Nobody had ever told him how she died, but it might have been from tuberculosis like Evangeline. In any case, he felt such sorrow for all the Negroes in *Uncle Tom's*

Cabin and in the world in general that he kept on sobbing in bed, but softly with his head under the pillow so *Aita* wouldn't hear. Nevertheless, life was worth living as long as there were people like Uncle Tom, people who died forgiving everyone— including the slave trader Legree, the one who'd whipped him to death—in the arms of his former master and friend George, who arrived too late to buy him his freedom. But then, in an aside, Planicio confessed to Don Román, *"Ené,* Don Román. It was so sad." And the don relived the sorrow he himself had felt for characters who could have existed.

"Do you really think Uncle Tom existed?"

"He could have."

"But it wouldn't have been as bad," said Planicio to console himself.

Don Román thought that it could very well have been even worse, but he smiled with his dark eyes to alleviate the boy's pain.

"You don't read?" the don asked his assistant, meaning did he like to read.

"No, sir," replied the other, meaning he didn't know how to read.

"But you should read," advised Don Román.

"You don't say," replied the Galician roguishly, knowing what the don meant but amused by the misunderstanding. He played along but not because it mattered to him whether or not Don Román discovered he couldn't read. He didn't have anything against reading and understood that times had changed, although he wasn't so sure after seeing how it could make a thirteen-year-old boy snivel.

One day when they were alone, Planicio told Don Román, *"Aita* doesn't know how to read. He says that in his day kids didn't learn. They worked as cabin boys."

The don felt terrible, thinking he'd offended his assistant. As soon as he could he begged his forgiveness and offered to teach him.

"A man as intelligent as you are could learn in less than a month."

Pachi was appalled at the suggestion and cut him off right there. "Thank you very much, Don Román, but reading should be left to men like you."

To men like him? Paralyzed and no good for anything else? No matter how well he took his illness, he was sometimes afflicted with doubts of the kind. That's why he was so specially attracted to Planicio, who was always overjoyed to see him.

"Don Román! . . . " Planicio cried from the top of the mountain, drawing out the *a* just so he'd turn his head and smile.

He could tell the boy's happiness at seeing him was not affected in the least by his circumstances; the boy didn't even look at him strangely when he had to contort his body, trying to find a more comfortable position in the wheelchair.

"Can I help, Don Román?" he asked.

And when it was the boy who asked, the don did let him help a bit.

"Listen, push my left shoulder over this way a bit. There, there. Not too hard, mind."

During long walks his huge body had a tendency to lean to the left for no apparent reason, and he had to counter the movement by hanging on to the right arm of the chair. He let himself be pushed back lightly by the boy who looked as though he'd been given the most important job in the world.

"How's that, Don Román?"

He'd say fine even if a crease had appeared in his pants between his legs because the boy was so proud of himself.

Pachi, at the time of the bridge challenge, broke down and accused his son, "Any dumber and you wouldn't even have been born."

It was the same thing that infuriated him when Planicio let someone else win a pelota game he could have won hands down at Urbistondos under the pretext that it didn't matter, that they were just playing for fun. In other words his son didn't attach importance to the most vital issues—a pelota game, a race one had been challenged to where money was involved, between the Station Bridge and the Hierro Bridge. And yet he could get excited about the little bit he did for Don Román, who, poor man, did need help as he, Pachi, was the first to recognize, but within reason. Within reason and with certain prospects in mind. And he didn't mean Señorita Menchu by this last remark, although she did have a good foundation and even lately a much better face. Because the whole thing would just be much too complicated. Simply put, the prospects he'd envisioned were being fulfilled. Their meal out every day was a big help because in the garret room of 10-B Miracruz food was still a touchy issue. That bitch of a milk lady kept selling them milk that just got more watered down with each passing day. "It must be the rain," said the old hag, and although it didn't matter to him because he never touched the stuff, he knew Planicio was a growing boy. Of course he discussed all these problems with Don Román, who increased his pay by five duros a week. These were the prospects Pachi was referring to—having an employer who knew how to understand one's problems.

"Thanks very much, Don Román. This will be a big help. It doesn't take much for the two of us to get by."

Bad times, truly bad times they were, with the added complication of the ration card.

"*Aita!*" said Planicio with the excitement minor matters inspired in him. "Francisca told me they're distributing cooking oil in the store. I need the card."

"I lost it," replied his father in a curt tone.

"But, *Aita!* How did you lose it? . . ." asked the boy, astonished.

His father told him he lost it, but what he didn't say was that he lost it playing cards, a rare occurrence because all in all he won more times than he lost. As luck would have it, however, he lost the day he bet the ration card playing *siete y media*.

The boy looked into the matter and advised his father, "*Aita*, they told me we have to go to the Supply Department to say we lost it, and they'll give us a new one."

"Stop already with the card! For all the good it does us, I'd rather not have one."

It was a matter of principle. He would rather not have a card. When he'd lost it he'd said scornfully to the winner, "For the four stringy beans it'll bring you, you're welcome to it."

Fine, thought Planicio, maybe the beans were stringy, but the bread was good enough to eat.

"You call this bread?" said the Galician who had always been poor but who knew good food when he saw it. "These yellow balls made from leftover pig slop?"

Then to reinforce his position he brought politics into the discussion. "Is this what the war was for?"

He phrased his question in a way that made it clear that who actually won the war meant nothing to him. He was only referring to the outcome.

The next time Don Román paid him, Pachi bought a loaf of white bread (although the bran darkened its whiteness somewhat)—a round loaf they called farm house bread that weighed a kilogram—on the black market.

"There you go," he said to Planicio, as though showing him that this was the type of food he wanted for his son and not leftover pig slop.

Planicio made the bread last a whole week, but he was hungry, starving actually. He cut it into ultra-thin slices and food became his obsession. With the little money they earned, they couldn't afford to buy much, and he kept himself going with the thought that it would soon be summer, and Jacinto the countess's manservant would start visiting them again with the casseroles *Aita* managed to find fault with as well but that solved a lot of problems.

"There's no chance of your uncle ever going hungry. They started out as smugglers and now they're robbers."

His father was referring to the Garmendías from Alza. He regularly reminded his son that his grandfather had been a smuggler. Planicio said nothing, but he thought it was neat to have a smuggler for a grandfather. In fact, Dick Turpin, in his interminable fights with the hated English constables, was helped enormously by the smugglers who'd saved his life on more than one occasion.

The milk lady, with her white mustache and the watered-down milk, also sold black market bread from her horse-drawn cart. The old woman still arrived every morning wearing the same black dress but with the addition of a rough, very thick, black wool jacket and an equally thick small bonnet. When it rained she used a huge umbrella and covered the horse with an oilcloth. She complained bitterly. "*Ené,* times are tough!"

But people in the neighborhood knew her grumbling was only for form's sake and that she was elated to be making a lot of money.

The contents of the two-wheeled carriage, rain or shine, were also covered with oilcloths in separate compartments, and she allowed no prying. Under the oilcloths in the first row were the innocent goods such as vegetables, and underneath those was the black-market merchandise—bread, cooking oil, flour and sugar. She was kind to Planicio since she felt sorry for him because of his father, who everyone knew had gambled away his son's bread in a card game and who made a living exploiting the poor invalid from Calle de Ramón y Cajal. She showed her kindness with large loaves of bread she had trouble selling because they were so hard. Planicio moistened the bread, and then put it in the oven. It was only so-so, but it was good for making milk soup.

His father watched the operation scornfully and commented, "It's not even worth the coal you're using."

This wasn't true because Planicio gathered the coal along the train tracks that ran behind the house, and so it cost him nothing. It was really slag, but he knew how to choose pieces

that hadn't burned all the way and could be used again, enough
to cook the little they ate. His father, in his own words, preferred leaving his portion for his son and always managed to
eat out somewhere. In any event, the Galician was thinner;
he'd almost completely lost his paunch, and he looked younger
and more lively. With summer around the corner, he had made
a number of resolutions—in practical terms, no more card
games. Serious matters couldn't be left to the hazard of any
old thickhead winning at *siete y media*. Since Don Román had
increased his salary, Pachi had begun going to the Gros fronton where a team of high-ranking women racket players played.
As luck would have it, he thought, the Gros fronton was next
to the don's house so that on leaving there he still had enough
time to watch the last game. Lately Don Román had noticed
his hurry to be off but said nothing.

At first Pachi only played the daily double, which didn't
involve much risk-taking because once the game had begun, no
matter how excited you got, you couldn't up the wager. This
was important since it prevented him from playing the ration
card in a moment of folly—not that he missed the damn
thing, but the incident hadn't gone over very well in the district. As though he'd sold his soul to the devil. Materialists,
every one of them. Nothing but materialists. All they thought
about was food, even if it was pig's food. It was also important
to get to know the racket players and their potential in the different combinations of the daily double, although, being
women, there was little hope they'd show much common
sense, and so the results came as a constant surprise.

Once he'd gained the gatekeeper's confidence—the man
was from Irún and they already knew each other somewhat—
he began to smuggle Planicio in with him for free, naturally.
At first the boy was in awe of how hard the women hit the ball,
but *Aita* soon pointed out that it was nothing special and that
compared to hand pelota, pelota played with a racket was a
lesser art.

"Pelota, to be real pelota," he explained, "has to be played with this," and he opened his hand, which was still powerful, "and with these," and with his other hand, he showed another part of his anatomy.

He meant that hand pelota did not allow for deceit and that women, both to enhance their beauty and to play on the fronton, had to resort to subterfuge. This advice seemed sound to Planicio, although he was a bit embarrassed to see *Aita* point to that part of himself in public.

In spite of his words the Galician did think highly of *remonte,* the two-a-side form of pelota, which he felt was something out of the ordinary, especially when played by the Salsamendi brothers. *Remonte* was played on the Urumea fronton for large bets but with a system of brokers and a minimum amount—always in duros—that was too high for him. As well, the games were usually held after lunchtime when Pachi was busy as an aide-de-camp. But he was sure that one day his luck would turn, and he could experiment in the "pelota cathedral."

Although public morality was strict in those days, every once in a while disturbances broke out in the Gros over the allegedly dubious behavior of the women pelota players. There was one in particular, Chechu Larrañaga from Eibar, beautifully strong and powerful, who was the top player on the team. She had a light covering of down on her face, but it was very attractive because of her strength.

"I've always liked strong women," Pachi would say to his friends who'd laugh, although Planicio didn't really understand why.

"Ones with a good foundation, isn't that right, Pachi?"

Planicio had already noticed that his father's friends had a special language they used when talking about women, a language he couldn't seem to grasp. Larrañaga had to win all her games or else, when she didn't, people yelled the strangest things at her, like "Who did you sleep with last night?"

Planicio was surprised by their interest in such specifics.

Someone shouted back, "It can't have been with your mother!"

Planicio felt sad on hearing this because he thought that perhaps the girl was an orphan like himself.

Someone else, taking advantage of the ruckus, shouted out the terrible epithet, "Slut!"

The butt of these remarks looked unhappy, and her companions consoled her and told her to ignore them. The winners were especially understanding and consoling. But sometimes Larrañaga couldn't stand it, especially when they hurled the epithet at her, and she faced the public and made a gesture similar to the one Pachi made when he was explaining what hand pelota was about. Then all hell broke loose, and the pair of policemen on duty usually intervened. In those days a couple of policemen were enough to calm down a whole fronton in fury. When the rumpus was over, Pachi and his friends laughed and chatted together for a while. Planicio, on the other hand, felt awful. It made him feel so sad that he quit going.

PLANICIO LOVED being with Don Román because he felt the don was there for him alone. It was a little like when *Amá* used to wait for him in the doorway of the Miracruz house on summer nights—although he only remembered one summer in particular—thinking he'd be starving because for his mother it was extremely important for him to have a big appetite and eat lots of food. No matter how many people were on the doorstep, he felt his mother was there for him alone. When she died, the countess, who took particular pains with him, explained that his mother was there for him more than ever. Day and night, *Amá* never stopped watching him for a second. He studied the stars constantly—and still did— because it only seemed logical that from the garret room of one of the tallest homes in San Sebastian, it would be easier to establish contact. Moreover now, and this he'd become aware of after learning his catechism, *Amá* was with the Virgin Mary, and so his two mothers were together, watching over him. Wonderful. In any case—without it being the same—it was important to him that he have Don Román to himself. Once in a while he thought of bringing Ramoncho along with him to have him meet the don, but then he decided to keep him to himself. Because with Don Román, it was like with his mother—he never forgot a promise. If *Amá* said, "Tomorrow I'll make you custard," his favorite food of all, there was no way she would forget, and once—she was already sick by then; it was shortly before she died—she got up from bed just to make him some. If Don Román said, "Tomorrow I'll bring you such and such a book," you could be sure he would.

Whenever Planicio arrived late, he could see the don, as he drew nearer, craning his neck left and right until he saw him.

"Here he is," said Don Román, showing his relief that the boy had finally arrived.

With *Aita* it wasn't the same because *Aita* sometimes said tomorrow we'll do this or that, but you could never be sure it would happen. Or *Aita* asked him, "What did you do today?" and you couldn't be sure he'd listen to the answer either. Or he'd say, "Go on home. I'll be there shortly," and then he wouldn't come home at all that night. When they trotted together in the street—he trotted; *Aita* always walked very slowly—he felt that if he lengthened his stride and disappeared, his father wouldn't notice, or he'd find it normal that his son had left. If Planicio met another boy and said, "*Aita*, we're going to go play," for sure his father would say fine. If his father met up with a friend, Planicio waited; if they got into an involved discussion, he usually stood off to the side a little because *Aita* had friends who cursed and swore constantly, never failing to shock Planicio. When he knew the friend was one of those kind, he backed away immediately and trotted back and forth, looking in store windows he knew off by heart because he hardly ever left the Gros quarter, and the walks were always the same. The Berridi pastry shop window was always of

great interest in spite of the shortages because they still had
Berlin cream puffs. They didn't have bread though. On the
other hand, the shop had quite a good assortment of pastries,
although Planicio wasn't as interested in them because the
price of each pastry was way too high, and anyway they didn't
last. In any case, he hadn't gone back there since the day he'd
invited Ramoncho, at the end of winter, because he couldn't
afford to anymore. His father had insisted that times were
truly bad. "If we catch the flu," he complained, "we don't even
have enough to buy aspirin."

Aita could spend forever talking to a friend on the street,
even though once he'd said good-bye, he usually said, "What a
bore!" While Planicio waited, he did his own thing but without
taking his eyes off his father. In the Melchora shoe store, there
were boots with cloth soles and tacks that would be great for
winter. Plus, when they were new, the tacks clicked against the
sidewalk with a metallic ring that was very satisfying. The kids
who had a pair slid on the pavement with them on and made
sparks fly.

If he saw that his father was deeply engaged in conversation,
he went up to the Miner bicycle shop where he could kill a lot
of time. The only problem was that it was slightly off the main
street on a narrow side road, and if he wasn't careful his father
disappeared. If the conversation was over and *Aita* didn't see
him, he just left. Afterward he'd say, "Where were you hiding?" or he didn't remember to ask him anything. The delivery
boy for the grocery store had a bike with high handlebars and a
rack over the front wheel that was used to put the delivery basket on. He was sixteen and no matter how full the basket was,
he always jumped on the bike at a run. That is, he put his left
foot on the pedal and with his right foot pushed off, as though
he were skating, until he got up enough speed. Then he swung
his right leg over the seat in one elegant sweep, and if he was
going downhill, he took his hands off the handlebars right
away. When he had one, he did it all with a cigarette in his

mouth. Planicio watched the whole operation but not openly because the boy never waved to him even though they'd played together at Urbistondos. Another boy from 8 Calle de Miracruz also had a bike with racing handlebars, but he took it out only in the summer. He was a student and unfortunately was not friendly either. Planicio never daydreamed, not even about stuffing himself with Berlin cream puffs, but he couldn't help imagining what would happen and how his life would be different if he had a bike. He could run Señora Asun's errands at lightning speed, but there was one insoluble problem—what would he do with the bicycle when he reached his destination? Leave it in the doorway while he went upstairs to make his delivery? Impossible. He wouldn't leave a bicycle on the street, not even padlocked. He also thought about going to see Don Román, how he'd ride up to the wheelchair like an arrow and screech to a halt just next to the don, and how the latter would be taken completely by surprise because he wouldn't have even heard him coming. Another possibility was to build a harness to hitch to Don Román's wheelchair so he could take him on long rides. This was not Planicio's own idea but one he'd got from an illustration in *Around the World in Eighty Days* by Jules Verne in which a Chinese man is doing just that. But he doubted whether the don would agree because he wouldn't strike a very dignified figure in the wheelchair being pulled by Planicio on his bike. Aside from that, in China it was a normal sight, but in San Sebastian people were pretty leery of anything out of the ordinary. His father had had a French bicycle, a Peugeot, once, but he didn't have it anymore and hadn't told Planicio what had happened to it.

To keep up on the latest in fashion and people in the news, Señora Asun bought an illustrated magazine every Sunday. Planicio wasn't as interested in the magazines as he was in Don Román's books, but he read them too while waiting for specific instructions on his deliveries. The instructions were usually very complicated because his employer discussed at great length with her nieces whether he should go to one place or another first or which delivery was most important. Planicio had noticed that his employer was having a tougher time of it too. There was little work and she longed for summer with its influx of elegant customers. He noticed it because they didn't need him as often, and when they did it was for several deliveries at a time, combined so he didn't have to take the tramway.

"Take the Avenida," she explained, "and leave a package there for Ganchegui. Then go on to Buen Pastor and leave this corset for Señora de Goitia. After that . . . "

And she kept on explaining how he could easily cover several kilometers without having to take the tramway. Planicio agreed because he wouldn't have taken it anyway, but he realized it also meant he wouldn't have the forty centimos for the trip there and back. The señora always finished with the same admonition.

"Make sure you get a tip!"

Planicio tried, he really did, but without much success since he couldn't stand still, waiting until they gave him a tip or until the door was closed in his face. On the measures to be taken to obtain a tip, Señora Asun had hardened her position to such an extent that sometimes when he returned empty-handed, he said that yes, they had given him one, so as not to have to hear one more time that he wouldn't get anywhere in life if he kept this up. Ever since he was a little boy, many different people had predicted that Planicio wouldn't amount to anything because he didn't have what it took to accomplish anything. And so he had already resigned himself to the inevitable.

Consequently, many times over that particularly beautiful spring, he didn't have a single peseta in his pocket at nightfall, and he had to wait for *Aita* to get back to see if he had anything left. One never knew what was going to happen with *Aita*'s earnings, although one thing was sure—it would have something to do with the Gros fronton. Lately Pachi had made friends with one of the pelota players' boyfriends who gave him inside information on upcoming games. The *Cimarrón* flew into a terrible rage a number of times because what he'd been told would happen never happened, but the boyfriend always had a reasonable explanation for why things hadn't gone as planned, and Pachi always went back to him for advice. Sometimes his predictions were right on, and then Pachi had to celebrate and repay the favor, meaning that *Aita* got home very late or not at all or with no money at all, and Planicio went to bed on an empty stomach. But when Pachi did have money, he gave it to his son, who ran outside to see what he could buy. At that time of night all the stores were closed, and he had to go as far as the port in hopes that the black marketeer would still have stale slices of leftover soldiers' bread for sale. When the old woman said, "I don't have any left. What are you doing out at this time of night?" Planicio had no answer to give her. The most he could do was insist, "Don't you have something else?"

What on earth could be left at this time of night? Planicio understood the old woman's position and was embarrassed to have to insist, but he was ravenous.

Sometimes he thought she suspected him of something because Don Román had already explained to him that there was a law against black marketeers that provided for the death sentence. Maybe the old woman was risking her life when she sold him a stale slice of bread, just as he would be when he ate it, although it didn't make sense. Under the circumstances and because of his growth spurt, bread seemed to him to be the most desirable commodity on earth, and he couldn't believe that at one time any bakery, for ten centimos, would sell him a fairly large loaf and that he hadn't taken advantage of it to buy a whole armful. Even today, he said to his father, "*Aita,* when we get paid we have to buy food and keep some at home."

He meant that they should keep some kind of food around for when he suffered such terrible hunger pangs. For instance, someone had told him there was a cookie factory in Rentería that sold broken and misshapen cookies—the taste would still be the same—for one peseta a kilogram. They should buy five kilograms, put them in a tin box so they wouldn't go all soft and use them in emergencies. Having a big box with five kilograms of cookies in it must add an element of security to life. And in the summer he'd be sure to store away apples— obtained gratis—spacing them out on the kitchen shelves because even though they got all wrinkled with time, they'd still be good to eat. He was sure he could hold up well on a diet of cookies, apples and water. He just had to look at the Swiss Family Robinson. This was a great consolation to him too— the fact that all the adventurers in the novels Don Román let him borrow had gone through great tribulations and managed to get by with very little. Sometimes he thought that if he looked hard enough on Mount Ulía, he would find the bread tree that saved Salgari's heroes in so many extreme situations. For the time being, the most practical approach was to buy five kilograms of cookies in the Rentería factory. *Aita* agreed but they never got around to it because the matter of money was quite a complicated one. Planicio, because of Señora Asun's newfound discipline and her insistence that he come up with a tip, wasn't even scraping together an average of two pesetas a day. As for his father, the day he was paid was never a good time. Or more specifically, when *Aita* was paid, Planicio usually didn't see him, and when he did see him it was too late and Pachi got angry.

"Anyway, who says they'll sell you a kilogram's worth of cookies for one peseta?"

Francisca the concierge had told him because she used to work in the factory when she was a young girl and knew it well.

"Don't tell me you believe what that old fool has to say?"

Planicio insisted that yes, he did believe her, and he reminded his father that Francisca had worked in the factory when she was young.

Then his father interrupted him sarcastically. "Well then it must have been sometime last century. There've been a lot of changes since then." Since his joke went right over the boy's head, Pachi presented his other argument. "What's more, you'd spend more on the tramway than on the cookies."

In any case, Planicio didn't give up on his plan to find out exactly where the factory was, and even if he had to walk there—Rentería had to be about seven kilometers outside of San Sebastian—he would make his way there to replenish their larder.

In one of the illustrated magazines Señora Asun bought, Planicio saw a picture that opened new vistas for him. Two men who looked like mailmen but turned out to be human taxis were posing beside a tandem bicycle, in other words a two-seater that pulled a carriage big enough for two people. The carriage looked lightweight and was in the shape of a small car. The caption underneath indicated that it was a taxi-cycle, a rental vehicle pulled by humans that had begun operating in Valencia. In fact, the carriage door boasted a sign saying, NO. 1 TAXI-CYCLE. VALENCIA. The journalist predicted a rise in its popularity since the outlook for gasoline supplies to the Peninsula was increasingly poor. In passing he insinuated that the fuel shortage was the result of the stance adopted by one supposedly civilized nation, which hadn't been civilized until its discovery by Spain, that nevertheless couldn't forgive Spain its recent defeat of communism. Obviously, as long as there were men strong enough and swift enough to pull taxi-cycles in Spain, there was no need for concern about the international blockade that one nation wanted to impose because it couldn't forgive you know what.

Planicio didn't understand the political implications very well, but he did understand how he and his father, perched gracefully astride the tandem, could pull the carriage with Don Román safely ensconced inside. In other words, once more Jules Verne's drawing had been a sign of what science was to produce in the twentieth century. The taxi-cycle had certainly been well thought out. The body was painted black, and it had a roof, windows that could open and mudguards on the wheels. The tandem bicycle with two sets of pedals guaranteed a reasonable speed. He thought that for *Aita*—who had single-handedly guided the Fuenterrabía crew through three miles of madcap seas—pulling such a light aerodynamic vehicle would be a breeze. He, Planicio, who was used to running all the time, would also be a big help.

He thought about cutting out the picture without telling anyone but didn't dare, so he asked Señora Asun for permission. He was very embarrassed, but he had no choice. His employer vacillated because an illustrated magazine was, at the time, an object of value that had to last and be read by many people and exchanged for one's friends' magazines. She looked on the other side of the article to see if anything important was there and finally agreed when Planicio said it was to show Don Román. He'd show it to his father too but to the don first because his father was skeptical about everything except gambling because he knew there had to be a system that made it possible to chalk up more wins than losses, although he hadn't yet discovered it.

The picture just kept looking better and better. The two men who resembled mailmen—wearing broad flat caps—looked proudly into the camera, full of self-confidence. The one in front was holding on to the bicycle handlebars and had his right foot on the pedal, ready to push off, just like the grocery store delivery boy. He had a small mustache. The one behind him, more relaxed, stood at the back of the bicycle with his left hand on the seat. He held his head high. Curious onlookers in the street stayed at a respectful distance for the picture-taking. Planicio thought it would only make sense for his father to be in the front, in the pilot's seat, because he already knew how to ride a bike—before the war he had had a French bicycle, a Peugeot—with him behind but pedaling hard. If the carriage was big enough for two people, like the article said, then Señorita Menchu could come too, although he wasn't sure about that because he didn't think there would be enough room since Don Román was pretty fat. It didn't really matter because it was meant for Don Román so they could go on stupendous excursions together. There were parts of the city—the Concha beach, Onarreta, the Amara suburb, the Hierro Bridge—that they had talked about but couldn't even hope to reach with Don Román's wheelchair because of the distance involved. Sometimes the don talked to Planicio about a farmhouse in Martutene, on the riverbank, that had a small dock where he, Don Román, and other children had had adventures similar to Huckleberry Finn on the Mississippi River. He also told him about things that had happened in Usurbil and in Hernani, always close to a river with crystalline transparent pools—this was at the beginning of the century— and freshly cut fields. Don Román didn't talk much, but Planicio listened to him attentively; he could imagine it all and even smell the gentle aroma of the recently mowed fields that must surely be different from the ones he knew. Planicio didn't quite dare ask, but by the way the don spoke, it was obvious that in those years he was a child who could run with the others, although Planicio had trouble imagining it. At Christmastime, they used to go to Astigarraga to pick mistletoe to decorate the house with because the English said that if you came upon a girl under a branch of mistletoe you could kiss her.

"But that can't be true," interrupted Pachi the *Cimarrón*.

Don Román specified that this was what boys from Bilbao, shipowners' sons who had studied in England, said.

"Bah!" said the Galician. "People from Bilbao are even worse than Madrilenians." Pachi made this type of remark as a matter of form since regional differences meant nothing to him. After all, he was a Galician who, according to the Basques, were the worst of all—Last one in is a Galician!— although ever since his namesake and fellow countryman from Pardo had won the war, people were a bit more careful about using that kind of insult out loud. In any case, even though he was a Galician, he allowed that people from Bilbao were different, always boasting about the strangest things. Kissing a girl required certain special circumstances—the first being darkness—and the story about a branch of mistletoe was another one of the Bilbaons' nonsense.

What was clear, however, in Planicio's mind was that these places—Martutene, Hernani, Usurbil, Astigarraga, with their meandering rivers, their corn plantations, their gently waving prairies wafting their own special scent—existed, although he hadn't seen them because *Aita* never wanted to go on excursions. With the taxi-cycle they'd be easy to reach because none of them was further than twenty kilometers away from San Sebastian, and the article said one could "easily" do an average of twenty kilometers an hour on "gently rolling" terrain. Even more on the flat. It only made sense to think that the don would welcome the chance to return for a visit since just talking about it all made him excited.

Furthermore, Planicio was attracted by the idea of cycling in such a fashion along San Sebastian's streets where there was hardly any traffic in those days. He wasn't sure about the cap—not because of himself (he thought it looked great) but because of his father—then decided it wasn't essential and that the two of them, he and *Aita,* could wear berets. Big berets, nice and flat in front to form a visor. Actually he didn't want to have Señorita Menchu along because he could imagine Don Román sitting comfortably, very dignified, basking in the view as long as he was alone in the coach, but with his sister there, Planicio imagined him all curled up and looking a bit ridiculous. Another thorny issue was whether they could climb hills, although the article said that there was some allowance for climbing, according to a list of slope percentages that Planicio didn't understand but thought looked pretty impossible. The taxi-cycle was made for travel on flat terrain, and as soon as the going got steeper, he couldn't see it being possible. But when he looked more closely, he noted that the bicycle in the picture had a gearshift. Now that was exciting. It meant it was a real model of efficiency. A neighborhood boy—not the student—had a bicycle like that and had climbed Jaizquíbel with it.

In the afternoon, he shared his discovery with Don Román. It was a strange afternoon; it wasn't raining but gusts of wind from the interior carried an offish smell and made the possibility of an unexpected treacherous storm likely, one coming from the interior and not from the sea where storms normally started. In the street, Don Román and Pachi sought refuge under the pillars on Plaza de Guipúzcoa. First the aide-de-camp did what was expected of him, taking the don through the Plaza park and showing him the swans in the pond. He also took him to the small wooden bridge that spanned an artificial creek so he could watch the trout swimming. In this environment the fish were slightly lusterless, having lost so many scales it seemed like they'd be left completely naked. Both the don and his assistant were gloomy because they had had other plans for the day. As soon as a couple of drops fell and Pachi said that he'd guessed right, they took shelter under the pillars. He pushed the don's wheelchair up against the wall for better protection from the elements and began looking to see if anyone he knew was walking by; surely there'd be someone for him to talk to. He also watched the nannies dressed in white aprons and checked dresses. Some even wore hair nets or high buns covered with lace, but these ones didn't interest him as much because they were usually old, although one couldn't generalize about women. Some could be getting on in years and still have a good foundation. On the other hand, many young girls were attractive because of their bright faces, but afterward, when one looked more closely, they were like young tunnyfish— nothing but bones. Don Román had decided a long time ago not to look at the women so he watched only the children. They watched him too. They came up to his wheelchair and

stared at him, out of curiosity, but it didn't bother Don
Román because it was only natural for them to be interested in
his situation. He smiled at them and sometimes spoke to
them, but when he did, they generally ran off.

As usual, Planicio started up Paseo Nuevo from the Kursaal
Bridge, but since he didn't see them once he reached the second breakwater, he turned inland without breaking his stride—
splat! splat!—and in a few short minutes was at Plaza de
Guipúzcoa. It was hardly raining at all, but he assumed they'd
have gone under the pillars for shelter. He found them right
away. His father had met an acquaintance and was talking.
Don Román, poor man, looked defenseless, alone against the
wall. People passing by looked at him but skirted around him
as though they didn't want to bother him.

He greeted *Aita* softly so as not to distract him and came
right to the point with Don Román. The don might not be
interested in the idea of a taxi-cycle, but Planicio's explanation
did interest him because since that first morning, Planicio had
had time to imagine further what they could do with the vehicle. Pachi continued talking to his acquaintance, who of course
was a bore, but kept an ear open to their conversation and
soon realized what nonsense it was. He failed to understand
how the don could take the boy seriously and ask for particu-
lars while clearing up certain matters for Planicio. In fact, Don
Román was able to confirm that the road to Martutene was almost flat, and that they would have no problem getting there.
He supposed the dock would still be there, and of course he'd
love to see it again. Hernani? It was nothing, a small hill just
off of the main highway, but surely climbing it would not be a
major task. Afterward, mindful of his greatest fear, Planicio
asked, "Will it be very expensive, Don Román?"

The don didn't know of course, but all they had to do was
find out. The don knew he would never be able to get into the
taxi-cycle since it would be impossible for his huge body, which
kept getting bigger and bigger and more and more sluggish, to

fit through the tiny carriage door. And even if he could have, he wouldn't have. Then again, if he could, maybe he would because the boy's excitement made it all worthwhile.

"Shall we tell *Aita?*"

"We'd better think it over first. In particular, I'll find out how much it costs and how we could buy it. What do you think?"

In other words, they'd better act as conspirators and ensure the success of the venture. Planicio was alone no more. They kept on discussing all the possibilities, oblivious to what was going on around them. Pachi, when he saw that they'd hidden away the picture, lost interest in the matter and had time to change acquaintances twice. Not very interesting acquaintances, but he could talk to them about the nannies' anatomies without being cut off the way the don cut him off. One of the men provided him with what might be a scoop on games being played in the Gros fronton that afternoon, although the *Cimarrón* was increasingly convinced that you couldn't predict anything with any certainty when women were the players and that he had to find a way of gaining access to the Urumea fronton where the Salsamendi brothers had turned the game of *remonte* into a science.

DON ROMAN had felt the first symptoms of paralysis in Madrid when he was preparing for the liquidators exam in a boarding house on Calle de la Montera. One of the other lodgers was a medical student who also wanted to be a bullfighter and had managed to obtain his papers as a matador with the name *Niño de los Caireles*. He was the one who took the don to the General Hospital where his condition aroused a great deal of interest since paralysis was rarely seen in cases where there was no family history of the disease. One of the examining doctors was Don Gregorio Marañón who was just beginning to make a name for himself. He admitted that it was in fact exceedingly rare, especially since he noted that the boy's parents—Don Román was still a boy at the time—had never suffered from a serious venereal disease, but it was obvious where his muscular problems would lead. Marañón cheered him up by saying he could live many years, maybe fifty. What he didn't specify was what his life would be like during those years.

Fifty years had already come and gone so he had already had three bonus years. Lately they really had been bonus years in that he had experienced things such as Planicio's taxi-cycle, things that wouldn't come to pass—he already knew he'd never return to that particular bend the river formed as it passed through Martutene—but that gave him hope. Planicio's interest in him was unlike all the others, including Doctor Marañón, who was very kind and gave him good advice on what his greatest enemy would be—obesity. Don Gregorio had explained that he was thinking of writing a book on the subject, and in fact, when he published his essay entitled "Fat and Thin People" in 1926, he sent Don Román a signed copy. But when all was said and done, he was just one more patient despite the rare nature of his case, although it had been a nice gesture. But Planicio was different, and although the don thought no, afterward he thought yes and was ready to climb into the taxi-cycle—perhaps they could special order a bigger carriage door to accommodate him—so as not to dash the boy's hopes. Yet instinctively he didn't bring the subject up with his aide-de-camp because Pachi would surely bring down such fancies like a house of cards.

His aide-de-camp was a practical man who wouldn't agree to riding tandem but who did have ingenuous ideas of his own that could be carried out on the spot. One notable occasion was when he demonstrated to Don Román nothing was stopping him from going to a movie theater. The first time, they went to Trueba to see the movie *Raza,* almost out of a sense of patriotism because the movie was about what had happened during the war and about how logical the Nationalist victory had been. Planicio and Pachi carried him over the steps at the entrance, and then, although there was no need, an usher helped them carry the wheelchair to a parquet box where the three settled in. The usher took a personal interest in them and prepared the box as though it were their own suite. He moved the chairs around and found the best spot so the invalid didn't have to strain to see the film. Don Román gave the usher a tip, but it was obvious the man had helped out of a sense of professional duty. Planicio was in seventh heaven because the few times he'd gone to the movies, he'd been sitting up in the peanut gallery; having a seat to himself was like a dream come true. He cried a lot during the movie, especially during a scene where some monks—they were all saints—were shot to death on the seashore, and he thought he wouldn't have minded being one of them. Don Román was touched as well, and once in a while he had to take off his glasses surreptitiously. The *Cimarrón,* as always where the war was concerned, was careful not to show his feelings one way or another, but he had to admit that the film was very well done. There was one scene at the beginning of a frigate leaving the dock, which was really a marvel because he, as a boy, remembered those same boats, and that was exactly what they looked like.

It wasn't their last time. They were also lucky in that, at the Miramar theater, which was on their way to Paseo Nuevo, one of the ushers worked mornings as an office boy at the Revenue Delegation and had worked under Don Román. He did them all kinds of favors. They paid only for Don Román, and the Galician got in as his attendant. He made sure to reserve a box for them alone so no one bothered them. Of course, whenever Planicio went along he didn't pay either. Although she was a bit older than he was, he fell in love with Deanna Durbin in a movie called *Mad About Music,* which was to be expected because she sang like a goddess. Even *Aita* agreed to see it more than once because she really knew how to sing.

When the three of them were seated on the parquet, watch-

ing true marvels on the screen, the actors speaking Spanish so
perfectly that you'd never have thought the film had been
dubbed—the last films that Don Román had seen were silent
films—the don realized that these last years were his best. He
was quite sure they were his last because Don Gregorio had
mentioned fifty as an outside limit, and he'd already gone past
that. Furthermore, he could tell; he even started to let Pachi
help him move from one chair to another because the effort
involved in pushing himself up on his own was becoming truly
agonizing.

He bought a package of peanuts for Planicio, one of the few
things they sold at intermission, and the boy wolfed them
down; his hunger pangs were out of this world. Don Román
didn't realize it though; if he had, he would have done something to help, even though he didn't have all that much money
himself. His brother-in-law, who still lived in Salvatierra, was a
miller and sent them flour. Señorita Menchu was very careful
not to waste it, however, because everyone said it had been a
bad year for the crops, and next year would be even worse.

They, Pachi and Don Román, continued to travel in the old
quarter, discovering small taverns where they had a light meal
instead of their dinner—in Don Román's case, so he didn't
put on weight (although he was already slightly discouraged in
that area in spite of Marañón's advice) and in Pachi's case
because he couldn't afford dinner. Sometimes he arrived at the
Gros fronton with nothing but a duro and so had no choice
but to play a single combination on the daily double, which
meant he couldn't experiment and find a winning system. He
too suffered from hunger pangs because the small casserole he
had with the don was nothing more than an appetizer for him,
but he didn't want to take advantage of the situation. The don
said, "Go ahead, Pachi, have some more. You're young and
have room to spare."

Sometimes he did but not always; he saw that Don Román,
by the way he took his money out and counted it, did not have

money to throw away either. Or rather the don wanted to spend his money wisely in order to put some aside for Señorita Menchu, for when he was no longer there.

DON ROMAN had one sister in Salvatierra, who was married to the miller there, and another brother in Bilbao. He didn't see much of them. Menchu, his habitual companion, acted listless—at least with him—always angry at the maid whom she wanted to dismiss and, above all, enormously preoccupied with provisions to feed them. She kept all the supplies in a locked pantry, one of the reasons for the constant friction with the servant because even to take out some salt, one needed a key, and she was the only person who had one. Their sister in Salvatierra sent them flour and cooking oil clandestinely, which Señorita Menchu kept carefully stored away. Despite her pains, mildew got into a sack of flour once and she was inconsolable.

When Don Román returned home from his outings, Señorita Menchu usually had sad tales to tell. Or more to the point, ordinary tales but narrated with such laments that they were sad. Then she invariably asked him, "And how are you feeling?"

But her tone was such that Don Román felt she already had her answer—how could you feel, poor man, given that every day your condition worsens and that this very morning, just getting you out of the bathroom was an accomplishment in itself?

"Just fine. I feel just fine," he replied in spite of everything.

"Is that so?" said Señorita Menchu with such doubt that he was vexed. "And your stomach, is it better now?"

"I've told you, it was just a bit of heartburn. It went away as soon as I took some baking soda. You know I have a stomach of iron."

"Well, just as well," sighed his sister.

Meaning it was just as well that the poor man had something that worked properly. Don Román wasn't suspicious by nature, and he appreciated having people—particularly his younger sister—inquire into his health, which he realized was an affliction, but it wasn't going to get better just because they asked him every five minutes. That's why he so loved being in the box at the Miramar theater with both Louridos, father and son, watching *The Prisoner of Zenda,* starring Madeleine Carroll. The Galician said in an aside, "Now that's a real woman, hey, Don Román?"

The don agreed because there was no denying it. At other times he remarked, "It's always the same thing, Pachi. It's as though you have nothing else on your mind."

Pachi would occasionally have an off-color joke to tell, but if it was vulgar, Don Román didn't let him finish. Because for one thing, that type of conversation excited him, his stomach not being the only part of him that was still in perfect shape. So was the other. Sometimes he thought he would like to have seen the atrophy start with his digestive and reproductive systems. But such was not God's will. He resigned himself to his fate, which is why everyone called him a Christian gentleman.

He loved sitting in the box, and when Ronald Coleman was in a sword fight with some unscrupulous subject who, against all reason, wanted to dethrone the king, he liked watching Planicio's face more than the screen. It was worth it. The bonus years were worth it, and he thanked God for them but only with his heart because if he spoke out loud, people tried to label him.

IT WAS A VERY dry spring and looked like it would be another summer of drought and hardship. There were showers but untimely ones, which according to the farmers damaged the crops more than anything.

One afternoon in early June, at the usual hour, Pachi arrived for Don Román. He'd been caught in a downpour on his way there and arrived at the house drenched to the skin. The señorita showed concern for his condition.

"Look at you! Is it raining that much?"

"It is raining," said Pachi.

His jacket was wet, but it wouldn't do to take it off. Señorita Menchu invited him to sit next to the brazier; the charcoal was lit because Don Román had cold fingers and toes. Pachi always remained standing in the don's house, but that day he sat down.

"It's an ugly afternoon out there, Don Román."

"It looks like it."

"Windy too," continued the Galician.

Don Román was a bit sad, enjoyably so. He had learned how to combine the two. He enjoyed it because of the heat of the brazier, which helped him snooze; the nap did him good since he was having an increasingly hard time sleeping at night. He enjoyed it because from his seat in front of the mirador, he could see the sea, and if a steamboat passed by he imagined all the things that might be happening on board—sailors scurrying, crying out, swearing—as they sailed north to the Gran Sol cod-fishing grounds where nothing was the same, and on calm nights one of them would play the accordion while the others sang. In his house no one ever sang. The ships, which were lost to view in the space of three or four minutes, went on to exotic ports where things happened that even Pachi didn't dare tell him about, although he could imagine them and they alarmed him.

"You'll be cold from your drenching," said Señorita Menchu. "Would you like a liqueur? At this time of year, it's so easy to catch a cold."

Pachi accepted because he had no desire to come down with a cold. The word liqueur was suspect, and his fears were confirmed when she brought out an unlabeled bottle containing a liquid made out of mint by nuns from Azpeitia and another ingredient they wouldn't disclose. Not that they needed to, thought Pachi as he tasted it. He'd already noticed that the quality of liqueurs made by monks and nuns was far from being legendary. What's more, for virtue's sake the alcohol content was kept low, and the drink had no effect whatsoever. He drank it down in one gulp and said, "Very smooth."

Señorita Menchu considered this a compliment and added, "And very good for the digestion."

This was another of the legends about monastic liqueurs. It was as though the monks suffered from terrible digestive problems and so had specialized in finding a remedy with medicinal brews like this one that always contained an ingredient known only to them, which seemed very un-Christian of them. Besides which, the only thing Pachi needed for his digestion was food, and just that noon Planicio and he had polished off some roasted yams, the lowliest of sweet potatoes, and so he had no digestive problems.

Don Román was content, happy to see his sister invite Pachi to sit down. If she hadn't on such a languid day as today, he'd have felt very lonely listening to Señorita Menchu quarreling with the maid in the background. Halfway through the afternoon, his sister would have served him some tea, but weak tea because strong tea wasn't good for him, with saccharine because sugar was fattening and without milk for the same reason. They obviously couldn't go out on this slightly wet but very windy day. Whenever this had happened before—not too often, thank goodness—Pachi, after giving his weather report, had left until the next day—without sitting down because he was a servant after all, although afterward in the street they were friends. But that day, Señorita Menchu invited Pachi to sit down and even offered him a glass of mint liqueur, although Don Román already knew it wouldn't be to his aide-de-camp's liking. He, on the other hand, quite liked the cloying taste and licorice smell of the sweet drink, but he wasn't offered any. He was used to it.

He'd have liked having Planicio there with them, sitting around the table, but he knew it wouldn't happen. Halfway through the afternoon when the boy had finished his last errand for Señora Asun, he'd start up Paseo Nuevo at first and, given the weather, veer over to the arches in Plaza de Guipúzcoa. When he didn't find them there, he'd go back to the garret room at 10-B Miracruz alone.

"Tell me, Pachi," inquired the don. "Does Planicio have friends his own age?"

His assistant stayed quiet for a minute and then said, "Because of his job he doesn't have much time for friends."

"Poor boy!" said Señorita Menchu in a remorseful tone lacking in conviction.

"He has one friend," said Pachi as consolation. "Ramoncho. They're always together." He thought a bit longer and added, "In the summer, he has more. He's a good pelota player, but," and here concern crept into his voice, "he doesn't really care whether he wins."

The don became serious. "Pachi, next year we have to make sure the boy continues his studies."

The Galician agreed, although he didn't understand what studies Don Román was referring to because Planicio could already read beautifully—even upside down and sideways—and he had no problem whatsoever adding and subtracting.

Señorita Menchu mentioned that the Jesuits held evening classes at Luises for working boys and that she'd ask the parish priest for more details. It seemed a fitting task for a woman from the church women's group.

"I think it would be better if he went to the Peñaflorida Institute. He could audit classes toward his baccalaureate."

Those were Don Román's words, and they didn't sit well with Señorita Menchu. It was typical of her brother to say something of the kind. He never faced reality. In this case what the poor man's son needed was a basic education to help him learn a trade. Señorita Menchu wanted to help the poor man but within reason. The poor man was handsome. Perhaps his hands struck a discordant note, broad and powerful as they were, and slightly deformed by the game of pelota. They didn't quite fit, but that didn't mean they weren't attractive. Not only were they broad but long as well, with knobby fingers, the veins standing out on the still-youthful skin, with very short nails that could have been a bit cleaner. "How old is he?" she'd asked her brother one day.

"Thirty-five," he'd replied.

"But he looks older," Señorita Menchu had said.

Right then he didn't though. His hair was receding at the temples. It would have been barely noticeable if he didn't have the habit of leaving his beret on all the time. That is, his face was tanned by the long years at sea, but along his temples his skin was white, and one could see the mark left by the beret.

"But why a baccalaureate?" asked Señorita Menchu with a certain amount of irritation.

"He's a quick study," her brother explained to justify himself. Don Román had a tendency to make excuses for what he said to her because he felt he was a burden on her and that she had remained single to look after him.

"But he can study at Luises too," insisted his sister.

Of course he could, but Don Román wanted to see him graduate from Peñaflorida, which was the official secondary school, and he, in his spare time on the many long sunless winter afternoons, could help Planicio with the homework he didn't understand. Or even if he understood everything because he was very bright, the don could help him study. He liked the idea because it was increasingly difficult for him to go out every afternoon. He could tell. Of course, it was a seven year program. In other words he, Don Román, would be sixty when Planicio finished, and of course Don Gregorio had told him that just living to fifty was an accomplishment. He hadn't mentioned sixty. But the don could help him during the first few years, which would be the most difficult ones.

"What do you think?" Señorita Menchu asked Pachi.

"Whatever you say," responded the Galician without committing himself one way or another since he could see they didn't agree on the matter.

"You see," said Señorita Menchu to Don Román.

His sister obviously wanted to be in the right, at least this time, and that's why she interpreted his response in her favor. Don Román kept quiet and looked out toward the sea. He saw a small launch with a single rower who, given his stance and the time, must be rod fishing for calamary. The don was lost in thought for a moment. Then he said to Pachi while pointing at the launch, "It must have been a tough row for him all the way out there."

The *Cimarrón* calculated the distance and passed judgment. "A mile and a half. Not more than an hour without rowing too hard."

"Do you think so?" asked Señorita Menchu in admiration.

Then Pachi explained about the regatta in September of 1931 in the Concha Bay, with him in the bow wearing the Fuenterrabía blue jersey, which was stained red with blood along the bottom by the time he'd finished.

Don Román had heard the story before, and he let his thoughts wander. He thought about Planicio, who, when he didn't find them, would probably go up to the garret room alone to read a book. He read them in no time at all, and Don Román was running out of provisions. He would have to look in a big wicker chest he kept in the cellar room; it was full of other books he couldn't find a place for in the apartment. For example, there should be some books published on newsprint that he'd bound himself. Surely there would be the book about the knight Henry de Lagardière whose secret fencing thrust had got him out of many a tight corner. Once he'd even managed to fight a duel to the death while holding a baby girl in his left arm. She later turned out to be the daughter of his rival who, if the don remembered correctly, was the Count of Nevers, who had his own secret thrust, although he wasn't sure whether it was the same one as Henry who had copied him or vice versa. In any case, it was a family secret, and whoever mastered the thrust could live in absolute security during the complicat-

ed reign of Louis XIV of France. If only Planicio could read
them and then rehash the stories with him once he'd finished.
He knew the boy would be so moved that Don Román would
have to remind him they were only fiction. Naturally the boy
would rather they were real. As did he. Of course, if he asked
his sister whether it wouldn't be possible to bring the big chest
up from the cellar, she'd have all kinds of excuses. . . . Why on
earth did he want that chest? And he wouldn't dare tell the
truth. Moreover, she'd explain, the chest wouldn't fit in the
elevator, and the doorman was getting quite unpleasant and
less inclined to do favors. One more thing—the light bulb in
the cellar had burnt out and with so much junk, they'd have a
tough time finding the chest. And finally there were rats down
there, and Señorita Menchu was terrified of all rodents. That's
what they'd say of course, but he kept thinking of how Planicio would love the story of the Count of Nevers and the
Knight de Lagardière. He himself wouldn't mind finding out
again who the secret thrust belonged to originally.

Pachi the *Cimarrón* was telling Señorita Menchu how the
Fuenterrabía, Orio and Pasajes de San Juan crews were racing
bow to bow at the buoys and how that was where they finally
pulled ahead, taking the turn so sharply that you would have
sworn God himself was rowing. The expression quite shocked
Señorita Menchu; they weren't used to taking the Lord's name
in vain around their household. If Don Román had been paying attention, he'd have spoken up—"Pachi, please . . . " But
he didn't because he was still thinking about the wicker chest.

And so Pachi's crew had a small lead coming out of the
turn, but the trip back was even tougher. Every wave had to be
used to gain another tenth of a second. The coxswain yelled
out, *"Champa!"* and the oarsmen—especially he, Pachi, who
was in the bow setting the pace—brought it up, giving seven or
eight short swift strokes to put the boat on the crest of the
wave and precipitate it down the other side. That's what it felt
like. But the extra strokes were a killer. When they crossed the

sandbar between Santa Clara Island and the port, there was an especially strong surge, and a side wave engulfed the Pasajes de San Juan boat from starboard, dashing its crew's hopes of winning. It couldn't have been better. The yellow jerseys from Orio were having their own problems bailing water, so Pachi's crew was the first to enter into the din made by all the Fuenterrabía fishermen who went wild sounding their sirens. It was the first time they'd won the banner in five years of humiliation, and he, Pachi the Galician, was in the bow. When they disembarked at the port, he saw blood running down his legs because—and here he stood up to show Señorita Menchu the base of his spine—he'd ripped a gash in his skin from pressing back so hard against the side of the boat.

Once again the señorita was somewhat shocked to see him pointing to a part of himself one usually didn't point to, but her eyes shone and she asked, "But weren't you sitting on the bench?"

No, by God, it was impossible. This was how you had to sit—feet firmly pressed against the seat ahead, knees bent so your rear end pushed against your seat. Extending your legs, waist and torso gave you that extra push that could be transferred to the oar blade, the blade you never let out of your sight because of the importance of placing it just so in the water. No deeper than ten centimeters. And that's when the sea was calm. When it was rough they had to guess at its placement. So they only sat on the bench during warm-ups, which is why calluses formed you know where.

"Listen, Pachi," interrupted Don Román, "could you do me a favor?"

"Whatever you like, Don Román."

"Well, there's a wicker chest in a storage room in the cellar that I need, and I wonder if you couldn't bring it up for me."

Señorita Menchu's reaction was just as he'd expected.

What did he want the chest for?

Response: he needed some books from it.

But what kind of book could be in a chest that had been stored away for more than ten years without ever once being opened?

Some books from the time he'd been preparing for the liquidators exam, books he needed for his morning students. (Although he wasn't used to lying, this one came naturally to Don Román.)

And you need them right now?

"Especially now," argued Don Román, "because Pachi's here. He's so strong he could carry it up with the doorman's help."

"That man's help," replied Señorita Menchu with six months of scorn accumulated in her voice. The same number of months that they'd been angry with each other, ever since the doorman had quit offering to help Don Román and had made a remark her brother had already forgotten but not she.

"Is it very big?" inquired Pachi.

"What? The chest?" Señorita Menchu asked, answering her own question in the same breath. "Huge."

In other words it wasn't big, it was huge, and of course he couldn't expect any help from the doorman, for one thing because he wouldn't be there. He was never there when he should have been. Well then, Pachi the lady-killer's interest was now aroused. He said, "Maybe I can carry it up by myself."

Don Román felt a twinge of conscience thinking about his aide-de-camp's lumbago and was on the point of giving up on the idea. His sister had nipped it in the bud. Why bother pursuing it further? He wasn't even sure that *The Hunchback* was in the chest. There was a moment's silence broken by the *Cimarrón*.

"In any case we can try. There's no harm in trying."

"To make matters worse," insisted Señorita Menchu, "there's no light down there."

"Oh well, we can get by with a candle," said Pachi.

And so it was "we." In other words, he would look after the chest, and Señorita Menchu would hold the candle.

Don Román said, "The servant girl could go along to help Pachi."

He said it to spare his sister, but she vetoed his suggestion. "That girl? She never knows where to find anything. There's no way she could find the chest with all that mess down there."

"Fine, fine, just leave it."

But it ended up that they didn't just forget the whole adventure because that day Señorita Menchu felt like being a martyr. She combed her hair first because a señorita, even if it was just to go one floor down, could not walk out in the hallway looking the same way she did in her own home. She had no trouble finding a candle and candlestick because, with all the rationing of electricity, they always had some on hand. On their way out, Pachi took his beret, holding it in his hands instead of putting it on. In the hall, Señorita Menchu felt a certain satisfaction upon seeing her predictions borne out.

"You see? I told you the doorman wouldn't be here."

In any case, so there would be no doubt about it, she called out loudly without actually yelling, "Paco! Paco!"

Paco did not appear and Señorita Menchu insisted, "You see?"

This type of repetitiveness in a woman didn't bother Pachi. It was to be expected. In this regard, women were all more or less the same, all repetitious, quite needlessly so. Generally speaking, when females predicted that someone wouldn't do something and then were proven right, they got immense satisfaction out of it.

They lit the candle for the trip down the stairs to the cellar, and in the weak flickering light, Señorita Menchu didn't look bad at all. He'd already seen for himself that she was a woman with a good foundation and a powerful build, none of which was reflected in the lackluster quality of her face, not that she was ugly but more that she had the look of a spinster. The spinster part was more noticeable in her because of the constant complaints and sighs common to all women that were nonetheless more apparent in single women and widows. Pachi was very cynical about such things. To his mind, all they needed was a man.

The cellar smelled of mildew, and Señorita Menchu let herself be frightened by the smallest things.

"We're going to open the door? Oh, Lord!"

I'll give you "Oh, Lord," thought the *Cimarrón* while he forced the lock, all rusty and moldy. It took a lot of doing to maneuver the bolt. He managed somehow, but the wood, dilated from the humidity, kept the door from opening.

"It's always the same in the winter, you know. We've told the doorman a thousand times."

Then she repeated two things—that the doorman was a good-for-nothing and that she didn't understand why her brother wanted this chest after ten years.

The door was really stuck, which was fine with the *Cimarrón* because it had a kind of obscure symbolism for him. He wanted to show off for Señorita Menchu, who smelled good or anyway had a scent he liked. To top it off she said, "You won't be able to."

"You think not? We'll see."

He gathered up his considerable strength and threw himself at the door, which gave way on the first try, all except the bottom door jamb that he had to knock out of position with a kick. He was pleased with himself.

The señorita said, "Good God, Pachi! . . ."

I'll give it to you by God, the Homeland and the King—the *Cimarrón*'s unspoken intentions were clear, although he still felt that however propitious it might be, this whole affair could be awfully complicated.

"Did we break the door?" she asked, concerned.

"I don't think there was much to break. It's useless. Look at this panel." And he tore it off with a single blow. He then put it back in place so the señorita wouldn't worry because the door was the main entrance to the cellar, and she was afraid the other neighbors would complain.

"Are we going in there?" she asked, her fear somewhat ambiguous.

Of course they were. That's what they'd come down there for.

"Watch out for rats. . . ."

"Which locker is yours?"

It was at the back to the right, and they had to go down the hall, its cement floor humid in spots with even a puddle of water here and there. Spider webs hung from the ceiling.

"How awful! I haven't been down here for such a long time. You'd think they could keep it cleaner."

That's what was wrong with women; no matter how well-disposed they were, they let the slightest little thing upset them. He was sure that if he tried to make love to her, which he hadn't yet decided on, she'd have a number of objections to make about the cleanliness of the place.

The door to the Aldaiz's back room was no problem. It looked better inside and was relatively neat, although Señorita Menchu would have to say, "Good God, look at this! What a mess!"

Not that big a mess, the proof being that they found the square wicker chest right away. Pachi tried it out—it weighed a ton. It wasn't very big but the books were heavy.

"Do you think you can manage?"

"I've seen worse."

He lifted it up slightly to gauge how much it weighed, thinking that if he got a proper grip he should be able to make it.

"It'll be tough to get out of here because I can't get at it from the other side."

"Maybe I can help," said Señorita Menchu, and she placed the candlestick with the lit candle on an old dresser.

Just in case, she'd brought along a dust rag, and she began dusting the chest. Pachi watched her at work. Her hair had a blondish tinge, and a long lock had fallen onto her forehead. In this light her lips didn't look too pale; they looked appetizing. When she finished dusting, the señorita had to squeeze around the chest until she was facing Pachi, not an easy task because of all the junk in the way. It meant she had to do some swaying of the hips to get in position. All the while Pachi didn't take his eyes off her.

"Fine, now I'm set," said the señorita. "Let's see if we can lift it up between the two of us. I'll count to three, all right?"

"Pardon me?"

"We'll say one, two and three, and on the count of three we'll both lift at the same time, all right?"

Although she was a spinster, she still had a little girl's ways about her. Not that there was anything wrong with counting to three. It was just the way she'd said it.

"Sure," said Pachi. "One, two, three! Heave!"

Señorita Menchu's end lifted up slightly and Pachi's not at all since the handle had come off in his hand. They both laughed with unnerving complicity. Pachi's skepticism consisted in his not minding being the son of a Galician in a Basque town because as a pelota player he had very few equals. Just as in the blue rowing crew they ended up putting him in the bow despite the fact that that bastard the coxswain called him a Galician shithead, with *sh* for shit. This gave a balance to his life that was reflected in his lack of respect for words—when he didn't like them, he let them go in one ear and out the other. Because of his skepticism, he had trouble falling in love. Obviously he was not in the least bit interested in falling in love with Señorita Menchu. Moreover, he had no intention of doing so, although he could feel how in the dark room she neutralized the surrounding mustiness with her perfume. A perfume different than the one the girls in the house on Calle de Zabaleta used, the house he went to when he had no other choice. It wasn't that he liked Señorita Menchu's perfume more or less. Simply put, it was different.

She, clever woman, said, "Look, there's a rope behind you. We can put it under the chest, and between the two of us I think we can get it out of here."

Between the two of them again. The objections the señorita had wisely voiced minutes earlier in her brother's presence were nothing compared to the actual situation. It was becoming devilishly hard to get this chest, which felt like it was made out of iron instead of wicker, to budge an inch. And yet the señorita did not for a minute entertain the possibility of giving up. To put the rope under the chest, they had to draw closer together and even touch hands, something the dark made even more noticeable. Finally they decided to move all the junk in front of the door out of the way and drag the chest along on the ground. Pachi pulled on the rope and she pushed from behind. Pushed for real too. Pachi, however little he liked physical exertion himself, was a good judge of such things. She was a strong woman, and he'd always liked strong women. He thought that in spite of her finickiness, she could have been an excellent pelota player, like Chechu Larrañaga from Eibar. When they were outside the door, he said, "Hold it there."

Now he had enough room to maneuver, and he could strut his stuff, just in case. In case he changed his mind about what might happen between Señorita Menchu and him.

He stood the chest on its end, put his beret on after asking Señorita Menchu's permission, fed the rope through the only working handle, tied a knot, placed it on his head protected by the beret, knelt down and with both huge hands hitched it up from the bottom, and then in one motion propelled himself to a standing position. He adjusted the chest slightly so it sat square on his back, its weight evenly distributed between both arms and supported by his head. The señorita followed the operation breathlessly, her chest rising and falling as she panted since she too had been exerting herself. Once five years ago, she'd had a suitor, a business professor working in the Revenue Delegation under her brother. Her brother had cautiously championed his case and tried to show her what a suitable match he was but to no avail. The man wore stiff collars and smoked filter cigarettes that he made himself in a machine. The war was on then, and he'd been militarized in the procurement department. With his uniform on he looked even worse.

Pachi started up with a firm step, Señorita Menchu preceding him and lighting his way with the candle. In the doorway Paco the doorman—whose specialty was being around when he wasn't needed—asked them if they needed any help, and Señorita Menchu told him it was too late for that. Pachi, on the other hand, smiled at him. He had no desire to make an enemy out of the doorman.

Señorita Menchu entered the apartment triumphantly. Don Román was still contemplating with a melancholic air the triangle of sea he could glimpse through the mirador.

"There you are!" she said. Then she added, "Lord above!"

That day she prepared them a snack to shore up their forces. She herself had tea.

THE NEXT DAY Señorita Menchu was feeling doubly triumphant since she'd fired the maid. A feeling of euphoria enveloped her.

"Who does she think she is?"

It never failed. Every maid, no matter who, always ended up acting as though she were indispensable, especially in this house because of the don's paralysis. And yet, when Menchu suddenly fired her—what a relief!—nothing happened, and life went on as usual.

"You know what I think?" she explained to her brother. "I think we'd be better off with live-out help. She'd do her job, leave when she's through and we wouldn't have her around night and day, prying into our lives. What's more, it wouldn't cost as much."

Don Román didn't much care one way or the other. All he knew was that the good-for-nothing they'd just fired had understood him quite well and at least knew how to move him around the house in his wheelchair. It was going to be increasingly difficult to move him around.

That afternoon Don Román and his assistant went out for their usual walk. It was cloudy out as they walked along the sea toward Mount Ulía. Planicio joined up with them, and the don told him that he had asked for more information from Valencia on the taxi-cycle. He also gave him *The Hunchback* by Paul Féval—just as he'd thought, it had been in the chest—and assured him he'd like it. As luck would have it, in the same volume, bound with stiff cardboard binding and a cloth backing made by a craftsman from Calle del Pez, Madrid, in 1930, there were some other interesting novels: *Ivanhoe* by Walter Scott; *The Attack on the Lyon Post,* which gave no author because it was a "rigorously historical tale"; *Fabiola* by Cardinal Wiseman; *Life's a Dream* by Calderón de la Barca . . .

"This last one," warned Don Román, "you won't like. It's for grown-ups."

He always said, "Take good care of them for me." This was so the boy would appreciate them more.

Planicio always replied, "Don't worry, Don Román." And as proof of his zeal, he held on to the book with both hands, and if it was raining, he kept it under his sweater so it wouldn't get wet.

When they got back home, Señorita Menchu's euphoria was wearing off as she realized that the apartment was too big for one woman to look after alone. She'd looked into reliable live-out help in the area and gotten very few references, none of them encouraging. As always they all wanted something for nothing. The next day she'd go to the parish church and try to find a woman in need with the opposite attitude, in other words one whose desire to work was stronger than her pretensions.

In any case, she smiled at Pachi and asked him to do her a few favors while she tried to solve her problem with the help.

She had a package to be picked up at La Burgalesa bus station, something her brother-in-law, the miller in Salvatierra, sent every month. Could he go? At the same time—it was on his way—she asked him to withdraw some money from the bank since it would be difficult for her to get out the next day, for one thing because that good-for-nothing she'd had to fire had left the house in an absolute mess. The woman's talent for concealing dust in the furthermost reaches of the house was boundless. She, Menchu, was blind for not having seen what was under her very nose all these months. Not only was she blind, she was overly trusting, the proof being that she gave Pachi a check for 300 pesetas to be drawn on the account her brother had opened for her to cover household expenses. Pachi agreed to everything and headed off to his ruin.

In the morning, he picked up the package at La Burgalesa, weighed it in his hand and decided that it must be flour. He never once entertained the idea of opening the package. Then he went to the bank—it was the first time he'd been in an establishment of its class—where everything seemed so very easy. He handed the check over at the wicket that the receptionist indicated to him, and there he was given a number. The employee said, "When they call your number, go over to the cash wicket."

In effect, a few minutes later that's exactly what happened. The cashier asked, "How do you want it?"

"Pardon me?" asked Pachi, uncomprehending.

"Do you want it in bills of one hundred or smaller."

Pachi didn't know, and for want of anything better to say, he asked for bills of one hundred. They gave him three bills so new they stuck together, making it hard to tell that there were three of them. Those were days of waste not, want not, and even bank bills circulated for months, sometimes years at a time. They finished up in a sorry state, held together with glue or scotch tape because each bill, as long as its number was still legible, was still legal tender. He left the package in the garret room and went off to the bar since Señorita Menchu hadn't told him to come right back with the money.

It was a grim unpleasant day with no real rain. The farmers were growing increasingly pessimistic. Given the weather, the don wouldn't be in much of a hurry for his walk, and so Pachi had time to take a walk over to the Urumea fronton after his lunch. He'd already heard that Salsamendi III was playing in a combination of games that was a shoo-in as a money winner. The way he used the racket as though it were a natural extension of his arm, the third Salsamendi brother would most certainly end up outshining all his siblings; he used the racket like a whip—God himself would have trouble seeing the ball once he let it go. It would have to be a pretty sorry day for him to lose a game. But that was the kind of day he had.

Salsamendi III was not just elegant on the court but out on the street as well. He always wore a jacket and tie, unheard-of for a pelota player. Women found him wildly attractive. He wore the best in clothes, and in spite of his youth, his hair had begun to recede at the temples, which might be a sign of impending baldness, but which for the time being only served to make him look even more distinguished. He easily measured 5'9" but stood so straight he looked even taller. The previous summer, rumor had it that a marchioness wanted to marry him, and although no one could actually say which marchioness it had been, no one was surprised to hear it. He wasn't stuck-up in the least and returned everyone's greeting in the street. People didn't give autographs then, but he had a kind word for any children who drew near.

Pachi's disillusionment with the female pelota players from Gros was growing daily, and this wasn't the first time he'd gone back to the cathedral. Not that he'd wagered anything the other times. He was up in the gallery and the brokers didn't accept wagers from that high up. Of course, there was always side betting going on. The banker was a fellow called *el Potro*—the Sting—who stood at one end in front of the gallery. Some gamblers said it was better to play in the gallery because *el Potro* worked on his own and so didn't have to pay a commission to the house, which made the odds better. *El Potro* had to take considerable precautions; he refused any wagers where the money wasn't put up front. In turn, he didn't put the money away; instead he set it in small piles on the bench in full view of the public. Pachi put twenty duros on red—Salsamendi's color—since Salsamendi was favored three to one in the odds. It was now or never.

The game was pretty even until half-time, but from then on Salsamendi's partner really started screwing up. The fellow was from Elgóibar, a near beginner, and was eaten up by nerves. The public's jeering at him only made matters worse. Pachi didn't say a word because, in spite of his proverbial cynicism, he realized it was going to be tough to get out of this mess.

In spite of it all, Salsamendi was clearly a master at the game, but he couldn't work miracles. Once the game was over he was quite the gentleman, consoling his partner despite the fact that he'd lost the game for them and ignoring the spectators who continued to taunt the poor boy.

There was obviously only one way to get out of the tight spot he was in and that was to try his luck one more time. The next game was played with long wooden bats, and he placed twenty duros on blue, trusting to the advice given by a betting friend. His luck didn't hold out there either. In the remaining games, he'd tried other combinations, and at seven o'clock he left the fronton with only five duros left in his pocket. He hadn't had time to play them.

Part Two

Life with *Aita*

THE COMING of summer was heralded by the return of the count's household to 10-B Miracruz on June 20. The return was made with even more pomp and circumstance than in 1933 when one of the count's horses, a French import mounted by its French jockey, won the Grand Prize of the City of San Sebastian at Lasarte.

The heightened grandeur was attributable to several factors. Finally, as a consequence of a 1939 decree granting the return of Army-requisitioned vehicles to their rightful owners "as long as such persons or entities had been supporters of the National Movement," the countess—thanks to Jacinto's tenacity—managed to retrieve the black-topped yellow Hispano-Swiss car, which had lost none of its class in spite of the intervening years. The car had spent the war peacefully since it had been in the service of a staff general and so was still in good condition. Much better than most vehicles on the road in those years. In his zeal Jacinto even managed to retrieve his authentic ostrich feather duster and once again went happily about his business on Calle de Miracruz.

Jacinto was still extremely fond of Pachi and his son—

admiring of the athlete and sympathetic to the boy—but there was a noticeable change in him now that the family trustee had delegated all tasks related to the grandeur of the count's household to Jacinto. It was a particularly busy year for the trustee. The whole country was in a bad way, and they were reduced to eating bread made of corn, but things could have been worse; at least Spain wouldn't be entering the world war. He recouped—or rather restated the family's claim to—all the shares belonging to the count's household in the bank founded by the first count, the late count's father. The latter had had such a knack that ever since then there were titles of nobility for all his descendants since, aside from his financial wizardry, the first count had blue blood ties that came to light when the bank's consolidation gave him the means of exhibiting his intrinsic worth. As for the countess, whose fortune came from more conventional sources, the trustee revived a mountain grove in Puente del Arzobispo in the province of Toledo, which originally was meant to be used solely for its acorn crop and for grazing sheep but which could be used to plant rye for making bread.

A considerable distance separated the trustee's position from Jacinto's position, but the former, who had been a loan shark in his youth, was careful to keep all his bases covered, especially with regard to Jacinto who, given his particular leaning, might be capable of some fairly unpleasant business. Things were going well, and there was enough to go around. Which is why he delegated the responsibility for the grandeur of the count's household and its economic spin-offs to the man who had been the count's valet de chambre. The former valet refused to doff the black and yellow-striped vest he liked so much, although he was clearly more than just a house servant. The proof being that, after a brief struggle, the dirty old cook, the one who made hake with a green sauce that looked like flour paste and parsley, was confined—in spite of her position as a third-generation cook for the count's household—to the farmhouse at Puente del Arzobispo. There was no rancor involved; the move was simply made for the good of the household.

Within twenty-four hours of his arrival, Jacinto knew everything there was to know about the 300 pesetas Pachi had gambled away at the Urumea fronton with such dire consequences.

"What on earth were you thinking of?"

In other words Jacinto saw nothing wrong with helping oneself to others' belongings—in his case those of the count's household—but in a judicious fashion and in exchange for one's services. However, he would never have dreamt that someone of no mean intelligence would just help himself to 300 pesetas to go gambling at the fronton.

Pachi needed Jacinto's help and so deigned to try to explain.

"Winning."

"What do you mean, winning?"

"Winning, coming out a winner. By betting on Salsamendi with the odds three to one in his favor so, naturally . . ."

The theme was a familiar one, and Pachi was able to explain in a suggestively convincing manner just how natural it would have been to come out a winner at the fronton, as long as, of course, one kept one's wits about one and had a bit of good luck. "I've always had my wits about me, but lately luck just hasn't been on my side."

Jacinto was of a different mind, namely that Pachi had already had more than his share of luck, given the things he'd done for gambling's sake, beginning with the incident last summer at the Atocha public fronton, from which he escaped with nothing more than a black eye when he should by rights have ended up with his head bashed in, followed by his taking the 300 pesetas, which only ended up costing him his job when normally, if it hadn't been for Don Román, who was a saint as everyone knew, he'd have ended up in prison. Not to mention in 1930 when he bet against a whole town, his own town, Pasajes de San Pedro, because he knew that his team—in which he was the bowhand—hadn't a hope of winning. The nerve of the man!

But Jacinto had his own weaknesses, and one of these was Pachi the *Cimarrón*. His weakness was in no way attributable to a deviant character trait; simply put, he liked the man, and Pachi's friendship—despite the fact that behind his back people called him a Galician *tranposua*—had always given Jacinto a certain prestige and even protection. When they gave Pachi a black eye in the tavern at Eguía, it had taken three of them to take him on because one man alone could never have gotten the better of the *Cimarrón*.

"We've got to settle this," Jacinto said.

"Settle what?"

"This whole business with Don Román. We've got to find a way for you to give his money back."

"It won't be easy."

The Galician could read something in Jacinto's eyes that needed translation. Jacinto's pupils shone with the light of power because he was a man who was in a position to lend 300 pesetas, which in 1942 was a great deal of money. He was in a position to lend that amount because in a world convulsed by war, the count's household was seated on the firm bedrock of the bank and the mountain grove in Puente del Arzobispo. Whatever was good for the count's household was good for him since he took his own small share of course and paid for it through his services. Lately he hadn't just been giving the young señoritas manicures. He'd also been giving them permanents using the accredited Solriza kits, a 100% domestic product. He'd been able to make the most of the kits because the young countesses—whose looks were nothing out of the ordinary—had very manageable hair that took well to his elegant bouffant hairstyles, symbolic crowns of their nobility. Perhaps French *coiffeurs*, whom he admired so much, would object to the mechanization of the process, but he was only an amateur, learning his trade as he went.

Despite the fact that the Galician read in his look the possibility of a loan of 300 pesetas, Pachi insisted, "It won't be easy."

It wouldn't be easy because Don Román would get over it, especially with Planicio thrown into the balance, but Señorita Menchu's reaction was of much greater concern.

IN JUNE the drought caused a series of dry violent thunder storms. The farmers had no words left with which to lament their lot. Any precipitation during these storms was usually in the form of hailstones. The apples on Mount Ulía were all shriveled and bruised, never having ripened, but even the *Cimarrón* himself had to make do with them because since he'd left his job as Don Román's aide-de-camp, he had no money coming in whatsoever. Planicio had been dragged down with him, losing his job as an errand boy.

The only thing they kept buying every day was milk for Planicio. The Galician thought it was the least a father could do for his son, even if it meant going back to smoking cigarette butts again. Planicio bought a peseta's worth of milk, which equaled a third of a liter. In the shops, milk cost three-fifty a liter, but the mustachioed milk lady, as a special favor, sold it to the boy for three pesetas. Planicio mentioned her gesture to his father, but the latter, a cynic, said, "I don't want any favors from anyone. Tell her to throw in half a peseta's worth of water and leave it at that."

The day Pachi left the Urumea fronton with five duros in his pocket, he headed off to Calle de Zabaleta since the outcome would be the same whether or not he gave the five duros back.

When the truth sank in in Don Román's house, there was a silence such as the one preceding the end of the world. Señorita Menchu had been having a particularly bad day, finding it impossible to look after the house and her brother on her own. To make matters worse, her brother was oblivious to the strain she was feeling and had already said several times, "I'd like to shave."

Each morning he managed to sit up in bed, pulling hard with both hands on the reinforced metal headboard that was slightly higher than usual to make it easier for him to pull on. Then the maid gave him a washbasin full of hot water and his shaving tools. He made out fine with the safety razor, always making sure not to cut himself because when he did, even if he staunched the flow of blood with cigarette paper, it usually stained his shirt collar, and then his younger sister chided him, "You're not careful enough."

Or worse yet, she showed him pity. "If it's too hard to do, I can help."

If it's too hard to do. Just starting each new day was terribly hard, and after making it through the night—something he'd been managing for many years—it was even harder to face the new day. He tried to make the time after dinner last and so listened attentively to everything his sister had to say. Usually she talked about the inexcusable behavior of their brother and sister to whom she'd written without receiving a reply; or if they had, the reply didn't answer her questions; or the miller in Salvatierra was announcing a poor harvest and indicating he might have to cut back on the amount of flour he sent to them; or her suspicions had been confirmed concerning their sister-in-law in Bilbao, a woman with no principles whatsoever, who was breaking her husband's heart. It went without saying that the latter's case was a downright disgrace. Two years had gone by since he'd been to see them, and the last time he'd only come to ask a favor of Don Román, who at the time was still the Revenue delegate, so they were all dancing attendance on him.

She also talked to him about her friends, and Don Román kept listening because he didn't want to be left alone at night, hoping against hope that he'd find a comfortable position in his bed, one so comfortable that he'd fall immediately into a deep sleep. But all that ever happened was that he ended up lying on his back in a fearful fitful sleep. At first, while Señorita Menchu and the maid were still up, he lay awake, their preparations for bedtime making him feel like he had company. Both women were tired by that time and didn't quarrel. Or else they didn't quarrel so as not to disturb Don Román who'd already been "put down." That's exactly the way his sister phrased it when talking to the maid.

"We're going to put the don down now."

By putting him down, they meant putting him to bed so he could begin his night. They stayed up planning the next day's meals down to the last detail.

"What should we have tomorrow for the first course?" the señorita asked, condescending this once to consult the other.

"We could cook some Tolosa beans."

"Are there any left?"

"Yes, Señorita."

There was a moment's silence, a moment filled with expectancy for Don Román—already in his hopeless position on his back—because he loved red beans from Tolosa.

"All right, that's what we'll have but without any pork."

He didn't like the sound of this last bit because red beans without pork weren't nearly as good. The maid was of the same opinion and tried for a compromise. "We could put a bit of pork in when we refry them."

The señorita said no and then added, "And we'll mash the don's up for him."

In order to make the beans even easier to digest, they diluted them at the last minute with a bit of hot water so that by the time they put the plate down in front of him, the mixture was lukewarm and tasteless. When he asked for a bit of salt, his youngest sister reminded him that the doctor had recommended he eat bland foods.

"What should we have next?"

Don Román couldn't be bothered to listen for the answer because whatever it was, it would be grilled, overcooked and stripped of any fat. In other words, one hassle after another, as his aide-de-camp would say, the same aide-de-camp he had lost because of 300 pesetas, which in 1942 represented a great deal of money but not enough to be worth losing a friend over.

The doors were locked, the shrill click of the bolt sounding at the front door, and yet Señorita Menchu still said, "Malen, did you lock the door?"

"Yes, Señorita."

And the night of silence began. Don Román glimpsed a light shining through the crack between the wall and his door, but it went out almost right away. Señorita Menchu slept on the other side of the wall. Her spring bed groaned slightly as she lay down and gave a last sigh. "Oh, Father in heaven!"

Señorita Menchu was quite a one for sighing imploringly. There was no escaping the silence now, and the possibility of this night ending and the light of the new day shining seemed highly remote. From time to time throughout the night, the water tank in the bathroom on the floor above started up, a noise that at times comforted him and at others irritated him, but any which way it didn't really matter because he could do nothing about it.

"If you need anything, just call," his sister said every night after putting him down. But he never did. He would when his time had come to die, certain as he was that it would happen at night. What's more, he wanted it to happen at night, without causing too much inconvenience for anyone. He assumed he'd die from suffocation when the last exhausted muscle could no longer keep his lungs going. Death would come at night, during his sleep, almost unannounced, leaving him just enough time to say, Dear God, or Jesus Christ my Lord, God and mortal both.

One day he asked his physician, "What will I die of?"

His physician was thrilled to have such a learned and compliant patient. Compliant in that he didn't require all sorts of evasive answers nor want to know more about his disease than the physician knew. The latter knew only that his patient's muscles were slowly atrophying without knowing why.

"Die? Who's talking about dying?"

He, Don Román Aldaiz, was talking about dying because it was a subject of interest to him.

"You know, you could still live to see us all die before you . . . "

And once again he went over everything Don Román must do in order to outlive them all—exercise his muscles, get out in the fresh air as much as possible, cut out all animal fats, starches, sausages, preserves . . . Since Don Román was not particularly interested in seeing them all in the ground before him, he insisted, "Fine, Doctor, but since we all have to die some day, I'm asking whether you can give me an idea of what I'll die from based on what you know of my disease."

The physician kept quiet for a minute, then adopted a festive air and like someone breaking good news said, "Perhaps from a heart attack. What do you think?"

Well, that was fine with him. For his part, he reckoned that the heart attack would be brought on by lung failure. In any case it would happen at night.

The arrival of daylight, with the first rays filtering in through the cracks in the Venetian blinds, was such a relief that he fell asleep. He'd just have dozed off when they came in to wake him up, or at least that's the way it seemed. That was when he felt that society as a whole expected him to lead a normal life—get up, work, go out, come home—and that even while shaving he was expected to be careful not to cut himself and bloody his shirt collar. The transition from night to day, day to night, dreaming to waking, all required such an effort on the part of his weary muscles that he welcomed the thought that heavenly beatitude might consist in the static contemplation of God. Sometimes at night he said to himself, All right now, I've freed myself from this crippled body, and the two of us are alone. *He* is watching me, and I am watching Him.

During the early years of his infirmity, in which the loneliness of his bed was even harder to bear, he felt his situation was sufficiently distressing for him to be compensated with a vision. With time he became more resigned and understood that with the background noise of the water tank, it was very difficult to reach a state of ecstasy. In compensation, however, he entered into a state of well-being that transported him into the dream world—the non-being—so fervently hoped for, so much so that he sometimes felt a twinge of conscience.

"I confess," he told the parish priest during confession, "that when I begin to think very hard about God, I fall asleep."

The parish priest marveled at how such a gentleman could act like such a little boy at times and felt like asking him whether he ever dreamed about angels.

That was another thing—Don Román didn't dream about angels per se but about a beautiful woman—not always the same one but always with similar traits—with whom he began gentle distant touching, which ended up in such a way that made it very difficult to explain during confession.

"Did you consent?"

"I don't think so because I was asleep."

"Well then, you don't even have to bring it up in confession."

He thought he was sleeping, but when it happened he awakened and entered into a state of lethargic daydreaming, thinking to himself that if this was what it was like in one's dreams, how much better it must be in real life. Afterward, in broad daylight, he had to fight the memory that rose to the surface every time a female passed by. On the Kursaal esplanade, there was a bosomy nanny who always greeted him warmly.

"Good afternoon, Don Román."

He responded, looking up and over her headdress toward the boundless sea because if he looked any lower, everyone would see what was going on inside him. Nevertheless, in spite of all the suffering, he thanked God that the paralysis had not affected his genitals. He fought; he lived. Even if at night he sometimes shed tears brought on by his rage, his affliction or his powerlessness.

WHEN THE TRUTH sank in at Don Román's house, there was a silence such as the one preceding the end of the world, so unthinkable was it that Pachi might have kept the sixty duros and the miller's bag of flour.

Until seven that night they had no news. Planicio, as usual, had run up and down the streets an hour earlier trying to find them. Not seeing them on Paseo Nuevo, he then reconnoitered the Plaza de Guipúzcoa without any luck. He asked the doorman at the Miramar movie theater if they were there, was told no and began at a stepped-up half-trot to make his way back to the Miracruz garret room. Stepped-up because if he hurried he could finish reading *The Hunchback* this afternoon and be ready to refresh Don Román's memory about who the real holder of the secret sword thrust was, Henry de Lagardière or the Count of Nevers. But when he arrived at the door, Francisca sent him off to see Señora Asun who'd already received three telephone calls about the tenant from the garret room.

"What's with your father?" asked the corset maker in a strange voice.

"I don't know."

"They've been waiting for him all afternoon at Ramón y Cajal."

Planicio didn't know what to say, and Señora Asun remarked, "What's he been up to now?"

Even without knowing about the check, the feeling in the neighborhood was that if the Galician hadn't shown up, it wasn't because something had happened to him. It was because he'd been up to something he shouldn't have been up to.

"In any case, you go off and explain it to them."

This so that Señorita Menchu—who was also a member of the church women's group—wouldn't call her a fourth time. Planicio did as he was told, although he had no idea what explanation he could give.

Señorita Menchu opened the door and spat out, "So finally someone shows up."

The vestibule was next to Don Román's sitting room, and the don made an effort to look around the door, saying to Planicio, "Come in, come in!" because he didn't want to leave the boy alone with his sister.

He still hadn't shaved but was resigned to it. The worst part had been tutoring his students with this thin raggedy beard that, it seemed to him, gave him even more of a porcine air. He ran his hand over his face and could feel the stubble. But his sister had already said a number of times, "You can shave later!" She yelled it at him because she'd had it with all the filth that sow had left behind. Don Román didn't like to hear her call Malen a sow in that tone of voice, but he didn't dare defend the girl.

Once his classes were over, he retired to his invalid's chair, like a half-wit always looking out to sea with only its inner movement visible from this distance. Like him. Although he was still enchanted with the idea of celestial beatitude being the ecstatic contemplation of God—the antithesis of having to get up, bed down, move from his chair to the wheelchair and back again—he hoped he would be granted one thing, that heaven was over there, where sky and sea met, not because the Earth was round and the horizon its optical consequence but because there was nothing more beautiful than the stretch of sky above the sea between Santa Clara Island and Mount Urgull. It was dark blue at sunrise and crimson at sunset. His hope was that when his lungs began to fail—followed by the cardiac arrest—he would be carried off to that heaven in a small fishing boat that would begin its journey with the first morning rays and travel slowly enough so as not to reach the heights until late afternoon when the horizon began turning crimson. Once he asked his aide-de-camp, "Pachi, how far away do you think the horizon is?"

"Pardon me?"

"Over there, where heaven and sea meet, see?"

Pachi answered, "Yes," but cautiously because abstract questions like this one made him wary.

"How far away would that be?"

"It's hard to know."

But Don Román wanted to know.

"Try and imagine how long a small fishing boat would take to go that far, then calculate the distance. You've been a sailor."

"Let's see . . . until it disappears from sight?"

Good point. Very good point because Don Román would be in heaven when it disappeared from sight. With his question asked, Don Román didn't pay much attention to the answer— whether it was five or six nautical miles, whether it would take three or five hours to get there—because he was thinking about what would be waiting for him on the other side of the crimson horizon. Sometimes with anguish in his heart. But whatever it was, let it be over there. That sad, sad afternoon while his sister kept repeating furiously that Malen was a sow who'd left the house in such a state that she'd have to call in the city sanitation department, he just kept watching more intensely than ever the triangle of sea he could glimpse through the mirador. From four o'clock on Señorita Menchu kept asking where on earth Pachi was, why he hadn't arrived yet. At one point she said, "To top it all off, I'd asked him to run a couple of errands."

"What errands?" asked her brother.

"Oh, to pick up a sack of flour from La Burgalesa and cash a check for me."

That was when he felt the tightening of his heart, not because of what might be on the other side of the horizon, but because he knew that Pachi the *Cimarrón* could not be left to walk around the city with 300 pesetas. Afterward, he regretted his words a thousand times over because, by giving voice to them, he cut off any possibility of a solution, but he couldn't help himself from exclaiming, "Whatever were you thinking of?"

"What do you mean?"

"Sending him to cash your check for you. Obviously you don't know the man."

At first Señorita Menchu didn't realize what he meant. If she even mentioned Pachi's late arrival, it wasn't because she was in a hurry to have the money or the flour; it was because she thought she could ask them to dispense with their walk that afternoon and have Pachi help her move some furniture around to see just what condition Malen had left the house in. She wanted him to help her the way he'd helped her carry the square wicker chest up from the cellar two days earlier. Efficiently and without incident but in a way she quite liked. And in enjoyable company. Which is why it was such a blow to go from this pleasurable sense of expectation to a terrible suspicion. The suspicion that he might have kept *her* money; the suspicion that his courtesy in the cellar and the parade of strength he'd put on with the chest, which was as heavy as lead and demanded an extremely strong physique in all respects, might only have been a bid to win her over. The transition from one state to the other was a difficult one, but once the transition was made she threw herself on the telephone to call 10-B Miracruz via Asun the corset maker.

Don Román was transfigured. All he could say was, "Now wait, who are you calling? I didn't mean it. What are you doing? It's not even six o'clock yet."

Please let her wait. Even if Pachi had kept the 300 pesetas, they'd come up with a solution. Moreover, it probably wasn't a case of his just taking the money. Please wait.

"And Planicio, is he there?" asked Señorita Menchu over the telephone. "I beg you, Asun, tell whoever gets back first to come right over."

When he heard Planicio's name, Don Román could see him in his mind's eye running up one street after another at his farm horse's half-trot, excited about seeing the don again to relive and rehash the adventures of the knight of Nevers. He felt helpless, as though he were going to cry. When his sister hung up, Don Román said to her, "If Pachi comes, let me speak to him first."

"What's this? Now I'm not capable of speaking for myself?"

"It's just that, please . . . "

Don Román didn't know what he was asking for, and he finished with an entreaty. "Please, if Planicio comes, let me speak to him."

But she didn't.

IF IT HAD BEEN possible to join together Planicio's and Don Román's sorrow, something special would have flowered that night.

If there had been the slightest hope that the whole affair might be treated as though it were a mistake, it was immediately dispelled by Señorita Menchu.

"So there you have it. Tell your father he's a thief, just that, a thief. The nerve of the man!"

What's worse, she looked at Planicio as though she suspected the sins of the father to be visited on the son. The boy had no doubt that what Señorita Menchu said was true because it wouldn't make sense otherwise. And then Don Román's silence was all the confirmation he needed. The level of indignation seemed to him to be proportionate to the amount missing because 300 pesetas was an enormous sum for someone from the garret room at 10-B Miracruz in 1942.

"You know nothing about the flour either?"

Don Román, when allowed to speak calmly, could express himself just fine, but in an argument he had to refrain from speaking because his tongue, which always stuck slightly out from between his fat lips, seemed to go all hard and he stuttered. So he said nothing and let her proceed with the brutal cross-examination. The boy didn't dare glance his way, and so the don couldn't even console him with a look. The most he could stammer out was, "L–leave him be, Men–Menchu. The b–boy is n–not at f–fault."

"So now he's the one I'm accusing, am I?"

But the "he" in question was quite sure that he too was at fault for having such a father.

Her anger was all-encompassing, although it revolved around what that thief had done with the 300 pesetas. Five hundred meters separated Calle de Miracruz and Calle de Ramón y Cajal, and nothing that happened in between was a secret. Everyone knew that while Pachi's wife was still alive his behavior had been questionable at best, but once he was widowed, after the initial mourning period—if there had even been one—he'd started frequenting Calle de Zabaleta, a real disgrace, those poor unfortunate women who needed her prayers, although even now those sickening women might be copulating with the *Cimarrón* for her 300 pesetas.

"Did I accuse the boy in any way? I'm doing him a favor by having him tell his father to bring back the money before I call the police."

Don Román stammered out as best he could, but softly since there was no way to check his sister's flow, that, "No, not for him to worry. She wouldn't go that far. Don't worry, Planicio. I'll speak to your father. Tell him to come see me. We'll talk." He spoke hesitantly and almost inaudibly. But the boy didn't hear him. It was impossible to hear over the torrent of words coming from Señorita Menchu. Moreover, she had him glued to the spot in the doorway of the sitting room, and the distant afternoon light from the window behind Don Román in his chair shone in Planicio's eyes—it was the time of day when the setting sun appeared in the triangle formed by the mirador—so it was impossible to see much less hear the don.

The don's sister's last words to him as she led him to the front door were "Remember now, or else."

Don Román murmured, "Planicio, Planicio," over and over, but the door had already closed behind him.

IF IT HAD BEEN possible to join together Planicio's and Don Román's sorrow, something special would have flowered that night.

The *Cimarrón* showed up in the garret room at eleven o'clock, calm, expecting some trouble but confident he could settle the matter. Planicio, whose eyes were dry but whose heart was weeping, said, "What have you done, *Aita?*"

The Galician looked at him, aloof. In those days, parents had no need to justify themselves to their children.

"What do you mean?"

"Señorita Menchu says you kept the 300 pesetas from the check she gave you to cash."

The Galician's position was clear. "I needed the money, but I'll give it back to her."

Then Planicio, who still had engraved on his mind and his heart each word Señorita Menchu had uttered, said, "But *Aita*, that's stealing!"

He wasn't trying to teach his father a lesson in morality, just show him how Señorita Menchu viewed the matter. Nevertheless, he did say, "But *Aita*, that's stealing."

At that, *Aita* stepped up and, although Planicio instinctively took a step backward, hit him full across the face. In the Trincherpe district of Pasajes de San Pedro, parents routinely hit their children with more than symbolic blows.

"Go wipe your nose." This because the blood was flowing freely. Here again was another example of what worried Pachi about his son. Any child, when his father lifted his hand against him, knew what was coming and took precautions. In fact, his father—the Galician's father—had had to take his belt to him because it was so hard to hit the mark using just his hand. What's more he held the belt by the tip so the buckle could do its damage. Planicio, on the other hand, just stayed rooted to the spot so of course the blow hit him full across the face.

Actually his father had done him a favor because once *Aita* was asleep, Planicio could start to cry, something he desperately needed to do. The garret room was comprised of a bedroom and a kitchen—its shelves, the range, a cabinet, a table, four chairs, the count's old rickety armchair and an extension where Planicio's bed stood. When Planicio's mother died, Pachi took the master bed out of the bedroom, set it up next to his son's and left it there.

His father dropped off to sleep right away; sleep came quickly to him when he had worries. He'd told his son that he'd give the money back. But he didn't know how. Originally he thought the money could be docked from the salary Don Román gave him, but maybe they'd made such a big deal out of it that he was out of a job by now. Judging by the way his son had spoken to him, the latter seemed to be a distinct possibility.

When his father slept, nothing could wake him. Just in case though, Planicio went outside to unleash his grief. Sometimes he felt badly because he'd forget his mother for stretches of time, especially since he'd met Don Román, who was there for Planicio alone. Just like *Amá,* who had never seemed to have anything more important to do than wait for him to come home so she could say, "Where have you been? How come you're so dirty? Put that shirt back in your pants. What a mess you look! I've made you some custard. Would you like some? Come on, come over here so I can wash your face a bit. Now what have you done to get your hair all matted like that? Don't worry, I won't pull."

The Galician, who was a born cynic, watched and said, "Thank God one mother's enough."

His mother combed his hair out so gently it felt like a caress. Even though she had to use the steel comb for nits, it didn't hurt. Every week she washed his hair with water she'd heated up on the stove. The whole process took some time because they had to agree on a temperature first.

"Careful, *Amá,* it's burning hot!"

"How can you say that? Look, I've got my hands in it."

She added a bit of cold water anyway. The soap they used wasn't the best and took forever to lather. Planicio liked it better that way because *Amá*, with her short vigorous hands, scrubbed away as hard as she could into the hairline, starting at the nape of his neck and stopping every once in a while to scratch his scalp.

"There, that's the spot!" he said. "That's where it itches."

"Let's hope you haven't got lice," said his mother, but only for form's sake since she took great care to see that he never did get lice.

Meanwhile, another pot was on the stove heating up, this one with clean water to rinse the soap out. She poured it little by little out of a pitcher over the wash basin, using her hand to swish it through. He loved the feel so much it gave him goose bumps. Afterward, she wrapped the big towel around his head and began drying his hair so vigorously it made him dizzy. She rubbed hard because that way the hair grew in healthier. She lightened her touch to finish, holding his head against her chest. Then she pushed him back slightly and took the towel off to see if his hair was dry. But Planicio said, "Do some more."

He put his head back on *Amá's* chest, and she finished by scratching his back. That's why Planicio liked it better having his hair washed when *Aita*, who thought it was all a lot of babying, wasn't around.

Now he supposed that even if *Amá* were still alive, she wouldn't wash his hair anymore because he was too big. When she fell ill and couldn't get up from bed, he sat on the floor next to the head of her bed, and she ran her hand through his hair.

"*Ené*, look at your hair!"

"I can wash it, *Amá*," he said.

She gave him instructions on how to wash his hair, instructions he followed to the letter, although he already knew them off by heart. But afterward, when he finished wringing out the water, he went over to the bed, sat down on the floor again and

Amá finished drying his hair with a towel to help his hair grow in healthy, even though she couldn't rub hard anymore.

Sometimes he felt bad about forgetting his mother. At other times he felt she'd never died at all. That night early in June, it was hard to cry, not for fear of waking up his father, no fear of that, but because his heart was still so heavy. At times like this he still whispered under his breath, *"Amá, Amá,* I'm over here . . . "* so his mother would know the tough time he was having. The weather that day had been nothing out of the ordinary, but in contrast, the night sky was full of stars, beautiful stars that clearly showed the Ursa Major, the only constellation he knew. His father knew many more from his time as a sailor but only as helpful navigational tools that were of little use in a city, so he never talked about them.

Maybe if Planicio had dared look at Don Román, the latter would have said something to him, but an opportunity never arose because Señorita Menchu's nonstop talking gave him no choice but to stay nailed to the spot. Anyway, he couldn't see the don at the back of the room with the light of the window leaving him in shadow. During his thirteen years he'd realized that his father sometimes did strange things, like taking 300 pesetas, thinking he'd give them back. Or like what had happened at the Atocha fronton last summer when he went from being the expert to the Galician *tranposua*. Planicio always knew his father was different. Different from the others. When Pachi won the Concha regatta in 1931, there were thirteen oarsmen plus the coxswain, but when the crew disembarked on the Fuenterrabía quay, it was obvious that the real winner was Pachi—just Pachi, without the epigraphic Galician—sitting in the bow, alone, not paired up with the other fishermen, pulling them all along. "Heave!" he bellowed and the oar bent in his hands, driving against the wave as though it would break in two, but he managed to skirt the danger and have the crew skipping along on the crests of the waves. The other oarsmen had no choice but to fall in with the bowhand's rhythm. The coxswain counted the strokes in Basque, gesturing with his left arm, but the bowhand was really the one propelling them forward. That's why, when they drew near to the buoy, the coxswain yelled out, "Bring it around, Pachi!" because the trick was to cut the corner as sharply as possible, using a rhythm based on quick staccato strokes. The *Cimarrón* complied, forcing all the others to follow suit, and the coxswain, seeing that they were heading straight for the bay, had nothing but words of praise to call out to Pachi who, not as loudly, made reference to his, the coxswain's, whore of a mother. This because back on land, the latter had called Pachi a shithead Galician, with *sh* for shit.

Whenever anyone heard Pachi tell the regatta story, they were suitably impressed for a while, or even for much longer because his fame as a bowhand was legendary. The Orio coxswain himself, whose name was Olaizola, had said in public that with a man like him in the bow he could have won the regatta too. Eventually, however, they forgot his feats and couldn't forgive him some of his other antics. Planicio would never forget because during the regatta, even though he was still just a little boy, he'd followed behind in the shipowner's boat with *Amá,* and everyone in the boat kept exclaiming over his father. That's why his father had misunderstood him when he'd said, "But *Aita,* that's stealing." What he'd meant was that he wanted *Aita* to go clear up the matter as quickly as possible, especially with Don Román, so they could still be friends. But after the blow he'd received, it looked like they were all angry, that nothing would be that simple, and that, once again, he was in for a stretch of loneliness.

THE SAME LONELINESS created a lump in Don Román's throat while his sister explained that now finally everything was oh so clear and that she meant business. Either Pachi brought the money back the next day or she'd report him to the police.

"You shouldn't have spoken like that to the boy."

"What did I say to the boy? I have nothing against him."

But in the very next breath she said, "Like father, like son."

The don's tongue had gone all stiff between his lips, and he couldn't argue anymore.

"When you can, please help me to bed," he asked Señorita Menchu.

Which she did after a short while, and to comfort her brother she told him she'd talk to Paco the doorman the next day about taking him out on walks the way he used to while they looked for another assistant. Don Román kept quiet, although he had a hard time imagining life without the *Cimarrón*. It was just the time of year when the blackberries were about to ripen, and Pachi had told him he knew a hidden place where the fattest and juiciest berries could be found. And that he, Pachi, had the perfect recipe for blackberries in sugar and white wine. The don couldn't imagine going back to the way things had been before. Paco the doorman would leave him on the Kursaal esplanade facing the sea, and Don Román would pray for the morning steamboat to appear soon and carry him off slowly, slowly enough so that he could see day's end, to the other side of the horizon. To make matters worse, the bosomy nanny would come up to greet him again, and he'd have to turn his gaze away without seeming to be discourteous. The children, as usual, would stand staring at him out of curiosity from a distance. When he smiled at them, they'd run away. Likewise if he spoke to them. One of the mothers would conscientiously scold her child and say, "Speak when you're spoken to." But the child would make a face because the don looked so strange, scary even. One child, braver than the others, on a dare or just for fun, would come up from behind, touch his wheelchair and run off. Paco the doorman would yell at them, and then he'd feel even more alone while waiting for his steamboat.

That's why he would miss the *Cimarrón*'s son even more than the *Cimarrón* himself. The *Cimarrón*'s boy was a child too, but when he saw the don, he picked up speed and cried out excitedly, "Don Román!" Everyone stood watching them, but the boy paid no heed and ran up to him, panting, to tell him some important news—that he'd read the book and liked it (there hadn't been a single one he hadn't just loved); that Señora Asun had sent him on an errand to Calle de Urbieta, and the lady of the house had asked him to remember her to Don Román since she knew that he, Planicio, saw him every day because she in turn, the lady of the house, had seen them walking by; that he'd found out they'd be showing a new movie at the Miramar theater on Saturday and—what luck!—it was a Deanna Durbin film called *It Started with Eve*. And above all, ever since the subject came up for the first time on a rainy afternoon under the pillars of the Guipúzcoa plaza, Planicio always asked, "Have you found out anything about the taxicycles?"

He had but he didn't have the heart to tell the boy, not all of it. The vehicle wasn't as stable as it should be, and on sharp curves it was apt to overturn.

"In any case," he said to ease the boy's mind, "this summer we have to organize a trip to Martutene. I know a taxi driver. . . ."

It wasn't a bad solution, but Planicio would rather make the taxi-cycle more stable so that *Aita* and he, both with their berets on just right, could parade the don through the streets of San Sebastián, pedaling hard on the tandem bike.

Being transported from this world of hope to the immobility of the Kursaal esplanade would, Don Román hoped, be the ultimate effort he'd have to make. Worse yet, Paco the doorman, for sole distraction, would read the newspaper to him when he thought the don was bored. As though the newspaper had anything left to say that could be of interest to him. At times like these, he felt he could learn to hate his sister. Señorita Menchu didn't report Pachi to the police, but on the slightest pretext, she'd ask who on earth that scoundrel thought he was and declare she couldn't be fooled that easily.

She always stressed the *she,* making the statement very personal, as though something were between them that made Pachi's
actions even more reprehensible. Don Román listened in
silence since there was no point saying anything. In any case,
he kept thinking that the money was his after all, and he knew
what Pachi was like. The Galician had always tried to do right
by the don and not take advantage of their forays into the old
quarter, even though, if it were left up to Pachi, he would
always have had twice as much—there was no mistaking it. He
ordered what Don Román ordered or only had seconds if the
don insisted. On the other hand, on the few times the occasion
had arisen, Pachi had kept Don Román's money. Once the don
asked him to buy a book for him and gave Pachi five duros.
The next day Pachi said, "They didn't have it in, but they said
they'd be getting it one of these days so I'll go back for it."
Don Román never did know if Pachi went back, but after a
certain amount of time he quit asking and gave the five duros
up for lost. The same sort of thing had happened on a few
other occasions, but Don Román accepted having a friend who
was like that once in a while. The business of the 300 pesetas,
in spite of the amount it represented, could have been worked
out if he hadn't gone and said to his sister, "Whatever were you
thinking of? What do you mean, sending him to cash your
check? You obviously don't know him."

In any case, Señorita Menchu's reaction had been out of all
proportion, a sign of a marked personal grudge. In other
words, her anger with Malen, the fired maid, was for esthetic
and hygienic reasons—the dirt the woman managed to accu-
mulate was offensive to her, to Señorita Menchu, and to anyone the least bit sensitive. On the other hand, what Pachi had
done was beyond description. This she said as though she'd
made a superhuman effort to describe the act and had been
confronted with the only logical conclusion, namely that what
he had done to her had no name.

THE SILENCE BETWEEN the garret room at 10-B
Miracruz and the apartment on Ramón y Cajal lasted the
whole month of June. It was during that time that the race
between the bridges was held. Planicio had no choice but to
agree to the race despite the fact that he was suffering so much
from a lack of nutrition that he just couldn't get any hungrier.
The stews and attention Jacinto paid to them counted for
something, but the food went through his system so quickly
that sometimes Planicio felt like he was hungrier afterward
than he'd been to begin with. *Aita* started going back to
Pasajes Ancho and bringing home fish scraps that they ate with
vinegar and salt.

"It does wonders for the digestion," commented Pachi contemptuously.

Señora Asun wrestled with whether or not the sons should
be made to pay for the fathers' sins. Either she felt she should
show solidarity with her fellow women's group member Señorita Menchu, or she had no need for Planicio anymore because
of a reduced workload; in any case, she let him go.

She told Señorita Menchu so in a meeting of the church
women's group.

"I had to let Planicio go too."

"You did? Was he up to something?"

"No, not with me, but, my dear, after what they did to you
. . ."

In actual fact, she didn't let him go. She just told him she'd
call him when there was an errand to run. And then she never
called him.

The grandeur of the count's household was more noticeable
because the fourth floor apartment at 10-B Miracruz, the one
that had been vacant since the beginning of the war, was now
occupied by the countess's niece, the daughter of one of the
late count's younger brothers. The daughter had married a
Cuban of Spanish origin, educated in England, who chose for
his wife and himself a marquisate, the Mata marquisate. Jacin-

to, elegant effeminate herald that he was, explained it all very well. Just as they had inherited a mountain grove in Puente del Arzobispo from the countess's side, they had inherited titles from the count, titles his father, the founder, had reinstated. Jacinto was referring to the founder of the family bank, a blue-blooded financier who had hired a professional genealogist to delve into the military exploits of his ancestors, exploits to which certain titles of nobility were ascribed. These were then grouped together for subsequent distribution. The Cuban drew from this field of titles, coming up with a marquisate, which in spite of its higher-sounding name, was inferior in category to the count's. The latter's household, although unobtrusively, due to the countess's simplicity, stood for the grandeur of Spain itself.

The marchioness's lineage was not readily apparent. With-out being homely, she was rather dull and excessively preoccu-pied with the education of her three children. In contrast, her spouse, the marquis, had a noble cosmopolitan bearing. His father had sent him to England for his schooling since his father had business dealings with the Yankees, all of whom were in awe of a Cambridge accent. Furthermore—and his son inherited his taste as well—he was wild about everything British.

Jacinto was truly devoted to the marquis and had been the one to convince him to spend the summer in San Sebastian. The marquis usually vacationed along the Riviera or in the south of England, but Europe was still at war and he had to be content with staying in an apartment on Calle de Miracruz. His American-sized fortune as a shareholder in the Cuban Telephone Company and the Havana Electric Light Power Co., which, now that his father, a distinguished emigrant, had passed away, consisted of monthly payments out of Geneva, was more substantial than that of the count's household.

With due reverence Jacinto introduced the marquis to Pachi on the occasion of a chance encounter in the vestibule. Jacinto was not just an expert on heraldry; he also knew the protocol to follow when making introductions. In other words, the distance between the marquis and the Galician was such that introductions had to be made so that both parties realized who the other was—without shaking hands—since it wasn't as though they would ever be friends.

"Señor Marquis, this is Pachi Lourido, whom I've already mentioned to you."

At the same time, Jacinto positioned himself so as to prevent Pachi from stretching out his hand. He didn't have to worry about the marquis, not because the latter might think it beneath him but because the marquis was very British in all he did, and in England people shook hands very rarely.

"Pleased to meet you," the marquis replied courteously. His accent was that of an Anglo-Saxon whose Spanish was fluent. It was only when he was very angry, something that never happened in public, that he let slip a few Caribbean idioms.

"Pachi was a great oarsman, and in 1931 he won the Flag of Honor for the Fuenterrabía crew."

"That's right, you'd mentioned that."

Jacinto had mentioned it because the marquis had also been an oarsman for an outrigger in Cambridge. The way the marquis spoke of those days, it was never really clear whether he actually did take part in the famous Oxford-Cambridge regatta. He always said, "I rowed for the Cambridge crew," but left it at that.

The marquis looked at Pachi with interest because Basque oarsmen had quite a reputation, and Sarasúa had earned his fame in an international regatta rowing in a single yawl despite the fact that he was more of a crewman. Sports played an extremely important role for the marquis. He was an excellent tennis player and showed a benevolent interest toward the popular sports played in the Basque region.

"What's more," continued Jacinto, "Pachi is a very good pelota player."

"Jai-alai?" inquired the marquis. He was referring to the game of pelota played with a wicker racket best known in Miami and Cuba.

Pachi understood what the marquis meant and explained that he played hand pelota. The marquis expressed amazement at this aspect of Pachi's personality, saying he found it hard to understand why one would bat a ball around with one's hand. The British were the ones who'd discovered the many ways a ball could be projected in order to create a situation of conflict for one's opponent—cricket, tennis, volleyball, soccer—but had never entertained the possibility of using the human hand as a percussive element. The human hand as a prehensile element, capable of catching the ball and throwing it to another player, yes, but using one's bare hand as a tool to bat the ball with, no. This is what he explained to Pachi, who answered, "Yes, Señor."

The Galician was having a rough time of it in a social milieu that refused to understand that the matter of the 300 pesetas was a personal affair he would resolve with the family from Ramón y Cajal as soon as he was able to. And so he agreed with the marquis, saying that "Yes, Señor," batting a ball with one's bare hand was barbaric.

"Does your hand not swell up from playing that way?"

"Yes, Señor, a great deal."

"I'm not surprised," said the marquis happy to have his suspicions borne out.

"But the worst part," continued Pachi, eager to please, "is when it splits open."

"What ever do you mean?"

"Look here," and he pointed to his right hand. "Sometimes it feels like my hand is splitting open," he continued, "not from the outside but from the inside—the muscles separate from the inside out and sometimes make it impossible to finish a game."

"Of course, of course," agreed the marquis, delighted to

find that the sport was much more barbaric than he had imagined.

Jacinto couldn't resist joining in the conversation. "Have you seen his hand, Señor Marquis?"

The marquis thought it looked slightly deformed though powerful. As for Pachi, it seemed to him that a gentleman who was willing to spend time standing in a vestibule talking about how to hit a ball just might take some interest in his, Pachi's, life, at least now when no one else took any interest at all, and he, conscientious father that he was, was beginning to worry about his son's lack of nutrition not to mention his own hunger.

"Well, it was a pleasure meeting you, Pachi," said the marquis, and he tipped the brim of his soft felt hat very slightly.

Pachi took off his beret and, improvising, half-bowed to the marquis.

The marquis took the stairs up the three flights because he didn't trust the elevator. The esthetic value of the stairway had changed with the arrival of the count's niece and nephew by marriage. A bare marble staircase still led to the second floor; from the second to the third—the countess's floor—the marble was covered in thick carpeting that they took up when they returned to Madrid. From the third floor up, the stairway was made of a blend of gravel and cement giving it an institutional look. The marquis mitigated its effect with another carpet, thicker and wider than his aunt's. The countess and her nephew-by-marriage got along splendidly although the latter sometimes felt his aunt wasn't doing everything she should to uphold the standards of the count's household. When he moved into 10-B Miracruz, he suggested to her that they lay carpet on the stretch of stairs leading to the corset shop as well. The countess disagreed gently but firmly, saying things had always been that way. The marquis insisted because it only seemed natural to have the carpet start at the ground floor and continue on up to the fourth floor. Diplomatically the countess suggested they'd see next summer. The marquis kept his peace, thinking there was very little likelihood of his coming back for another summer; the European war should be over by then, and if not, he could rent a villa somewhere close to Miraconcha. The Miracruz apartment was too small for him. His aunt's apartment was another story. Since her door was 10-B, it meant there was also an A as well as a C; the entrance into the countess's apartment was through B, but then the apartment spread out to A and C, occupying more than a thousand square meters and providing for sufficient living quarters, sitting rooms and social standing. The fourth floor, on the other hand, was just part of 10-B and had no A or C.

AFTER TWO WEEKS of silence, it seemed Planicio would never see Don Román again. He didn't dare go near Kursaal for fear he'd run into the don. Even on holy days he went to the Capuchinos church instead of the parish church to avoid bumping into Señorita Menchu and having her bring up the police again. The señorita had been categoric—"Tell your father to return the money or I'll call the police." And when she'd said good-bye to him, she'd repeated, "Remember now, or else." He, Planicio, had never said a word to *Aita* about the police; nor had he ever brought up the whole business again, not after *Aita* hit him.

Planicio spent his time alone. When the count's household arrived, he was entertained by all the commotion it caused, especially all the furniture they moved into the fourth floor apartment. One day he helped the movers, and one of the men gave him a peseta. Three children moved into the apartment, one a girl his age, the other two a younger girl and a baby boy, old enough to walk. They had a British nanny who always spoke to them in English. Francisca the concierge was slightly overwhelmed by such grandeur and didn't know how to act. She was particularly thrown off by the marquis who took the stairs, leaving her waiting anxiously next to the open elevator doors. She had specific instructions for Planicio: not to run

down the stairs, not to be constantly going in and out, not to
stay with his father any length of time in the vestibule, to
move out of the way and leave the marquis the railing if he met
up with him in the stairway, but as much as possible, to avoid
being there at the same time as the marquis. Planicio took all
kinds of precautions, carefully checking the stairway before
going up or down. Once, he did happen to be on the stairs at
the same time as the marquis, but it was a cloudy day and he
pressed back against the wall so hard, so as not to bother him,
that the marquis didn't see him. Officially he didn't meet the
marquis until the day of the race between the bridges.

He went back to Urbistondos, but nothing was the same
because his friends weren't there anymore. Just some little
kids. He didn't see Ramoncho much because his friend worked
as an apprentice in a printing shop.

"Jacinto," he asked the manservant, "maybe you could find
me a job."

"We'll find one, don't worry. I've talked to the shop owner,
and he promised to call you when he needs someone."

Planicio walked up to Mount Ulía looking for apples and
gazed over at the Kursaal esplanade, wondering whether Don
Román was there. In the bushes among the scattered rocks
close to the sea, he found wonderful ripe blackberries but
didn't want to pick any because they had no white wine to go
with them. Or sugar. Besides, they'd said they would eat the
berries with Don Román.

One sunny Sunday he went with Ramoncho to the Amara
suburb on the outskirts of the city next to the Urumea River.
With the rain, small ponds had formed, and the two boys went
sailing on old planks. Ramoncho didn't read much, but he
liked to have Planicio tell him stories. On their trip to the
Amara ponds, Planicio told him about Huckleberry Finn
crossing the Mississippi River. In one pond there was an old
abandoned car with water up to its windows. They used a board
to steer themselves over to the car, climbed up on the roof,

then pretended it was the deck of a boat like the ones on the Mississippi River.

Once they'd finished sailing they had foot races back, Ramoncho getting a head start but Planicio inevitably catching up to him. Planicio hazarded a guess that he could run around San Sebastian in two hours. Ramoncho pooh-poohed the idea—the whole purpose of the exercise—and Planicio insisted, mostly because he'd quite liked the bet made by Phileas Fogg who went around the world in eighty days in the face of great difficulties. Then they started to elaborate on the idea, deciding he could probably make it around the city in that amount of time but only if he caught the tramway for part of the way. They also discussed the meaning of city because if one had to go as far as Mount Igueldo on the one hand and the top of Ategorrieta on the other, it would be impossible to make it in that time, even taking the tram. The discussion started to wane when Planicio said, "I bet I can run between the bridges in less than fifteen minutes."

"Which bridges?"

"The Station Bridge and the Hierro Bridge."

"There and back?"

"Of course. Look, I start at the station, run along Paseo de los Fueros until the Hierro Bridge, cross over, then run back to the station along the other side of the river."

To Ramoncho it sounded like an awfully long way because San Sebastian ended at Paseo de los Fueros. The Hierro Bridge was for trains only and seemed awfully far away, which is why he said Planicio couldn't make it in fifteen minutes. There were other reasons too—on their way back they'd pass through the station anyway. Sunday was turning into a dull day, and they had no money and nothing to do. On the Station Bridge a few fishermen were trying their hand at rod fishing for grey mullet. Both boys leaned on the wall to kill time but not because they were interested in the fishing, which was nothing special.

"I bet you can't do it now," said Ramoncho.

Planicio knew he meant the fifteen-minute run. He thought it over for a few seconds and said why not. He'd nothing to lose and it would be fun. One thing though—neither of them had a watch. That could be a major stumbling block. They thought of maybe asking one of the fishermen for the time when Planicio set off and then again once he got back. But it was a bit embarrassing, and anyway the fisherman might leave before he got back. Afterward, they thought of using the station clock, but both of them looked up at it suspiciously because it didn't keep time all that well. Often it just stopped. They looked and checked—six-fifteen.

"I think it's working, don't you?"

"Looks like it. Let's see."

The two of them gazed steadily at the big rusted sphere. It felt like the hands had stayed put for an awfully long time, but it couldn't have been that long because they saw the big hand move to twenty.

"Seems all right. Doesn't it?" said Ramoncho.

"Yeah."

"How about you start at six-twenty-five and be back for six-forty. Sound all right?"

"Sure."

Suddenly Ramoncho wasn't so sure.

"What if you trick me? Like if you say you've run the whole way and it's not true."

Planicio wasn't offended by the question. In this type of situation it was expected that where one could get away with something, one did.

Both of them stood silently thinking, and after a bit Planicio said scornfully, "How can I trick you, stupid? If you stay here to wait for me and I start running up Fueros, the only way I can come back is to go over the Hierro Bridge."

That much was obvious, but since they were in no hurry, Ramoncho insisted. "Once you're out of sight, you could swim across the river to the other side." He was just talking for the hell of it because Planicio only knew how to dog paddle enough to keep himself from drowning. If he had to swim across the river, it would take him a lot longer than fifteen minutes. For that reason, even before Planicio could respond, Ramoncho gave in, saying, "Okay, let's get on with it, I trust you."

They decided to wait until six-thirty to make it easier to keep time.

Planicio started up at his usual trot, except he pumped his arms as if for a race. Ramoncho followed his progress along Paseo de los Fueros until he was lost from sight. There was a large vacant lot past the Amara playground where the circus set up in the summer. There the city ended and time started to drag for Planicio. It was even more boring than when he trotted up and down streets making deliveries. He still couldn't see the Hierro Bridge and thought about turning back, thinking he must have miscalculated. Not miscalculated really—he'd only said he could do it in fifteen minutes for something to say because he felt Ramoncho was bored being with him. The weeks were long, and at least on Sundays he could go out with Ramoncho. He felt he should give him a good reason for coming. So he'd have at least one friend. Not many kids didn't have a mother, but that wasn't his fault. However, it was embarrassing not to have any friends.

A couple who looked like farmers were out walking in the sun, pushing a baby carriage. The husband had his sleeves rolled up. Planicio saw he wore a watch and stopped to ask him the time.

"Could you tell me what time it is, please?"

In those days not everyone had a watch, and people who did were used to being asked the time. The man looked at his watch conscientiously and replied, "Six-thirty."

"Thank you," said Planicio and started running again, thrilled that no time had passed. What's more, now he could see the Hierro Bridge. As soon as he crossed the bridge, the race would feel like it was almost over. He had the impression that everything was downhill on the other shore. He liked crossing over the Hierro Bridge because it was really a railway bridge, not a pedestrian bridge, so the only place to run was on thin narrow sheets of metal that resounded loudly as he ran. If a train ever appeared, it was scary. Halfway back from the bridge, he got a stitch in his side—they called it a *limaco*—and stopped for a minute to see if he could get rid of it by breathing deeply. Afterward, he thought it best to keep running, only more slowly, holding his hand against his side. When he saw the station off in the distance, he stepped up the pace as much as possible because it seemed to him he'd been running for an hour and that Ramoncho, tired of waiting, would have left. But no. He was still there. Planicio was panting but not overly so. Between breaths he said, "Whoo-eee!" Then he asked, "How long did it take me?"

Both of them looked at the clock. It showed six-forty, but the big hand was moving to forty-five.

"You made even better time," admitted Ramoncho.

"It didn't take me fifteen minutes?" exclaimed Planicio.

His friend said no, only ten minutes. A fisherman, out of luck and bored, had been half-watching what the boys were up to.

"Did you go as far as the Hierro Bridge?" he asked Planicio.

"Yes, Señor."

"Well, there and back must be three kilometers."

They didn't reply, seeing no reason to, and both made their separate ways home. That night, Planicio told his father, *"Aita,* I made a bet I could run from the Station Bridge to the Hierro Bridge and back in fifteen minutes and I did it in ten."

"How much did you bet?"

"Oh, nothing. I just said I could, and Ramoncho said I couldn't."

His son's ways really had him worried. Planicio never took

advantage of the opportunities that presented themselves. When Planicio lost a pelota game he'd been winning hands down, all he said was, "It doesn't matter, *Aita;* we were just playing."

The Galician had already noticed that his son, in spite of his flat feet, was a very good runner, and the next day in the bar, he put out some feelers. Lately it hadn't been easy for him in the bar because he usually had to have someone else pick up the tab. Of course, debts were owed him since he'd always been happy to pay a round when he was in the money, especially if they were from gambling wins. He looked on it as his obligation. In any case, he'd come to realize that not everyone thought the same way. The barkeep let him run up a tab because he was a long-standing customer. But usually he had to make do with a couple of small glasses of red wine. He needed that amount just for medicinal purposes because every day he was more depressed. When he got depressed, he cursed his brother-in-law from Alza who overnight had become a Carlista and been appointed alderman on city council and who never took off his red beret, not even for God, and devoted his time to black marketeering. Of course, he did receive good news every once in a while. His aging bachelor brother-in-law had married a buxom young girl from Irún who was almost certainly cuckolding him. One thing for certain was that his wife drank and had already caused more than one public scandal.

Pachi put out some feelers because one of the bar regulars was a lathemaker who worked for Vitorio Luzuriaga and whose son had won the 1000-meter race in the provincial championships of the Youth Movement in Tolosa's Berazubi stadium. The lathemaker had told the story several times already, always stressing that the race had been held in Tolosa's Berazubi stadium, which at the time was just about the only track and field stadium in Spain. Pachi's plan worked because it was simple, because the climate was favorable and because the Galician was an old hand at getting people to wager. The lathemaker didn't

want the race to be too long because his son was not a long
distance runner.

"Well, my son is," replied Pachi, and everyone broke out
laughing.

The other man took offense and said, "Speaking of dis-
tances, have you money to go the distance with a bet?"

There was a minute's tense silence because the remark was a
low blow. The Galician simply responded with a yes and the
other man ventured, "How much do you want to bet?"

"Five duros," replied the Galician, affecting a careless air.

They settled on the following Sunday in the afternoon, the
race to be held on the same course where, according to the
Galician, his son had already shown his stuff.

Of course, Pachi didn't have five duros, but he was counting
on Jacinto. The manservant was appalled. "But, have you seen
the other boy run?"

"What's there to see?" said Pachi, offended. "He's not up to
speed. That kid can't cut it. Planicio has it won, easy."

"But when did you ever see him?" insisted the manservant,
distrustfully.

"Listen, they live hereabouts. How could I not have seen
him?"

Pachi didn't know where they lived and had never seen the
boy run, which was why he didn't mind embellishing the
story, the smaller the detail the better, to make it more convincing.

"How do we split the bet?" asked Jacinto, already half
resigned.

"Half and half."

"What do you mean, 'half and half'?"

"I put up the boy, and you put up the money." Before Jacinto could protest, Pachi went on, "We have to put up more
money. The boy's father is betting five duros, but there'll be
others from the bar who'll get drawn in, and we should gamble
at least another five duros."

Finally it was time for the clincher. "Have you ever lost when I've told you what way to bet?"

He was referring to the previous summer on the Atocha public fronton where, following the *Cimarrón's* advice, Jacinto had made a few pesetas. There was a difference though because Pachi knew pelota and knew the players, but Jacinto had never heard him talk about running races. Furthermore, the two boys weren't even real runners, and nothing pointed to either one of them being a serious contender.

"I'll have to think it over. Jesus, what a man. Always up to something!"

Wednesday was Jacinto's day off, and that afternoon Pachi took him to see Planicio run. Planicio protested, or rather he protested before he knew the whole story.

"But, *Aita*. I said I ran it in ten minutes but I'm not sure!"

"Well then, you shouldn't have said anything!"

"Ramoncho's the one who told me!"

Finally his father pointed out that Planicio had to run and win, or he, Pachi, would personally bash his head in. On Wednesday with Jacinto, Planicio was already resigned to his fate and knew he had to make a good impression. The manservant still called him Francisquito because he loved using the diminutive form. For all the running they made him do, it was impossible to tell what the final outcome would be, but Jacinto had a good time with the *Cimarrón*. The latter told a few highly off-color jokes, and Jacinto objected out of a sense of propriety.

"Oh, Pachi, the things you know! Go on, tell me another one but not quite as dirty."

That very night, Planicio saw there was a positive side to the race. They decided he had to be kept well-fed so he'd be good and strong on the day of the race. The idea came from the marquis who'd heard about the race and taken an interest in it. This type of money-backed bet was also very common in England. He didn't have first-hand knowledge of such bets, but he'd heard that many lords at the beginning of the century organized foot races in which their servants, and sometimes even they, participated. Once, the story went, the Count of Norfolk organized an endurance race in which runners could only drop out if they passed out. One of the count's own servants won, an East Indian who ran barefoot and lasted for three whole days. Jacinto knew how much the marquis was interested in this type of sporting event, which is why he told him about it.

"What day is the match to be?" inquired the aristocrat.

"Next Sunday, Señor."

"If I can, I'll be there." Then he added. "You'll have to be sure to feed the boy a hydrocarbon-based diet until the day of the race."

"What's that, Señor?"

The marquis explained that Africans and Asians were such good long-distance runners because they ate tuber plants and starch rich in hydrocarbons. He also explained the metabolic process involved. Jacinto translated this as best he could, and for four days they fed Planicio meat and potatoes. The man-servant brought the basic ingredients up directly from the count's pantry, and Pachi cooked generous amounts so there was enough for both of them. They also gave Planicio large glasses of milk with lots of added sugar because the marquis had recommended glucose as well. Planicio's stomach was a bottomless pit, and he devoured everything they put in front of him because he hadn't had a solid meal for almost a month. Jacinto took fright, saying, "All that food will surely be bad for him!"

"Man, what harm can it do!" replied the *Cimarrón* who knew all there was to know on the subject. In the Basque country, preparation for sports contests had always involved eating huge quantities of food. When he was on the rowing crew, for two weeks before the race, they'd eaten a kilo's worth of steaks every day.

"Bone in or out?" asked Jacinto with interest.

"Listen, there was so much I can't say. What I can tell you is that one plate wasn't enough to hold it, they had to use two plates. And if anyone couldn't eat the whole thing, it meant they were out of shape and had to be replaced."

Given all the attention he was receiving, Planicio was happy but worried at the same time.

"*Aita,* what if I don't win? . . ."

Jacinto, understanding, said, "Just do your best and don't worry about the rest."

"Except," intervened the *Cimarrón,* "your best means winning. Is that clear? Go on, go practice."

With everything that had happened to him, Planicio was becoming a fatalist. He'd lost his mother, and no one had ever explained what she died of. The following year his father had told him he couldn't go to Atocha anymore, once again without an explanation, and had flown into a rage when Planicio misinterpreted him. Señora Asun had said, "I'll call you when I need you to run an errand," and then had never called him again. Now his father was telling him he had to win a race without even saying whom he was running against. Above all, and worst of all, was the business with Don Román. When they'd been together, everything had seemed different, and now they didn't see each other anymore and clearly never would again.

Come Sunday he missed Don Román more than ever because he was sure the don would have liked to see him run, or if he hadn't liked the bet he would have convinced his father not to make him race. As things stood, Planicio would rather race because he felt well and strong. For the first time in a long time, people—Francisca, Jacinto and his own father—were looking after him.

"How do you feel?"

"Good. Shouldn't I?"

Besides, Don Román always used to say, "It's something to see that boy run. He never gets tired of running." In other words, it was almost certain Don Román would have liked to see him run too, and he, Planicio, would have wanted to win even more. In any case, Planicio had decided to do his best to keep on Jacinto's good side since Jacinto desperately wanted to see him succeed.

"This afternoon the marquis will almost certainly be coming," Jacinto had announced in a trembling voice.

But Planicio was more interested in making Jacinto happy because from time to time he heard him say to *Aita,* "Pachi, we have to solve this business with Don Román. You can't stay on bad terms with a gentleman like him."

Aita agreed but said it wasn't easy, not easy at all, and that the two from Ramón y Cajal hadn't tried to understand. In other words, *Aita* too was offended because there was no reason to get so worked up and call him a thief in front of his own son without even knowing what had happened to the 300 pesetas and how he planned to return them. What kind of behavior was that to say such things in front of a child? What must his son have thought?

They gave *Aita* a bicycle to follow behind the race. The lathe-maker had his own; it was agreed that the fathers would act as their sons' trainers and coach them during the race. The lathe-maker also brought a stopwatch along, one they used in the foundry to clock the workers. There wasn't much use for it because the race would be won by the first one in and time didn't matter, but having a timer made it seem more official. They gave the stopwatch to Raimundo the barkeep, who was also the judge since he hadn't joined in the betting because all the others were his customers, and he didn't want any trouble. At first they congregated on the Station Bridge but then decided to move because it was hot out, with only a slight wind from the south, and the sun was beating down on the bridge. Moreover, quite a few fishermen and passersby had started staring at them. All the regulars from Raimundo's bar were there, and the group of about twenty people stood out. They moved

over to Paseo de los Fueros, which had benches and trees for
shade. The lathemaker looked suspicious and said, "Look, if
the race is supposed to be from one bridge to the other and
back, they'll have to start at the bridge." He was referring to
the Station Bridge.

A brief discussion followed. Then the Galician declared it
didn't matter—wherever they started, the course was the same.
This caused some further discussion, more because it was Sunday than anything else; the spectators had come straight from
the bar and had already had a drink or two. But they were all
in good spirits and looking forward to a good time, except the
lathemaker from Luzuriaga who seemed to be preoccupied.
Pachi tried out the loaned bicycle and had trouble at first staying on because he hadn't ridden one in more than ten years.
Everyone laughed except the fellow who'd loaned it to him,
who called out, "Hey! Watch it with that bike or you'll be running just like your son."

They sat down on benches at the end of the Paseo under the
shade of the chestnut trees, most of them smoking cigars—it
was a Sunday—all of them content and amused by the Galician's caustic humor as he organized the bets, although he did
point out the bets wouldn't be final until Jacinto arrived since
Jacinto was going to be the bank.

"You and Jacinto are pretty cozy," said one fellow.

"What can I say? When there's no choice . . . I should tell
you it doesn't take long to get used to, and it's not really all
that different. I'm sure you'd like it."

Pachi made it sound like something it wasn't, but everyone
laughed because only he could have such a quick comeback,
which was also a put down.

Planicio sat on the wall overlooking the river, suffering from
a mild stomachache because the wait was making him nervous.
The other boy was also off on his own but closer to his father,
who spoke to him every once in a while. The Youth Front
champion for the province of Guipúzcoa was wearing short

pants and white running shoes. Planicio was wearing his blue cotton long pants because he didn't have any others. The same thing with his fiber sandals; he was wearing the only ones he had. This too had helped shape Planicio's character in that he didn't have any material options—he had *one* shirt, *one* pair of pants; he had shoes or sandals but not both at the same time. In other words, when his father said, "Let's go to the race," he didn't have to think to wear this or that so as to be more comfortable and run better. He put on the only things he had. Life was simple, which is why his fatalism and his resignation added up to the same thing.

The lathemaker asked, "What are we waiting for?"

They explained again about Jacinto and also that the marquis might be coming. In fact, the marquis did arrive at the wheel of his car, quite an elegant brand new Citroën. Jacinto sat next to him. The marquis stopped a little way off, and Jacinto got down to see what was happening. He had thirty duros in his pocket because the marquis had asked, "How much is the bet?"

Jacinto didn't dare say five duros, but he didn't put more than thirty in his pocket just in case.

None of the people present had any idea who the winner would be, but bets were placed—mostly in the lathemaker's son's favor; after all, he did hold a title—and Jacinto only gambled ten duros. He went back to speak to the marquis, who of course hadn't come to bet but instead to participate as a simple spectator of one of the popular games so rooted in the Basque way of life and so characteristic as well of his beloved England. He got out of the car and greeted the others courteously.

"Good day, Señores."

Without hesitation they all stood up, removed their hats and returned his greeting. The nobleman was of medium height but of a good build. He wore a white sharkskin twilled jacket, a blue raw silk tie with red stripes; his shirt was also made of silk, cream-colored; he had dark pants and white summer shoes with black trim, and to top it all off, a soft grey felt hat and, in his buttonhole, a sprig of tiny blue flowers.

He was a man who knew how to impress since he had conscientiously and successfully prepared for his role as a marquis. His wife was the one with the blue blood, and he was the one with the prestige. The prestige of having rowed in the Cambridge crew, of being an excellent tennis player, of having very pleasing features, a lightly bronzed complexion, not too much so, blue eyes and a highly attractive smile.

When he said, "Good day, señores," everyone stood up without Jacinto having to say who he was; they knew without being told.

Then he said, "Good day, Pachi."

The latter quickly got off his bicycle to return the greeting.

"Where are the competitors?"

Planicio, who was still sitting down because he wasn't sure where his stomach ache was leading, didn't move since he hadn't heard the marquis. The slight made Jacinto nervous.

"Francisquito, come over here!"

Those gathered together would have laughed at his saying Francisquito but didn't dare in front of the marquis.

Once the elementary courtesies were dispensed with, the marquis went back to his car since it didn't befit him to become too involved in something he was watching as a simple spectator.

It wasn't easy, but at last the start judge managed to get everyone to agree, and the runners set off followed by the two fathers and two other cyclists who wanted to see the race from up close. The lathemaker's son got off to a good start, running on the balls of his feet, slender and graceful. He made a good impression on the group, and they commented, "He's running well."

Not that they all spoke at once, but it was the general feeling. In no time at all he had a 100-meter lead on Planicio, and the collective wisdom was that the race was as good as over.

Someone said slyly to Jacinto, "Jacinto, how about another bet?"

But Jacinto couldn't, for one thing because he was seeing to the marquis, who, once the runners had disappeared out of sight, said, "Take the wheel. We'll follow them."

Which is what they did. They let them run out front, and by the time they were half a kilometer away from the Hierro Bridge, the Berazubi champion had an even bigger lead on Planicio. The marquis said, "That boy," referring to Planicio, "has a funny gait, but he's a steady runner."

"Yes, Señor," admitted Jacinto. "I've already told his father he should take him to see a doctor, but he won't listen. The boy has flat feet."

Jacinto knew already that the fifteen duros were lost and it was breaking him up inside, but in front of the marquis he wanted to show that he knew how to lose like a gentleman because, in compensation for this disastrous race, he was driving the car that belonged to his beloved marquis, something that made him dizzy with emotion. If it were up to Jacinto, the marquis would be a Grandee of Spain.

"Don't get too close," recommended the marquis.

Jacinto was happy to comply because he could imagine the things the *Cimarrón* was saying to his son, and it was better they didn't reach the marquis's ears. For starters, the lathe-maker who used his bicycle every day to go to work had no trouble riding and could keep up with his son without losing his dignity. On the other hand, the Galician looked completely out of control on his, missing the pedals and constantly having to put his feet down on the ground. One time when he missed a pedal, he hit his ankle with all his might against the chain wheel and swore so loudly he could be heard from the car. Jacinto blushed. They could also hear Planicio complaining, "But I can't run any faster, *Aita!*"

In other words, the two camps were worlds apart. The lathe-

maker was pedaling smoothly at a slow pace adapted to his
son's gait; every once in a while he'd circle back so as not to
overtake his son and glance over at his rival. He told his son,
"Good going, son; you've got it made."

Planicio ran the way he always had—splat, splat!—with his
toes pointed out, all the while arguing with his father. The
marquis observed, "He shouldn't talk to his son so much; it
makes it hard for the boy to breathe properly. You should tell
him so."

"Yes, Señor."

Jacinto pulled the car up to the *Cimarrón*'s bicycle and sig-
naled for him to stop.

"Listen, Pachi, don't make the boy talk while he's running
because he'll run out of breath."

The manservant noticed that the Galician, in his fury, was
about to say something inadvisable, and Jacinto cast him a
pleading glance, at the same time motioning with his head
toward the marquis to make him understand. The other caught
on and said, "Yes, Señor."

The marquis had been looking out the window absent-
mindedly since he didn't think it befitted him to intervene,
seeing he was just a spectator. But when he saw the boy's
father understood, he thought it only right to say, "Your son is
a very sure runner but perhaps he lacks in velocity because of
the way he runs. He should have his feet examined."

"Yes, Señor."

Meanwhile, the race continued, both boys having crossed
over the Hierro Bridge, and the *Cimarrón* hated having to keep
up a conversation on the state of his son's feet when he should
be egging his son on. By that he meant, just like in pelota,
insulting him, generally with references of an obscene nature.
The same was true of the rowing crew where oarsmen worked
in pairs and rhymes were made out of "guts" and "nuts," mostly by the coxswain whose job it was. Which is why he said,
"Yes, Señor," to get it over with and because a marquis who

took an interest in a bet such as this one had to be, in some way, a useful man to know.

"Yes, Señor."

"Go on back to your son; he's still going strong."

From where they sat they could see the two runners perfectly on the other side of the river. The provincial champion still had the lead, but perhaps in perspective it didn't seem quite as big a lead or at least it hadn't grown. The afternoon, though hot, was pleasant and quite a few people out walking commented as the boys ran by since they could tell it was a race.

Pachi had to pedal hard on his bicycle, zigzagging as he went, to catch up with the runners. The marquis remarked, "I'm afraid your friend's son . . . What is his name?"

"Who? The boy?"

"Yes."

"Francisquito," the manservant thought it over for a minute, then added. "Actually I call him Francisquito, but everyone else calls him Planicio."

The marquis laughed lightly and continued, "Well, I'm afraid that Planicio doesn't have enough velocity for the finish. If it weren't for that, I don't think his would be a lost cause."

Jacinto didn't know what velocity meant, but he was quite happy to see the interest the marquis was showing in the race.

"Carry on, but don't get too close. We don't want to crowd them."

What really complicated the final result was the additional bets, which, uncontrolled, were being placed among the bar regulars when the runners passed in front of them on the other riverbank. The runners could be seen quite clearly, and some people thought that the lathemaker's son had an unbeatable lead and others not, and that furthermore, the Galician's son was having an easier go of it. Even so, said the former group, there was only a third of the race left and therefore there was nothing Planicio could do. So the bets were three to one in favor of the lathemaker. At any rate, they were in for a rollick-

ing good time because if the Galician lost, it would be good for
a laugh since the man, when he was angry, came out with the
strangest things. Likewise if he won with the added advantage
that if he won he'd pay them all a round.

Cries urging on one or another of the runners went up from
the spectators' side of the river.

To Planicio they yelled, *"Alza Pilili!"* It was a kind of war cry
for those from Alza, and the boy raised his arms in response,
excited and gratified.

"See, see!" said his fans. "Look how easy he's running and
how he responds."

And they started up again, "Go get 'im, Planicio!"

Once again the boy raised his arms. It even seemed like he
let himself be distracted from the race for a minute, giving the
lathemaker's son a chance to increase his lead slightly.

When the boys reached the Station Bridge, the group got to
its feet and took up positions from where they could see the
whole final portion of the race. Some more daring than others
climbed onto the wall, but the others told them to be careful
not to fall into the river and mess everything up. However,
they didn't see the last part of the race because the provincial
champion ran into some difficulty. Just after the Station
Bridge he began to run much more slowly. It was then that the
Galician, with a genuine bellow, shouted for his son to run
harder, which was fine with Planicio because he could see he
was catching up. That is, he couldn't speed up that much, but
it didn't bother him to keep up the same pace, his usual pace,
the same one he'd run Señora Asun's errands at, and even at
that he realized he was catching up because the other boy
seemed very close. When the two were side by side, the lathemaker's son made a couple of strange noises, almost stopping
as he staggered and said, "Oh, no!" several times. His face was
drained of all color, he crouched down and began to vomit, at
first just saliva, then everything. Planicio stopped, naturally,
and held him by the shoulders so he wouldn't fall over. He also

asked him how he was, and when his father, Planicio's father, yelled, "Keep going!" the boy didn't understand what he meant. The lathemaker had dismounted from his bicycle, somewhat shaken by his son's condition.

The Galician, in an amazed stupor, his eyes rolling out of their orbit, yelled at his son, "Keep going, *gilipollas!*"

In those days, this variation on the word imbecile was not very common and less so in the Basque region, but it wasn't the first time the Galician had used it. The boy, like his father, was utterly amazed but for a different reason. He said, "But, *Aita*, how can I go on? Don't you see how sick he is?"

Aita turned him to face the finish line and gave him a push. The bettors, seeing the crowd forming around the fallen boy, moved in closer. What was going on? What had happened? Even the judge, who had just finished drawing a thick red line for the finish with a piece of brick, left his post and drew nearer to the group. The marquis had seen everything clearly and told Jacinto to stop the car since it was no longer a question of interfering. He was there to help. As soon as he drew near, the others made way for him. He took a look at the boy on the ground, then rendered his decision.

"He's fainted," then turning to the lathemaker, he said reassuringly. "It's nothing serious. Jacinto, there's a blanket in the trunk of the car. Bring it here. In cases like this it's important to make sure he doesn't catch cold, what with the way he's perspiring."

"Yes, Señor."

That is everyone said, "Yes, Señor," except the Galician who was determined to make his son continue the race. Jacinto returned with the blanket, but under his breath he pointed out to the marquis that it would get dirty because the lathemaker's son was covered in vomit. The marquis replied quite audibly, "It doesn't matter. It will wash off."

"Yes, Señor."

They sat him down on the wall, covered in the blanket, and

the marquis asked when the boy last ate and what he had eaten. It became obvious that he had eaten too late and too much. For future reference the marquis gave some advice to the lathemaker on a runner's diet, for which the man thanked him. Then the marquis turned to Planicio who, off to the side with his father, formed a conflict-ridden duo and scolded him, "Your obligation was to keep on running to the finish."

THAT SAME NIGHT Jacinto lent 300 pesetas to Pachi to settle the matter with Don Román. It was a special night because to celebrate the fiasco, which was eventually resolved, the bar regulars themselves had invited Jacinto to Raimundo's bar. Up to that point, he had refrained from going out of fear. Being a homosexual was identified in the Criminal Code as an offense—public mischief—and it was dangerous for him to go to taverns where men had had one drink too many and might accost him on the weakest pretexts. But the regulars had begun to question whether he really was a homosexual. Effeminate and full of mannerisms, yes, but of the other there was no proof.

"Isn't that so?" they asked Pachi.

"Hell, I can't say from personal experience."

In any case, that afternoon he'd done himself proud. When the marquis said to Planicio, "Your obligation was to keep on running to the finish," it was clear that if no one had crossed the finish line, properly speaking there was no winner.

Instinctively the *Cimarrón* hit his son who, as usual, didn't think to duck, but Pachi didn't lift his hand a second time out of respect for the marquis. Then those who had bet on the lathemaker's son said, "What happens with the bets?"

But by that they meant that nothing would happen with the bets, other than that everyone would get his money back, peacefully.

"That's right. What happens with the bets?" replied the others, meaning that the winner was clearly Planicio, although he'd been stupid enough not to keep on to the finish. A minor detail. Were they gentlemen or brutes?

Things were taking a turn for the worse; it was one thing to show respect to the marquis and another to lose duros. The lathemaker said to Pachi, "For my part, I've lost and my five duros are yours to keep."

It was a commendable gesture, and there was a minute of respectful silence, which was broken in a most unseemly manner by those who had bet on Planicio, thus poisoning matters further.

"See, see! Even his own father admits it."

So? Who was the father for his admission to mean something? He was just paying for having given his son too much to eat too late. The marquis had clearly said that Planicio's obligation was to continue on to the finish line even if the other boy was dying. If he didn't, then there was no winner.

The marquis realized he had unwittingly violated the principle of nonintervention learned in Cambridge, and he called Jacinto over to speak to him in private. The latter, after learning the marquis's wishes, took Raimundo aside since Raimundo was the person holding all the bets. The *Cimarrón,* who had a consumptive's hearing for this type of exchange, intercepted Jacinto, "But don't be a simpleton about it."

In other words, the marquis had given the manservant forty duros to solve the dispute since he had spent an enjoyable afternoon, his intervention had been most appreciated by these simple townsfolk and he didn't want his image to be spoiled for 200 pesetas, which didn't even amount to ten dollars.

"Silence, gentlemen," said Jacinto with authority. "All those who are owed money will be paid."

The marquis took his leave with an affable gesture for all, except for the two boys, whom he clapped on the back and congratulated on their performance.

And so they invited Jacinto to Raimundo's bar because he had been in a small way the protagonist of the afternoon and especially of the end result.

The subject of the race kept them going for several days. When the lathemaker wasn't there, Jacinto pointed out that the marquis had specifically said to him—he underlined the fact that he had been the one the marquis had confided in— that in any case, the other boy was pushing himself too hard. Translated, it meant that even if he hadn't passed out, Planicio would probably have won because the other boy had been pushing too hard from the start. It was even possible that he'd fainted due to overexertion. On the other hand, the marquis had himself, throughout the race, remarked on how Planicio was keeping a steady pace. Many people encouraged the *Cimarrón* to train his son as a runner to compete in the town bullfighting rings where long-distance races were usually held—one race equaling a given number of laps around the ring—since he'd surely be good at it. The *Cimarrón* had had the same thought himself, but his son's temperament and attitude toward matters of the sort were definite minuses. He didn't see how he could make a career out of it for Planicio no matter how strong his legs were. On the other hand, he felt some consolation because his remark to Jacinto when the marquis gave Jacinto forty duros, namely his saying, "Don't be a simpleton about it," had been very timely because Pachi was the one who took charge of paying off the different players in such a way that he and Jacinto each cleared ten duros off the top.

"See how things always end up for the best when you're with me?" Pachi pointed out once again.

That was when Jacinto loaned him the 300 pesetas to straighten out the misunderstanding.

DURING THE LAST days of June many things happened. Planicio, thanks to the marquis's intervention, was hired as a ball boy at the San Sebastián Tennis Club. His father hired on as a porter at the North Train Station. And most of all, the silence was broken with the pair from Ramón y Cajal but in such a strange way that it changed all their lives.

"Mind," said Jacinto with some concern as he handed over the 300 pesetas, "tomorrow you'll go over and pay them back, won't you?"

"Hell, don't worry," replied Pachi, unperturbed by Jacinto's lack of confidence. "I like to be able to hold my head up high too and know people aren't thinking something that isn't true."

He didn't go the next morning because he knew Don Román would be tutoring his students for the Revenue exam. The morning wasn't a good time since he, for one, wanted some explanations, and if he was asked for explanations he also had quite a few to give. He didn't go after lunch because he finished eating late. Since he had some money left over from the day before, it seemed only natural to treat himself to a substantial meal. It didn't matter to him either whether Don Román was there when he arrived—he'd already been told they took the poor man from five to seven o'clock to the Kursaal esplanade, planting him there like a tree facing the sea— because the one who really had some explaining to do was Señorita Menchu, who had called him a thief in front of his own son. He didn't think she'd dare repeat her remarks in his presence because, although a month had already gone by, he well remembered Señorita Menchu's heavy breathing as they pushed the square wicker chest full of books and her admiration when he demonstrated his strength for her.

As it was, it was around five-thirty when he went to the apartment on Ramón y Cajal, and in effect, just as he'd been told, there was poor Don Román facing the sea, his head falling slightly forward, and that bloody lump of a doorman at his side, not paying the slightest bit of attention to him. If a child drew near or passed close by, the don turned his head to watch him go by. Even from this distance and without seeing his face, the don looked different. First Pachi would ask for an explanation from Señorita Menchu, and then he'd straighten matters out with·Don Román, a much easier task.

The señorita herself opened the door to him, a sign that they still didn't have another maid. She gave a start when she saw Pachi and began smoothing down her hair and tugging at her dress, a dark brown Carmen habit attached with a black leather strap around her waist. This was another of her odd ways. She had made a vow not to take it off until her brother's condition had improved, since lately it had been deteriorating. Just taking him out for a walk every afternoon was a feat in itself, and naturally having him move from one chair to the other on his own with the gut-wrenching effort it entailed was now unthinkable. Between the doorman and herself, they had an awful time getting him up and into his wheelchair. That's why she'd started wearing a habit, very discreetly, without telling her brother why, but since he could guess the reason, it made him feel as though the calf-length brown tunic, without any adornment of any kind, was his own shroud.

That day, Pachi had a slightly stiff neck because he'd caught cold the night before on his way out of Raimundo's bar. This gave him, on his entrance, a haughty look. The vestibule was quite dark when Pachi said, "I've come to bring the 300 pesetas you asked me to pick up the other day."

And why not? Calmly state he'd just finished running the errand he'd been charged with a month ago. Was a month really all that long? With Señorita Menchu (with Don Román it would have been different) he felt like doing something out of the ordinary because he felt in control. It was worth a try. Pachi liked it when women wore perfume, and he had already noticed that he liked the perfume Señorita Menchu wore even better than most. In other words, in the semi-obscurity that made everything so much easier, the señorita's fragrance was much more perceptible than the stiffness the Carmen habit lent her.

"You do know what I'm talking about?" asked Pachi.

"Yes, yes, of course."

Furthermore, at this time of day, once the door was closed behind him, the silence was absolute, not just in the apartment

but in the whole building and practically in all of San Sebastian. Any sound that did reach them from the Kursaal esplanade—for example, a child's cry—only served to accentuate
the feeling of silence and solitude.

Whenever Pachi ate a substantial meal, he always had a bit
of wine to wash it down. Wine served to relax him, so this
business with Señorita Menchu, which he'd always detected
just under the surface and had always dismissed because of the
huge complications he'd envisaged, no longer seemed quite as
complicated. She didn't take the money. Pachi left it on a gilt
and painted desk that stood in the vestibule. Then the struggle
began. At first it might almost have seemed like a violation.
Of course, she wasn't completely unresponsive, but in spite of
that, she cried out, "No, not with the Carmen habit on!"

But her cry was so weak it didn't break the silence, the aid-
ing and abetting silence. Pachi found her objection reasonable
and offered solicitously, "Don't worry. We'll take it off right
away."

And he set his words to action, all the while looking for a
better spot than the vestibule to continue the operation. He
knew the house well, and at this time of day the same welcom-
ing silence reigned throughout. Once in the bedroom Señorita
Menchu said, "Good God in heaven. What are you going to
do?"

Although she kept feigning a struggle, maintaining the aura
of a violation, her question was put in such a way that it was
more like an invitation that required an adequate response.

THE SECOND TIME, when there was no way the act
could be looked on as occurring under protest, she limited herself to one resigned question.

"You're coming back for more?"

And the *Cimarrón* began to laugh at how this spinster could
sound so childlike at times. She put the question as though
they were eating a plate of cod sounds together.

SEÑORITA MENCHU'S confession was a pleasant surprise for the parish priest. He found it admirable that the most tiresome parishioner in the whole parish could be so matter of fact about having sinned. She usually came to him for confession but never headed straight for the confessional. First she had to visit the parish office, which she seemed to take as her own office or as a complaints bureau. The sexton, a hunchbacked and ill-natured man, couldn't stand her because she was always bothering him with her tales of woe revolving around the household help—how she wanted him to send her a clean, well-behaved, good Christian girl willing to do her every bidding.

"You do understand?"

Of course he understood what she wanted, but if he ever did find a girl like the one she described, you could be sure he wouldn't send her to Señorita Menchu. If the sexton put up with her at all, which he didn't really, it was out of respect for her brother, who had found a position for one of his nieces as a clerk with the Revenue Delegation. Not to mention the poor man's condition, a condition he nevertheless managed to bear with much more dignity than the hunchback bore his infirmity. Another sore point was the way she always objected to the mass times or just had to remark on activities surrounding the pilgrimage to the Sanctuary of Our Lady in Aránzazu or the Saint's Day—July 31—or a visit to Loyola. . . . Señorita Menchu had to have her say on them all, either to voice a complaint or to indicate where changes should be made. The sexton's response was to say that they were outside his purview and refer her to the priest who attended to her with admirable patience, this out of respect for her brother, a Christian gentleman who set an example for them all to follow.

That is why, when Señorita Menchu kneeled down in the confessional box this time, the priest didn't realize at first who she was.

"Hail Mary, full of grace."

"Untouched by the sin of conception, most Holy Mary."

"Father, I have fornicated."

"How many times, my child?"

Señorita Menchu was not sure whether to say once or twice but was reassured to see the priest had not jumped up scandalized and torn into her. He simply asked her softly, "How many times, my child?" Just in case, she said twice, although both were on the same occasion. In other words, she might be the most tiresome parishioner in the parish, but when her turn came to be a true sinner, she remembered her catechism and confessed by the book without beating around the bush. She'd hardly slept all night after what had happened, busy as she was going over the confession she'd have to make the next morning and wondering whether she should present it as an act committed under protest to which she only consented after the fact. But then the second time had been with her total consent. Total because she, from the first day she'd met Pachi, had found him to be a very interesting man who'd been terribly unlucky in his life, unlike the business professor who worked for the Revenue Delegation, wore stiff-collared shirts, smoked tipped cigarettes and led a charmed life—even during the war he served in the office of an intendant—but whom she couldn't abide no matter how much her brother tried to convince her otherwise.

Right up to the last minute, she wasn't sure what she'd say, especially because of the attenuating circumstances surrounding the event that, in its initial phase, made it look very much like a violation to which she'd only consented after the fact. But when she knelt down, her religious education prevailed and she simply said, "Father, I have fornicated."

The only thing that surprised the parish priest—who after all had been hearing confessions for thirty-three years—was Señorita Menchu's insistence that he exempt her from her private vow to continue wearing the Carmen habit. He agreed, gave her a severe penance, recommended she avoid other occa-

sions for sin and asked her to love her brother more every day;
lately he had seemed sad and loathe to go on living. The priest
kept this information to himself but made a point of bringing
up the other matter because Don Román, his exemplariness
aside, was a truly worthwhile man.

Perhaps the reconciliation was just that much too late for
Don Román. The day of the incident, when he returned home,
his sister said, "Pachi just left. He came to bring back the 300
pesetas we asked him to pick up the other day."

Just like that, as if it were the most natural thing in the
world, after a whole month of her repeating ad nauseam:

— everyone took advantage of him, Don Román, because he
was too good by far. She didn't elaborate further, but it was
understood she meant he was a fool;

— from the very first day, she, Señorita Menchu, had
thought Pachi was too big for his boots and had told Don
Román as much several times;

— if it had been up to her, she would already have turned
him in to the police. But of course, so as not to displease him,
Don Román, she had held her peace;

— to top it all off, that good-for-nothing hadn't sent the boy
by with the sack of miller's flour he'd picked up from La Burgalesa;

— and of course where the boy was concerned, she held no
grudges because in the final analysis, he was nothing but a
child, yet he hadn't returned the books he, Don Román, had
lent to him either and hadn't been by to give an explanation or
at least to thank them for not having sent his good-for-nothing father to jail.

Don Román had had to listen to it all for a month. At
times he got angry, at others he stammered out something in
their defense and, more often than not, he just stared straight
ahead, beyond the horizon, where surely the heaven he loved
was to be found. Of course it was foolish to think that way.
Heaven would be the same for everyone, and the thought that

he'd be taken there in a fishing boat was nothing more than poetic license, a pagan reminiscence of Charon's boat.

"So Pachi came."

"Yes."

"And what did he say?"

"Nothing special. That he'll be by to see you one of these days."

The presumed saintliness people insisted on attributing to Don Román during his lifetime was not as much due to his resigned immobility as to his ability to hold his peace. And so after this terrible month of imprecations, his sister, his youngest sister, could not be bothered to take the time to tell him why Pachi the *Cimarrón*'s absence—with 300 pesetas in his pocket—had gone on for so long. Then three days later, halfway through the afternoon on the Kursaal esplanade, Pachi arrived, followed by Planicio half-hidden behind his father.

"Don Román, did we ever miss you!" said the *Cimarrón* while he grasped the hand Don Román couldn't stretch out.

He then greeted Paco the doorman in such a way as to impart to the man that he was only here on a visit and not to take his place because doormen were known for their touchy disposition, and it was best to keep on their good side. And why he followed up quickly with, "I'm working at the North Station now."

That was all he said, from which it might be deduced that he was in the service of the National Railway System, which was true even though he worked for himself and only as an outside porter's helper. That is, there were inside porters who wore a uniform—a blue shirt and a numbered flat cap—and who only carried suitcases to the end of the platform. Outside, as the name indicated, there were outside porters who didn't need a uniform and could only be distinguished by a numbered plate they wore, usually on their beret. It so happened that one of the latter, a man they called Zurrido, another Galician from Trincherpe, was the one who had agreed to have Pachi help him with the rush of express trains in July and August, but he warned Pachi that come September his services would no longer be needed. That was fine with Pachi. Everyone knew he wasn't one to stick it out in the same job for very long.

In any case, in spite of not wanting to interfere, he did move Don Román because that imbecile of a doorman hadn't realized the don got cold in the shade. No matter how hot the day, Don Román was usually cold because of his permanent immobility.

"Should we move into the sun for a bit, Don Román?" and he maneuvered the wheelchair with the dexterity that comes from many hours of experience.

A spot could always be found that left the attendant in the shade—after all, the sun was hot—and his employer in the sun.

"Go on, Planicio, aren't you going to say hello to Don Román?"

The boy was feeling embarrassed again and had stayed behind his father, smiling and blushing slightly.

"Hello, Planicio!" said Don Román. Then he added, "How you've grown."

But almost immediately he decided it didn't make sense to say that in just a month's time—no matter how long the month had seemed to last—the boy had grown, so he corrected himself, "Well, you look older and sharper."

He said this because his father had bought Planicio, on credit, a new jacket and pants so he could work at the tennis club. That was why he looked older.

"I hear you're a runner now." Paco the doorman had told him about it, the news having got around.

"This one, a runner?" interjected Pachi, still smarting over what had happened. "If he doesn't end up a Sister of Charity or something along those lines, I don't know what he'll be good for."

And he recounted the race, explaining in great detail how,

after crossing over the Station Bridge, Planicio had caught up with the other runner and then stopped to watch him throw up.

"Well, what do you think of that," said Don Román. And Don Román, knowing Planicio, wasn't surprised in the least, but he shook his head slightly anyway, as if making a reproach but a gentle one because he wanted both of them, father and son, to be happy.

"What are you doing now?" Don Román asked Planicio.

"I'm working as a ball boy at the tennis club."

"Until we find something better," interrupted Pachi, so it was understood that he wasn't always going to have his son running after some fancy pants' tennis balls. "In any case, the tips are good. We're doing all right, Don Román."

He spoke in a tone of serene resignation, like a man who has always been faced with great difficulties in life, which with God's help he had managed to overcome.

The doorman said it was time to go back. Just what the Galician had been counting on.

"If it's all right with you, Don Román, maybe we could accompany you. That way we can say hello to Señorita Menchu. Actually I did say hello to her the other day. I don't know if she mentioned it, but Planicio hasn't seen her for some time."

Señorita Menchu blushed on seeing Pachi and became somewhat agitated. Even her brother noticed the change, especially because of the warm greeting she reserved for Planicio, even—something she never did—giving him a kiss, commenting on his elegant attire and telling him she'd give him a snack of bread and chocolate. Don Román had found his youngest sister's attitude over the past few days very disconcerting. All of a sudden, without his having improved one iota, she'd quit wearing the brown habit and black leather belt and started wearing her usual bright clothes, which by contrast seemed to be almost flashy.

The *Cimarrón*, in spite of what had happened, was nothing

but respectful toward her. He didn't make any asides and only glanced at her foundation from time to time to confirm that it was still excellent and that even the color in her face had improved. Cynical as he was, he thought this was what happened to many women. What they needed was a man. But his thoughts were only cynical to a point because Señorita Menchu didn't need just any man. She needed a man like him. The proof was that at the age of thirty she was still a spinster and a virgin in spite of almost certainly having had other opportunities; after all, she was a well-off woman. It wasn't her grumbling nature that would drive a man away. All women were alike and it was best just to ignore them. All in all, the matter wasn't as complicated as he'd imagined it would be.

Planicio was given his bread and chocolate as promised, and Pachi thought it better to say no, thank you, he wouldn't have anything.

Planicio told the don he'd already read all the stories from the large volume bound in cloth-covered binder's board that they'd taken out of the square wicker chest. Then Señorita Menchu, the same Señorita Menchu who for a whole month had kept reminding him that the boy hadn't returned the books that had been loaned to him, was the one who kindly suggested, "Well, I think there are even more books in that chest," and she added, speaking to Planicio, "Would you like to look for one?"

Of course he would. Señorita Menchu accompanied him and came back alone.

"We'll have to take that chest back downstairs because it's only in the way up here."

She spoke with no ulterior motive but was worried when Pachi offered, "If you like we can take it downstairs now."

What a different meaning every word held after what had happened! To Señorita Menchu, his meaning seemed glaringly obvious, but not to her brother, who through the open doorway was giving advice to Planicio.

"Look and see if you can find one with the same binding but smaller. The cover is reddish in color. Can you see it?"

"What's it called?"

"*Quo Vadis.*"

"What did you say?"

The don repeated the title, enunciating every syllable because naturally Planicio didn't know Latin. Don Román was used to being patient and repeating things over and over because after so many years of sitting or lying down, he'd had to make others understand him. And it was only getting worse. He could tell his stutter was becoming more pronounced. But Planicio was intelligent and a quick study. He, the don, would have to find some way of making sure Planicio could go back to school next term.

"Here it is!" cried Planicio jubilantly and could be heard enunciating slowly—"*Qu–o Va–dis.* Henry Sienkie . . ."

He couldn't finish the last name because he didn't know how to pronounce *w* followed by *i*, *c* and *z*. He appeared with the book in his hand, blowing off the dust.

"Stop, not like that!" cried out Señorita Menchu in her usual tone. Then in a gentler voice, "Not like that, child. Don't you see you're getting dust all over the place? Bring it here."

Planicio, who had stopped short on hearing her cry, stretched the book out timidly. She disappeared into the kitchen and reappeared in no time.

"There you go. I read it too when I was a little girl. It's a very sad story of Christians but you'll like it. Saint Peter is all right in the end. Isn't that so, Román?"

That night, a star-filled June night with no moon in sight, looking down on the garret room and all of San Sebastian, the bay off in the distance, with the weak light from the lighthouse reflecting in the low tide and the brackish sea air entering the Mount Ulía dell, Planicio said his three Hail Mary's from where he'd climbed up for a better view on top of the box that held the elevator machinery.

"Planicio. Aren't you coming to bed?"

"Yes, *Aita!* I'm coming."

AS THE DAYS PASSED, Señorita Menchu trembled—knowing intuitively what the consequences of that afternoon would be—the grandeur of the count's household grew and Planicio gradually adapted to the tennis club. The marquis always pronounced the words *tennis club* the British way, drawing out the *u* until it sounded like an *a* sound.

The Galician experienced no period of adaptation to his new job because his tendency was not to adapt to any job. He tolerated this particular job quite well because most of his fellow workers were from the same region as he. They had a Galician sense of humor he liked, and they usually brought their lunch pails and a mid-morning snack. He always said, "I'll bring the wine," and partook of the others' food. They knew that a widower with a son could not be doing too well in the meal department.

The job wasn't bad because between one train and the next was a lot of waiting around, telling of jokes and mutual kidding. There was a corner on the right side of the station where, although it was no great shakes, they could play a bit of pelota. It had quite a high wall separating it from the baggage claims area. On the left was a small wall, about two meters high, with a bench made out of old cracked cement. The ground was bare and the games were games of skill more than anything else.

At first the Galician, so as not to raise any suspicions, challenged the others. "Let's play for a glass of wine."

He didn't mind losing, but every once in a while they'd play for a duro and then he'd win. Mind, he'd win despite the fact that he was out of practice; it had been a whole year since he'd hit a ball. The platform porters, who tried not to associate with the outside porters, watched the games from a distance. But one young fellow from Azcoitia couldn't resist the temptation and took on the *Cimarrón*. Pachi won but with great difficulty.

He managed to win because the young man tried to play a game of strength, and on that court strength just didn't cut it. What counted was using the bit of masonry so that the ball, a soft one, cleared the side wall, rebounded once on the bench and fell dead to the ground. It looked like you could reach it first, but you never could because once on the bare ground, it could scarcely bounce the width of your hand. The fellow from Azcoitia caught on late in the game when Pachi was already well ahead and so couldn't catch up. But Pachi buttered him up afterward, telling him that his left hand was a gift from God and that on a standard fronton Pachi wouldn't dare play against him. From the first day, Pachi had resisted the friendly advances made by the outdoor porters since striking up a friendship with them seemed too impractical in that he was interested in winning some money and not in discussing the rights of this or that one. And so he made friends with the platform porters and even with the sleeping car attendants who were always so distant and aristocratic—dressed in their brown uniforms, gold buttons and French kepis—so much so that it seemed like they hadn't been through a war. The sleeping car attendants made purchases along the run—cooking oil, flour, sausage—that they then resold in San Sebastian. It was called the black market and operated quite a bit better than the official suppliers, one of the reasons Pachi attached so little importance to the ration card he'd lost and never bothered replacing. He bought one or two things from them but at a cut-rate price. That's what friends were for.

On one of his good days—he'd had several jobs and won a bet in the corner court—he bought a string of sausages from his friends and took it to the apartment on Ramón y Cajal. To ensure that Señorita Menchu didn't misinterpret his gesture, he went at noon when he was sure Don Román would be tutoring, and therefore there could be no repeat of the other day's performance. Not that he didn't want one—he would never have thought that a spinster, half forced against her will, could be so responsive—but he had to think the matter over because these things required careful consideration.

The señorita opened the door and was somewhat upset to have him see her dressed as she was, with an apron on, her hair in a bun and an unmade-up face. Pachi, on the other hand, thought she looked the way the mistress of the house should look, and he noted that her face now looked very different from before when, on top of being a spinster, she was still a virgin. It had more color, more life; she even seemed to have put on a bit of weight—he liked rounded edges—and yet she had circles under her eyes that gave her a melancholy yet attractive air. Pachi, although he was a cynic, knew how to appreciate a woman's finer points, and as things would have it she looked to him very much like the pretty girl from Alza he'd married, not just to spite her family, as rumor would have it, but because she too had been a comely complainer who, all the same, when her interest was piqued, could become soft and loving as he'd been able to confirm, before their marriage, in amongst the apple trees.

"Why, what brings you by at this time of day?"

"I came to bring you both a little present."

He knew Don Román would be listening in spite of the classes because the vestibule adjoined the living room where the mirador was, and listening to what was going on at the door didn't interfere with the students' recitation. From the doorway, since he hadn't been invited in, Pachi said, "Good day, Don Román and company."

"Come in, come in," said Señorita Menchu.

The don turned his head with difficulty—every day his neck felt shorter in amongst all the fat—to look at his former assistant.

"I brought you a bit of sausage from Aranda. It's butcher's meat."

Silence fell because in 1942 sausage—especially a string of sausages—was not to be taken lightly. Even in Guipúzcoa, where they boasted about everything, people admitted that sausage from Castilla preserved better and that the sausage from Aranda was something else again.

"Th–thank you ve–ry mu–much," stammered Don Román.

"Well, sorry for interrupting. I'll let you get back to your work," said the *Cimarrón,* like someone who doesn't have much time to spare.

"Listen, Pachi," said Don Román. "Come over this afternoon, and we'll have some together. I think I even have some white wine to go with it." Although Don Román no longer felt much like joking, he couldn't resist teasing his former assistant.

"Sausage with white wine? *Ené,* the things you come up with, Don Román. With sausage nothing but red wine will do. I've already told you."

Pachi had already told him during those days they'd surely never see again, on their forays into the old quarter's taverns when he could still lift himself up with one great heave at four o'clock in the afternoon because Pachi was coming for him to take him on some new adventure. During nights of what he thought of as permanent, incurable and resigned insomnia, he especially remembered the climbs up Mount Urgull when they passed in front of the British cemetery—which when one thought about it seemed an unlikely spot for it to be—and started resolutely up the steepest part that led to the cannon platform. On those warm afternoons—what a wonderful winter they'd had!—they'd climbed far up, and the sea in the hollows of the rocks along Paseo Nuevo could be heard as a deep rumble. The smell of pine, of fern, of moss along the rampart, Planicio's cries once he'd clambered up to the highest rock. "Don Román!" he'd called out several times. As long as the don hadn't made some sign with his forearm, the boy wouldn't give up. "Don Román! Can you see me?" Of course he could see him. The problem was that he had trouble moving his arm. They'd made many plans for the summer, and yet one month had changed all that. The shortest winter—and spring—of his life were followed by the longest month of his existence.

"I'm sorry, Pachi, I forgot. We'll have it with red wine."

"But red wine doesn't sit well with you."

This was his sister reminding him unnecessarily because he knew very well that wine didn't agree with him, nor did sausage, nor did anything other than waiting with dignity for what was to come.

"I'll just have a sip to keep you company." As though he'd just remembered, he added, "Planicio can come too, can't he?"

"If he comes, with the way he eats, there won't be any left for the rest of us."

IT WAS TRUE. Planicio's hunger was still ferocious. Once he'd finished eating in preparation for the race between the bridges, he was back to square one. The number of tips he received determined how much he ate. There was no counting on what *Aita* brought back because Pachi had to pay off the clothing he'd bought for Planicio on credit. Added to his hunger was Planicio's embarrassment because the two other ball boys always brought their lunch pails or a snack and some fruit that had been prepared for them at home, and when it was time for lunch, they kept a suspicious eye trained on him. Maybe because they were afraid they'd have to share with him. He went out onto the street and bought bread—black market bread—and grapes. He bought something filling too, like peanuts. The marquis said, using the Cuban term, "I see you like *manises*."

At the club the marquis was particularly dazzling. In the change room he had three lockers for his sports gear. One locker was exclusively for toiletries—a natural sponge, another fiber sponge for rubdowns, soap, shampoo, lotions, nail clippers and hair spray. No matter how long the match lasted, not a hair on his head was out of place. In the other locker, he stored his rackets. With the pro—a Frenchman who'd played in the Davis Cup but who was living in exile because of the war—he could spend hours on end talking about the tension or the handles of the rackets. Of course he was one of the best players in the club, if not the best. Once he'd even won a national mixed championship, paired up with Pepa Chávarri. The marquis had also trained Lilí Alvarez in Wimbledon, helping her learn the style of game one had to adopt in lawn tennis. He was seeded in the second national category and was on the point of moving up to first seed several times, but his obligations made it difficult for him to take part in the number of tournaments required to give the kind of results he needed to move on. This everyone knew, and those who didn't were quickly apprised of the fact by him. Of course the game he played was a first seed game, especially in pairs and mixed games. In the third locker he kept his robe and the slippers he wore to the shower. He wore a short-sleeved white linen shirt and long pants, as was the custom, white as well but more an off-white, in a light wool. Preparing for a game and cleaning up afterward were both part of a rite that took time. He spent practically the whole morning on it.

There was a player from Bilbao who competed with him in everything and who, to top it off, was a loudmouth. The marquis disliked him in a courteous fashion, and the other reciprocated but not as courteously because behind his back (but the marquis found out anyway) the Bilbaon called him the *Cubanito*. He'd also given him the nickname *manisero*, or peanut man. They often played against each other, and the marquis won more often than not, not that it was painless because they'd both start out being very courteous, graciously conceding hard-to-call shots and praising the opponent's good shots, but when the game started going badly for the Bilbaon—which was inevitable because he was heavy on his feet, playing the back court without any imagination whatsoever—the latter began to challenge every ball, and the marquis ended up with badly frayed nerves. Afterward, he usually discussed the matter with the French pro, who commiserated with him but insisted it was good for him to play against the Bilbaon, who was a tough tennis player and made the marquis concentrate on his game. This was the pro's main criticism where his most profitable pupil was concerned—that at times he let himself be distracted during the game.

"Surtout s'il y a une jolie femme près de vous." (Of course, they always spoke to each other in French.)

The marquis laughed graciously because he was very understanding of his little failings as long as they didn't affect his outward appearance. He admitted that his memory wasn't what it could be, that he lacked a sense of direction and truly at times didn't pay enough attention on the court. But if the pro tried to tell him not to serve standing on tiptoe like a whooping crane, it put the marquis in a fighting mood. The latter would show astonishment at the reproach and courteously but firmly insist he didn't stand on tiptoe to serve. Or if the flaw in question was an obvious one, the marquis conceded the point but then alleged that that was how Tilden hit the ball and that Tilden himself—the marquis tried to drop his name into the conversation as much as possible—said that what was a flaw in some players was a virtue in others. If the pro was tiresome and insisted, the marquis questioned whether he had ever really played with the French team in the Davis Cup and asked calculated questions to that effect. But this was a rare occurrence since what he liked best was playing with the Frenchman, a stubborn man from a modest background who showed his lack of education at times and had traces of *patois* in his speech, but an artist when it came to placing the ball in exactly the same spot as many times as necessary, making the training sessions a genuine show that club members gathered to watch.

"Now we'll try the backhand, Marquis."

All of this in French but without his ever dropping the proper form of address. And the pro would hit ten, twenty, fifty balls to the marquis's left so that once the rhythm was established, each return was a pleasure, each stroke harder, the ball always just barely clearing the net, at the right angle for the opponent until naturally a mistake was made. The pro symbolically wiped the sweat off his brow and said, "Ooph! If you could concentrate this much in your games . . ."

It was understood that if he were capable of that level of concentration, he could be playing Wimbledon. The marquis smiled, affable and modest, but pointed out that he had obligations other than tennis—he always pronounced it the British way—and that his obligations, both social and financial, were so preoccupying that at times it was difficult for him to achieve the desired level of concentration.

For Planicio, all the marquis's doings in the club were a source of great fascination. As soon as he arrived Planicio put himself at the marquis's disposal. In the change room, the marquis handed him the locker keys and said, Take out such and such a racket, or, No, today I'm going to use the Dunlop. Don't you know which one the Dunlop is yet? It's humid today and its strings will hold up better. Afterward Planicio followed him to the court, carrying the rackets—just in case, the marquis always brought more than one and took his time before the match deciding which one to use—the cans of balls and a small towel. The other ball boys didn't mind that Planicio had become the marquis's personal attendant because the *Cubanito*, while his behavior was always correct, tended to show the strain during his games. Now pay attention, boy. . . . Get that ball off the court right away. . . . Don't move until a point is scored. . . . Don't give me more than two balls at a time!

In actual fact, there were only four or five rules to remember, and Planicio learned them right away. He noticed that, although everyone said the games were friendly, the players were constantly getting angry. He didn't find this too strange though because the same thing happened on the fronton, the difference being that there people yelled and swore whereas in tennis the anger was veiled, seen only in the cold courtesies paid. Bitter comments were kept for the change room afterward, each player in his own corner.

The club groundskeeper, Julio, was a young married man with a two-year-old daughter whom Planicio was almost afraid to go near because of the suspicious looks her father always seemed to be sending his way. Julio used to be a farmer in the town of Igueldo and was always in a bad mood. Planicio helped him sprinkle the courts to the groundskeeper's amazement since he hadn't even asked Planicio to help. The other two ball boys were brothers, from Igueldo as well, who must have been related to the groundskeeper somehow, considering everything he let them get away with. They were always fighting, and when it was their turn to water down the courts, they did it grudgingly, leaving puddles of water behind. Planicio liked sprinkling the water in a fine spray so that it was evenly spread over the entire court. The other two left puddles on purpose, saying, "Screw them." They also talked about the opposite sex a lot, boasting about ways they'd devised of peeping into the ladies' change room. At that time, very few women played tennis, and Planicio couldn't understand why the other boys wanted to spy on the older women who did come.

The groundskeeper's wife looked after washing the towels, and Planicio helped her carry the loads of laundry. She was a pretty woman who was wild about her daughter, and since she'd noticed Planicio liked to watch her daughter, she made it easier for him.

"Look how big this boy is, Arancha."

Arancha looked at Planicio and said, "*Vewy* big boy."

Her mother was thrilled to hear her daughter speak and motioned her husband over to listen. He drew nearer, but the little girl refused to repeat what she'd said. Once again Julio looked at Planicio with distrust. On the other hand, whenever Planicio had nothing to do and Julio's wife had to go inside to wash the towels, she said, "Could you keep an eye on Arancha for me?"

She gave him instructions as well, mainly not to let Arancha put anything in her mouth or go near the tennis courts
because she bothered the players. Arancha didn't like to be separated from her mother, but when it was Planicio she didn't
mind. He took her to a place she liked because of all the dirt
there and let her play. Arancha went off into her own world for
the longest time, letting dirt slip through her fingers, and
Planicio loved every minute of it. With an old fluted brass tin,
they made mud pies together, which is what she liked doing
best. Planicio made very sure she didn't put any stones in her
mouth, and if she did he quickly fished them out.

"Mustn't eat stones."

When later on the little girl repeated the phrase, "No eat
'tonies," in front of her mother, the latter could hardly contain
her excitement.

If Julio saw Planicio taking the girl out for a walk, he asked,
"What do you think you're doing?"

"Your wife asked me to look after Arancha."

The groundskeeper was always amazed to hear that his wife
had made such a request, but he held his tongue.

In the evening, Planicio told Don Román all about his day
because the don liked to listen more than he liked to talk. At
sunset, when it was too dark for tennis, Planicio would start
out on the trip back to Ramón y Cajal at his farm horse's half-
trot, a long trip because the tennis club was at the other end of
the city at the foot of Mount Igueldo, even further than the
Ondarreta prison across from the beach. It seemed to him that
the prisoners must like being able to see the sea, but it made
him feel awfully sad, although he said nothing about it to *Aita*
who was sick of seeing him sad or embarrassed.

"What do you think life is?" yelled the *Cimarrón*. "The
priesthood is about all you're fit for." The *Cimarrón*, although
he wasn't very devout, did think well of priests, or at least he
thought it was only normal that they should show compassion
for their fellow man. But seeing his son cry over a novel or say,

"It's so sad, *Aita!*" about anything and everything drove him wild.

Don Román, on the other hand, understood and tried to help.

Planicio said, "Don Román, this morning on my way to the tennis club, I saw a prisoner looking out through the bars." And the two of them sat without speaking because they both knew it must be very sad to be behind bars.

If by chance Señorita Menchu overheard them, she said, "The man must have done something wrong, and now he's paying for it."

Well, yes, of course, but the Ondarreta prison was ugly and depressing enough from the outside; from the inside it must be even worse. They said it had a central courtyard where condemned criminals were executed, and Planicio, as he passed by in the early morning on his way to work, was always afraid he might hear gunshots. Don Román reassured him.

"Don't worry, it's not true."

"What isn't true, Don Román?"

It wasn't true that that's how they were killed. Moreover, there were very few executions. Perhaps there wouldn't even be any more. But they both still felt a twinge of sorrow and, realizing this, Planicio changed the subject. He told Don Román about Arancha because Don Román liked children even though he didn't have much luck with them since they were afraid of him and refused to go near him. It turned out that Señorita Menchu liked children too and she sighed.

"How old did you say she is?" the señorita asked.

"Two years old," answered Planicio.

And Señorita Menchu sighed, "Oh, dear!"

Some nights Pachi dropped by too but not for very long because at nine o'clock the express train from Madrid arrived, and it was one of the busiest trains.

Things weren't the same anymore. Planicio had to be more careful around Don Román than when they used to go on walks together to Mount Urgull because it wasn't the same now that they stayed indoors. Besides, Señorita Menchu was usually around. But it had its advantages too because now they were real visits, and when *Aita* came, the four of them sat around the table like friends. What's more, every once in a while *Aita* brought small presents.

Don Román said, "Things must be going well in your new job, Pachi. I'm happy for you."

It was news to Planicio since conditions around the garret room hadn't improved that he could see, but he thought it a nice gesture on his father's part to bring presents to the apartment on Ramón y Cajal.

IN 1912, while he was still a physician at the General Hospital in Madrid, Don Gregorio announced to Don Román that he could live for many years in spite of his disability. To the age of fifty or over. As though this were quite an accomplishment because Don Román was only twenty-three at the time and his fiftieth year seemed so far away that it needn't be of any real concern. As his fiftieth birthday approached, Don Román had tried to remember whether the doctor had said *over* fifty or *way over* fifty. Now, at fifty-four, his body told him on a daily basis that it was the former. At that time, Gregorio Marañón was a relatively unknown physician recently arrived from Germany who no one would have thought might have a gift for prophesy. Afterward he became so famous that, as childish as it might seem, Don Román accepted his prediction as a scientific and incontrovertible statement of fact. Every year, the don sent a Christmas card to the doctor, who replied in his own handwriting, expressing his pleasure at hearing that Don Román was doing so well. Don Román didn't bother explaining that he wasn't doing all that well. He assumed the doctor simply meant the mere fact that he was still alive was an accomplishment in itself. In 1930, Don Gregorio sent him a biography he'd written on Enrique IV of Castille with a kind dedication to him.

Don Román finally decided to leave the matter of his death in God's hands and quit worrying whether in fact he'd be taken away in a small steamboat past the sun-reddened horizon or whether it would be much simpler than that. By the same token he wouldn't spoil it for those who wanted to make him out to be a saint while he was still alive. Not that he didn't daydream about the horizon every day as the sun set. It truly was beautiful, and everything beautiful came from God.

Pachi was as much a skeptic as ever, as well as a cynic, and yet Don Román liked to confide in him.

"Pachi, this year of my life has been like a gift from God."

The *Cimarrón* kept a wary silence in case the don had an ulterior motive in speaking thus. Sometimes Don Román spoke of how he worried about his sister, still a little girl in his eyes, quite to the Galician's displeasure because, as things stood, he failed to see when he'd be able to bed Señorita Menchu again, and the older man, by confiding in him this way, was only turning the knife in the wound. Of course he replied quite calmly, "Don't worry, Don Román. God's will will be done."

After the events of that late June afternoon during which she, of her own free will, agreed to make love a second time, it only seemed logical that another opportunity should arise, especially considering how attentive and courteous he had been. Not only did no such opportunity arise, but worse yet, the *Cimarrón* was positive Senorita Menchu didn't open the door to him on purpose in spite of his repeated ringing of the doorbell one carefully chosen afternoon. Don Román was on the Kursaal esplanade with that imbecile of a doorman, just like the last time. Later on he went back for their evening get-together. Planicio was already there, and it was as if she couldn't do enough for the boy—treating him to bread and chocolate—while casting melancholy glances laced with a hint of reproach in Pachi's direction. It was beyond even God's understanding, he was sure.

One Sunday they took advantage of the doorman's day off to take Don Román back to the Miramar movie theater just like in the old days. They planned their outing ahead of time, and when they mentioned the movie they'd decided on, Señorita Menchu remarked, "That's one I'd like to see as well. Maybe I'll go with my friends some day."

But obviously she didn't have to go with her friends. Instead, she went with them. They seated Don Román sideways at the front so he could see the screen with as little effort as possible. Señorita Menchu made sure she sat next to her brother. However, she couldn't stop Pachi from sitting down next to her. During the newsreel he held himself in check, but after the intermission he made his move. As long as he stuck to casually brushing up against her shoulder or forearm, Señorita Menchu did nothing more than feebly attempt to move away, but when he started trying to touch her lower down, the rebuff was forceful. The whole movie was spent in mute and vain struggles, and the Galician left in an extreme state of agitation. Although he was tempted, he didn't head for Calle de Zabaleta because the only woman he wanted was that devil's spinster. And so, when they arrived at the doorstep at Ramón y Cajal, although she gave him a look pleading for understanding, the *Cimarrón* said a curt good-bye because he had just enough time to make the Madrid-Irún express train.

ON AUGUST 15, the Feast of the Assumption and the culmination of the San Sebastian Festival Week, there could be no doubt left in Señorita Menchu's mind. She must be pregnant since her first suspicions dated back to July 18—the day civil war had broken out in 1936 (holidays were her benchmarks)—and another month erased any possible doubt. Since the month of July, the priest who'd been party to her suspicions through confession had been saying, "Pray, my daughter, but pray not to be with or without child, which is up to God to decide. Pray for guidance in your time of trouble."

Señorita Menchu, contrite in the confessional box, asked, "Oh, Father! What shall I do?"

And the priest answered, "My daughter, pray and trust in God."

Sometimes he asked her, "And what is he doing now?"

"He's working at the station and seems to be doing quite well."

The priest sincerely hoped so but found it hard to believe because as a student of human nature, the impression left by this infrequent parishioner did not mesh with the idea of a stable, reasonably well-paid job.

"And what does he do?" he insisted.

Señorita Menchu didn't quite know herself. The priest seemed to vaguely remember that Pachi was a seaman, but he'd also said he was a shoemaker, a pelota player, and now he worked at the station.

As the days passed, Señorita Menchu's sighs spoke of her fear. Her fear that, in spite of such unequivocal signs, she might not be pregnant. In 1942, at a time when official morals had been established for the good of the nation, if a man was responsible for a single woman's being with child, he married her. It was assumed in the case of a pregnancy that the man was the cause and marriage the effect. By asking the priest, "What shall I do?" she meant what should she do to make sure it all worked out as it should so that she could marry Pachi. She could see why the parish priest advised her to pray, but she felt there must also be some more practical measures designed to make Pachi aware of the situation so he could meet his obligations. Finally on the Feast of the Assumption of the Blessed Virgin, when there could be no mistaking her condition any longer, the priest realized without any great surprise what Señorita Menchu's true aspirations were—after all, he had spent thirty-three years in the confessional box for an average of three hours every day. But his very experience made him state his case clearly. He, if the requirements of free

choice and mutual consent laid out by the Mother Church
were met, would agree to marry them, although he dreaded
weddings precipitated by a pregnancy. But in no case would he
become a marriage broker.

"Oh, Father? What shall I do then?"

By now the priest had begun to understand that these laments were due to the illusion of hope.

"Don't you have an older married sister in Alava?"

"Yes, Father."

"Well then, go to her. She'll understand and come to your
aid."

At first glance the advice seemed preposterous because her
older sister, who had married the flour mill operator, really just
a miller from Salvatierra, would never be able to understand
such a complex situation. Although, when one actually thought
about it, her husband wasn't really a miller, just a small industrialist who had a small flour mill, which, after the war, grew
in size, thus giving him more prestige in the family since he
was the one who handed out sacks of flour to them every
month.

After two days of reflection this piece of advice seemed to
make more sense than the others, and she wrote to her sister,
begging her to come to San Sebastian on a matter she mustn't
mention to anyone, and if possible leave her husband behind in
Salvatierra because the whole affair was quite delicate—a question of honor. A tear here and there smudged the ink to
heighten the dramatic content of the plea, although it was not
easy for Señorita Menchu to summon up tears since she'd
never felt better. Getting up in the morning, she did feel slightly nauseous, nothing to speak of, but on the whole she'd never
felt this good. Her swollen breasts lent her a natural whole-
someness, and she seemed to remember—or perhaps she'd
heard it from her grandmother—that this was a sign of a good
pregnancy and meant an abundant supply of milk. The idea of
breast-feeding a child, modestly covering her breast with a

handkerchief while the father, the child's father—in other words Pachi—looked on and her brother, Don Román, smiled, seemed to her to be the height of happiness. The only one who didn't seem to fit at all into this family scene was Planicio, but she knew he'd have to play a role somehow, and for that reason, to get him on her side, she gave him bread and chocolate every afternoon.

Planicio, thirteen going on fourteen, growing in spite of his diet lacking in nutrition, was experiencing such a hunger streak that the milk bun and ounce of chocolate they gave him in the apartment on Ramón y Cajal sent his stomach into spasms. He made it last as long as possible by taking tiny little bites, but it never gave him more than a brief respite. He dreamed of one day, one Sunday afternoon, sitting down all alone in the Miracruz garret room with the complete collection of Dick Turpin stories, a big one-kilo loaf of bread—he knew where he could find them for sale—several pounds of chocolate, and experiencing true happiness. You wouldn't think it would be impossible, but somehow he never managed to save enough money because his daily needs were greater than the dream of a Sunday afternoon.

Jacinto, whose power and influence were still growing, assumed now that both father and son were working that they wouldn't need his leftovers anymore. Besides, he lived in dread of the marquis coming upon him in the stairway, carrying a casserole. His heart, out of loyalty, was still with the main household, the countess's household, but he had a weakness for the marquis, whose elegance and distinction quite took his breath away.

Aita didn't bring much home either because he was still paying for the clothes they'd bought on credit, for his own needs and for the little gifts he continued to take to Ramón y Cajal in compensation, Planicio assumed, for the 300 pesetas.

The only money Planicio made was from tips, and the marquis was the one most likely to tip him, usually with a peseta.

On rainy days when there were no players, he often spent the day without a centimo in his pocket.

Early in the morning, even when the sun was out, no club members were around so the ball boys practiced. The Igueldo brothers had a couple of old warped rackets and were furious when the *Cubanito* gave a much newer racket to Planicio.

"You're a pig," they told him.

"Why?"

"Because you've got the best racket."

"The marquis gave it to me."

Planicio always called him the marquis just like Jacinto, but the others called him the *Cubanito* or the *manisero,* copying the Bilbaon and some other club members. At any rate, since Planicio wasn't all that interested in tennis, he gave the racket to the other boys but took it back whenever the marquis appeared so he wouldn't think he didn't appreciate it.

"What is this tennis?" *Aita* asked once.

Planicio explained the game to him, and the Galician made a gesture showing his contempt. It sounded like the games the female pelota players played on the Gros fronton, except that it made even less sense. To him, the logical thing, considering they were facing one another with only a net in between, would be for them to try to hit their opponent with the ball.

"Tell me, can they aim for their opponent?"

They could but there wasn't much point because the opponent could easily avoid being hit.

"Anyway, it's a soft ball," said the Galician, understandingly.

"But it stings if it hits you," his son pointed out.

The boys preferred playing on a kind of fronton without side walls, which made it harder, used by club members to practice their swing. For Planicio, used to playing with a makeshift ball that bounced every which way, using a racket to hit a rubber ball that always bounced back was nothing. Julio the groundskeeper didn't let them play on the real courts for fear they'd do some damage, but sometimes he'd let them on if they promised to sprinkle the court with water and drag the roller and mat over it afterward. They weren't very good at serves, but during the game itself they held their own since the other two boys had been pelota players as well and had no trouble handling a racket. Sometimes a club member showed up without a partner and asked one of the boys to practice with him. People laughed watching Planicio play because of the singular ways he had of returning the ball. He didn't know how to use the backhand, instead he switched the racket from one hand to the other with the greatest of ease, returning the ball just as easily with his right or left hand. With his characteristic toes-out run making him look like a duck, he ran tirelessly all over the court, forever entertaining, and when it seemed like the ball was going to hit the ground for a second time, he arrived—splat! splat!—just in time to get his racket underneath the ball and return it. He liked to see the occasional spectator laughing. It made him try even harder because he wanted to please.

There was one lady, the wife of the German consul in San Sebastian, who liked to play with him because he kept her on her toes with his untiring returns. One day they played a game, and even though Planicio served underhand because he didn't know how to serve any other way, he won the game hands down. The German woman was disconsolate. After all, she was an elegant player and one of the better-known women players in the club. She spoke Spanish quite well and protested, "You don't hit the ball hard enough, and you lob them too high! That's not playing tennis."

Since then, she hadn't wanted to play with Planicio again. He discussed the matter with *Aita*.

"Whoever told you to beat a lady who pays you a peseta for playing?"

Planicio found the question disconcerting. Usually his father bawled him out for not trying hard enough to win, but *Aita* tried to explain it to him, patiently.

"You've got to know when to win and when not to win."

He tried to explain the facts patiently although he doubted very much that the boy would understand. It had become apparent to him that, although Planicio had a great aptitude for reading, according to Don Román, he had little aptitude for life itself.

In spite of everything, the German woman did ask Planicio to practice with her again because he gave her a real workout, and she needed to watch her figure. Planicio asked excitedly, "Would you like to play a game, Señora?" thinking he'd let her win this time like *Aita* had told him to do, but the señora, just in case, always said no, they were better off practicing.

The Igueldo brothers, ever full of malice and mindful of one thing and one thing only, said, "The German's in love with you. If I were you, I'd screw her."

Planicio, who had his own problems in that regard, was taken aback by such a proposal. The situation seemed highly improbable with a woman so much older than he—she must be at least forty—who, when she played tennis, wore culottes that came to below her knees. No matter how much detail the others went into on how it was done and how easy it really was, he couldn't imagine any of it being interesting with the lady who wore culottes.

JULIO AND HIS WIFE earned 600 pesetas a month plus their house and electricity. The house was in a far corner of the club, hidden behind a hedge fence next to the piles of red brick dust they carried over in wheelbarrow loads for the courts. Behind the house was a small garden they grew vegetables in for their own needs, it being hard to get by on 600 pesetas. That's why the groundskeeper's wife took the club's towels in for washing, since it paid extra, as well as any player's clothes. She was forever working, and sometimes she took it out on her husband.

"Is this what you brought me here for? We were going to go back to the farm!"

At other times she said, "It looks to me like you've chosen a loafer's job."

This because her husband spent his time going up and down, sprinkling and rolling the courts, not what anyone would call hard work, while she spent all day scrubbing the laundry in cold water, even in winter, looking after both the house and the ladies' change room as well as dealing with the women themselves, a tedious lot, always asking for a needle to stitch something up with. Arancha was some compensation, but her mother couldn't stand how the child was such a picky eater. If they gave Arancha meat, she kept adding bits to her mouth, chewing away until she had one big wad, which she then spat out.

"What on earth are you doing, damn you! I'll kill you!"

But of course her mother didn't kill her. Instead, she prepared something else to see if it would go down better. Arancha looked on, entertained by all the fuss and by her parents' arguments when her father accused his wife of having no patience.

"Give it to her yourself then!"

Julio started giving her the purée or the pap, sometimes without a hitch. Then he said to his spouse, "You see, woman?" But at other times, she started blowing bubbles, getting food all over her clothes, and it was her father who stomped off in a fury.

What Arancha liked best was playing with the comb. She combed her doll's hair, her own hair and, sometimes even, Planicio's hair because he let her. This they did in hiding because her mother called it a dirty game, not because Planicio's hair was dirty, which it was, but because the child put the comb in her mouth. In fact, there was only the one comb in the house, and she did have a point; it was about as dirty as they come.

"Besides, you keep losing it and then we can never find it again!"

For that reason, Planicio bought Arancha an imitation tor-

toiseshell comb for ninety-five centimos in the Olaizola drug-
store on the Boulevard. He went up to her mother and said, "I
bought this for Arancha."

He brought it one day when the groundskeeper wasn't
around because the latter still looked at him with a great deal
of distrust.

"*Ené,* the things you do!"

But the woman was obviously pleased with his gesture, especially seeing how happy it made her daughter.

"Me comb Tithio."

In other words, she wanted to comb Planicio's hair, and her
mother let her because every time she heard her daughter make
a sentence that made sense, she felt a great thrill. Aside from
being a picky eater, Arancha hadn't started talking until she
was over two years old, and the groundskeeper's wife, who was
pessimistic by nature, had begun to think that her daughter
would never speak, even though the ladies in the locker room
assured her, from experience, that this was common and that
some children took longer than others to say their first words.
But she was happy to see for herself that they were right.
That's why she agreed to let her daughter comb Planicio's hair,
although once again she warned him not to let her put the
comb in her mouth.

The drama unfolded at mealtime in the following manner.
It was an unpleasant morning, cloudy, with a strong northwest
wind that threatened rain, and no one came to play tennis.
The little girl was so excited about her comb that she wouldn't
let go of Planicio's hand. She made him take her to a hidden
corner where there was a small fountain she used to wet the
comb, and so she began to comb her doll's, her own and Planicio's hair. Planicio was very careful to see that she didn't get
wet herself since she wasn't supposed to go near water in case
she caught a cold, another of the things her mother worried
about. He managed to ensure she hardly got wet at all or in
any case so little that it wasn't even noticeable, and in compen-

sation he let her fill the fluted tin pan they used to make mud pies and dump its contents over his head. Then she ran the comb through his hair—he crouched down so she could reach, keeping very still because it was like a caress—and chattered on in the way her mother loved. "Stay still, you! Eh! Me comb." She combed his hair, and he stayed still except for gently tickling her ribs that were so soft to the touch. He also brushed his hand against her small legs but very lightly because she was sick of having people all over her, which was why she got along so well with Planicio. He had to bring his face up close for her to be able to comb his hair, and he could feel her breath tickling his ear. Arancha could spend forever combing away, and Planicio, to change positions a bit, would whisper secrets to her, another thing she liked, and she said, "Yeth" but almost right away she made him return to his crouched position and scolded, "Don't move, you bugger!" She swore with ease and since everyone laughed except for her mother, she swore often. The ladies in the change room, the ones with experience, told the groundskeeper's wife that it was better not to scold her because the child didn't know what she was saying but that she mustn't laugh either so the child wouldn't think she'd made a joke.

In other words, it was a perfect morning because with Planicio around, Arancha wouldn't be up to any mischief. When her mother called out to bring her home for lunch, things took a slight turn for the worse. Planicio had trouble convincing her that she had to stop combing his hair and that they had to go in for some "yum-yum." It was a Monday and her mother was overworked, Monday being the big laundry day. She'd prepared a nutritious pap of corn starch and egg for Arancha. But there were problems. At first Arancha wanted to eat inside, then, no, outside on a small wooden table that stood next to the entrance, sheltered from the wind.

Her mother said, "That child. With everything I have to do!" but she took the pap outside and sat her in a chair on some cushions. Arancha took two spoonfuls distractedly, without letting go of the comb, and on the third spoonful started to blow energetic bubbles. Her mother yelled, "If you spit it out I'll kill you!"

The child considered throwing a tantrum but simply said, "Tithio feed me."

"*Now* what do you want?" her mother cried out in desperation because Mondays were always bad days and this one more than most. Because of the humidity and the cloud-covered sky, the laundry wouldn't be dry, and the next day she'd have to explain it to the tennis players.

The child repeated, "Tithio feed me," and there was no mistaking that she wanted Planicio to feed her, Planicio who stood slightly off to the side because he knew that mealtimes were not the best of times.

Her mother repeated in a loud enough voice to be heard, "You want Planicio to feed you?"

She spoke loudly enough so that he could hear and understand the invitation.

"Now she wants you to feed her. That girl!"

Planicio drew near and told Arancha he'd feed her but only if she ate it all up. Inside he felt a rosy glow because her mother and father were important people, and yet the child wanted him to feed her. In spite of everything, he made his big mistake. He started out fine, telling Arancha stories she liked to hear and talking about hairstyles they'd do with the comb once she'd finished eating, if of course she ate it all because little girls who didn't eat their food all up were in for an unpleasant surprise. Arancha, recently turned two, sat there with her brown hair and fair complexion, her black eyes staring fixedly, her mother inside the house, so Arancha wouldn't see her since that's when she was impossible. The dish was a very large old porcelain dish, and the little girl ate half her meal just fine and another quarter with some difficulty. Planicio was quite pleased with what he'd accomplished and wished Don Román could see him. He was pleased with himself, but at the same time he was suffering from severe hunger pangs since he hadn't eaten a thing since eight that morning and then only his usual watered-down milk soup, which didn't amount to anything. The chances of his eating anything at noon looked poor because all he had were copper coins in his pocket. The corn starch and egg looked smooth and tasty, yellow in color, like the custards he didn't remember having had since *Amá* died, and there was still a quarter of it left. Sometimes a trickle oozed out the corner of the child's lips and Planicio painstakingly scooped it up saying, "Careful, don't waste any." He was starving, Arancha didn't want anymore and he threatened her, "Watch out or I'll eat it." He pretended to eat the pap with the spoon. His reason being of course that the child would say no and eat it herself. But Arancha liked Tithio's idea and laughed because he was so funny pretending to eat the pap, smacking his lips in satisfaction, inflating his cheeks. The fact was that Arancha wasn't going to eat anymore, her mother was still inside, he was so hungry that he couldn't stand it any longer, the pap reminded him of his *Amá's* custards and that's when Julio the groundskeeper saw him hastily finish off the last of the pap in a few huge spoonfuls. Actually Julio arrived just at that instant and didn't see everything that had gone on before. All he saw was Planicio eating his daughter's food, and he cried out so loudly that his wife came out to see what was going on, and even the two Igueldo brothers, who hadn't given a sign of life all morning, appeared.

PLANICIO SPENT all that afternoon walking the streets of San Sebastian because he didn't know how to explain what he'd done, and he was too old to cry. He just left the club and started running. He ran along Ondarreta beach—splat! splat!—which on such a drab day was almost empty, with no canopies out. On sunny days he and the two other ball boys hung out there, watching the girls in their bathing suits, which, although they had little skirts on them, still showed off their breasts. At first he tried to explain how Arancha had eaten almost everything and that it was only at the end . . . But he didn't know how to explain what had happened at the end. What's more, it was a difficult thing to do because Arancha's father had never trusted him and seemed happy to have his suspicions confirmed. His wife screamed at her husband, "What are you saying?" and the two brothers laughed.

That's when Planicio started to run, even though at this time of day he couldn't go home because if *Aita* happened to be there and asked what had happened, he didn't know what to say. Things like this just couldn't be explained. He couldn't explain it to Don Román either, not because the don wouldn't understand but because Planicio wouldn't know how to explain. What's more, he didn't have any friends left. He didn't see Ramoncho on Sundays anymore since Sunday was the day he had the most work to do at the club. It didn't matter to him since he was used to being alone and waiting for evening to come so he could go see Don Román. Planicio got along all right with the other two ball boys. In fact, they were getting to like tennis and were learning how to serve. The problem was that they always wanted to talk about the same thing. It was so pointless. There was no reason why they couldn't go to Ondarreta beach to watch the girls in their bathing suits, but why talk about it? At the Hotel Londres he turned on to Calle de Urbieta toward the Amara suburb, intent on getting as far away as he could. From time to time the French pro gave them tips on their serves, the most difficult skill to master. He also told Planicio he should learn the backhand because changing his racket from one hand to the other when the ball was on his left wouldn't work when he had a half-decent player as his opponent. It only worked for defending himself against fat ladies—he must have meant the German woman—but that wasn't the way tennis was played. The marquis told Planicio the same thing, although he enjoyed watching the ease with which Planicio switched hands.

Just the thought of the marquis hearing about his eating Arancha's pap brought Planicio to a halt, and he started to cry out of anger, alone, next to the lagoon where the car they'd used as a boat had once been. But it wasn't true, swear to God. He'd given it all to Arancha, and when she hadn't wanted anymore, he'd insisted, told her stories, and he'd almost had her finish it all, and only at the very end, when hardly any was left and the child was spitting it out, had he finished off the last spoonfuls. Oh, God! He'd started crying tears of anger because they hadn't let him explain, and he ended up crying softly because he didn't know what to do. The only sure thing was that he wouldn't go to Ramón y Cajal that night. He didn't want them to think he only went for the bread and chocolate. Anyway, there was nothing for him to do here because the car that he and Ramoncho used to play Tom Sawyer and Huckleberry Finn with had been taken away, so he counted the coins in his pocket and went back to the city to buy himself powder candy and peanuts.

By seven he couldn't stand being on the street any longer, and he went to the garret room where time continued to hang so heavy that he even considered going downstairs to talk to Francisca. He didn't though because it made the concierge extremely nervous to have people other than those from the count's family in the vestibule. It used to be, last summer, that she knew when it was she had to be on the lookout for the countess's return from her walk, at around nine-thirty in the evening. Just before nine-thirty she opened the elevator doors and stopped everyone else from using it. The expansion of the count's household to include the fourth floor and the arbitrary ways of the marquis, who hardly ever used the elevator except every once in a while, were almost too much for Francisca. She'd become anxious and unsure of herself. She also worried about how to treat the marquis's daughters, who were still children but children from the count's household, and whether she should do something about the way they slammed the elevator doors. Perhaps she simply didn't have a vocation as a concierge in a house equipped with an elevator. And so Planicio didn't go downstairs. Francisca liked to listen to the boy's stories and was always asking him questions, especially about Don Román's household and the poor man's health; but given the present circumstances, it wasn't easy for him to talk to her because the woman wouldn't let him stand in the vestibule. She stayed in the doorway and he had to stand out on the street to talk to her, ready to vanish as soon as the count's relatives appeared.

At nine-thirty, to Planicio's surprise, *Aita* showed up with some provisions.

"Have you had supper?" he asked the boy, and without waiting for an answer, added, "Even if you have had supper, you won't say no to another one if I know you."

He was carrying a small bag of potatoes and a small can of cooking oil he'd bought from a sleeping car.

"At two pesetas a kilo, all you get is old potatoes, the kind we used to feed to the pigs."

He loved to harp on the fact that nowadays people had to settle for what only used to be good enough for pigs. He'd also managed to unearth some mussels, some pitifully tiny sorry-looking mussels.

"Just so's to add a bit of taste. Here, put them under the tap and wash off all the sand. Then start peeling potatoes. We've got salt, don't we?"

Everything else—parsley, onions and garlic—he'd brought with him because he knew there was nothing in the garret room except salt. And if there wasn't any salt, he could always ask a neighbor for some. He put the cooking oil in the earthen pan and fried the onions lightly so they wouldn't brown. He was quite put out when he discovered he'd forgotten to bring some green pepper.

"Jesus, how could I forget that!" he scolded himself, finding no solace in hearing Planicio say it didn't matter. His son's words only made him angrier. "How can you say it doesn't matter if there's no green pepper to go with the potatoes and mussels!"

Since there was nothing he could do about it, he kept on sautéing the onions, stirring carefully all the while. Then he threw in the mussels and sautéed them too. Lastly he added the crushed garlic and a generous helping of parsley. The concoction was beginning to smell quite appetizing and the *Cimarrón* cheered up.

"I brought a bit of bread too. Now we have to let it cook."

"How long, *Aita?*"

"Half an hour."

It was a horrendously long time, but *Aita* said, "Hey, good food takes time. Half an hour and then it has to sit for a bit."

Even as he gave this advice, Pachi couldn't work up much enthusiasm because his son had what must be a cast-iron stomach and never seemed to care what he put into it. All that counted was filling the vacuum. But Pachi was wrong because Planicio truly admired his father's culinary skills and would have liked to be able to sample his cooking every day. Planicio could see how it was worth waiting half an hour and a bit, time to let the food sit, no matter how hungry he was.

While they waited the *Cimarrón* sat down in the chair that used to belong to the count, staring steadily at the pan. From time to time he stood up to give the ingredients a stir. He also tasted the dish a couple of times to make sure he'd gotten the salt right. As long as the food was still on the stove, he'd worry about whether he'd gotten the amount right and wouldn't breathe easy again until the dish was on the table.

"I think the salt's just right. Listen, Don Román asked about you. Why didn't you come by today?"

Although the potatoes and mussels were some consolation, Planicio had been feeling sad because no one from Ramón y Cajal seemed to miss him. So he was happy to hear his father's unexpected remark.

"I had a bit of a headache."

"A headache?" asked his father, surprised because he himself was never sick. His lumbago (or rheumatism) was more a problem for certain types of work than anything else. He stood up again and tasted the sauce with the wooden spoon. "It's going to be good, mind, but it would have been even better with green pepper. Anyway, Don Román wondered if something had happened to you. Can you believe that!"

The *Cimarrón* knew that life held its surprises and so saw nothing strange about his son's absence at Ramón y Cajal, among other reasons because it had never been spelled out that he had to go there every afternoon. On the other hand, Don Román worried about everything. For example, he was still worried about Señorita Menchu's future, and every time he mentioned his concern to Pachi, it put a damper on Pachi's plans to repeat that late June afternoon encounter, which without any forethought had turned out so well. Moreover, the damned woman spent much of her time sighing and casting glances his way but gave him no opportunity whatsoever to repeat their encounter despite the fact that she'd obviously enjoyed it.

"What did Don Román say?"

His father didn't answer because he was busy taking the pan off the burner. Once he was through, however, he got back to the subject at hand.

"I bet your headache comes from reading too much."

"No, I wasn't even reading. What did Don Román say?"

"What I just told you. He asked where you were two or three times, and then he said he wondered if something had happened to you."

Something had definitely happened to him, but it wasn't something he could talk about or even think about now because the potatoes were truly delicious.

"It would have been better with green pepper though."

In any case, *Aita* was happy because his dish was a success.

In cooking, you never knew no matter how careful you were. The mussels, although sorry-looking because of their small size, still held in the spirals of their small shells an aftertaste of garlic and sea, and were a pleasure to suck on.

"Slowly, boy, eat slowly. How many times do I have to tell you? There's lots left."

He stressed to little avail that everything had to be done slowly in cuisine, both cooking and eating.

"What's the rush anyway?"

"Nothing, *Aita*. It's just a habit."

"Well, it's a bad habit. That's how you get headaches afterward."

He was horrified anew to see his son empty a whole glass of water in one gulp.

"Take some wine, for Christ's sake! How can you drink water with these potatoes?"

There were very few foods that Pachi didn't think it was scandalous to drink water with.

"All right, give me a bit of wine in my water."

This was even worse. It only served to ruin them both. Planicio helped himself to a bit of wine and after tasting it thought that maybe his father had been right.

"*Aita*, we have to do this more often."

"What?"

"This."

"Potatoes and mussels?"

Not that exactly. What Planicio wanted was for them to do this, eat supper together, sopping up the last bit of food from the pan and then going out under the stars to belch.

"Fine, we will. But, God, times are tough! Two pesetas for a kilo of potatoes. It's highway robbery!"

Whenever they ate a substantial dinner, *Aita* liked to sit back and relax afterward with a couple of small glasses of wine before going to bed. It was then that Planicio usually told him about the day's doings at the club—about the German lady, the way the French pro spoke, the marquis's elegance—and *Aita* had questions for him and asked for details. But when Planicio had nothing to say, like that night, for instance, because what had happened was better left unsaid, *Aita* didn't find it strange. Don Román would surely have asked, "What's wrong, Planicio? You're so quiet. Don't you have any stories for me?" And if Planicio still hadn't said anything, then the don would have told him about the time when he was still a boy that he went to the bend in the river in Martutene and set off on some adventure or other. Anyway, the next day Planicio would go to Ramón y Cajal to show the don that nothing had happened to him.

ON THE OTHER HAND, Planicio didn't go back to the club—he couldn't—but it just so happened that when he came back the next night from Ramón y Cajal, in spite of all the concierge's precautions, he bumped into the marquis in the lobby. The marquis said, "I didn't see you at the club today! What happened?"

"I had a headache, Señor Marquis."

"You don't say. Is it better?"

"Yes, Señor."

"Well then, see you tomorrow."

God had to have had a hand in it because all day long Planicio had been extra careful not to be seen on his way in or out, precisely because he was afraid of running into the marquis, who might have heard about Arancha's pap. And yet, just when he should have been especially careful—even if only out of respect for Francisca's repeated instructions on how he had to enter the lobby after nine o'clock at night—he hadn't been paying attention and had come face to face with the marquis, who'd said quite naturally, "See you tomorrow," and so he had no choice but to go back to the club. It was a relief in a way because, if not, he didn't know what he'd have done.

The next day he arrived at the tennis club expecting the

worst. The groundskeeper was busy sprinkling the courts and barely returned his greeting, but that was nothing unusual. Shortly afterward the two brothers arrived, and Julio told the three of them to take out the roller. The Igueldo boys, as usual, called the groundskeeper a bastard, always giving them the toughest job. The roller was made of stone. It was big and took two people to pull; the third person walked behind with the mat. The two brothers didn't say a word about the pap— why would they?—and in any case, they saw no reason why Planicio shouldn't have eaten it. The only thing he did wrong was to get caught. Then the German consul's wife arrived for a game, but first she wanted to warm up a bit with Planicio. The eldest ball boy, who was sixteen and whose mind was forever stuck in the gutter, said could Planicio ever give her a warm-up, and since Planicio knew full well what was implied, he told the other boy to go to hell, not because it bothered him but because that was the way they talked to each other.

After the warm-up session with the German lady, the groundskeeper's wife called him over. He'd planned to stay away from the house and not even talk to Arancha, whose fault it was that he was suffering such humiliation, but if her moth-er called him over, there was nothing he could do about it.

It was about eleven o'clock by then, and she asked him, "Are you hungry?"

Planicio didn't answer in case this was a trick question lead-ing up to the pap incident, even though he knew she wasn't like her husband.

"Do you like cornbread?"

He answered yes, he did.

"Come on in."

She put a wooden bowl on the table and told him to have a seat. Arancha came in and cried out, "Tithio, comb!" She dis-appeared and came back shortly with the comb, now missing a few teeth. The little girl thought it quite a feat to have kept the comb so long without losing it, which is why she showed it to

Planicio, who pointed out that it was broken, but she replied, "Me bweak, no me good."

Her mother was overcome with emotion.

"Did you see? She can say everything, absolutely everything. But the things she says!"

She poured some milk into his bowl and gave him two pieces of cornbread on the side, two big, flat, oval, crusty ones. Planicio was grateful for Arancha's presence because it helped him hide the fact that he felt like crying.

"Me sit, Tithio."

They had to pull a chair up to the table, and Planicio had to give her a bit of his cornbread.

"Would you look at that? If I give her cornbread for breakfast, she refuses to eat any, and now she has to have some of yours. That girl doesn't know her own mind!"

Planicio made it clear that he was quite happy to give her some. It was a relief to have a pretext to talk and clear his throat a bit because a knot had formed there and he was finding it hard to swallow. He broke the cornbread up into small pieces, threw them into the bowl then spooned them up, sipping a bit of milk at the same time but not too much, so he'd still have enough left. Arancha put her fingers into the bowl and brought out a piece of cornbread. Her mother told her not to use her fingers, that it was dirty, but once again Planicio insisted it didn't bother him. When he finished he stood up and thanked Arancha's mother. Arancha grabbed onto his hand and wanted to leave with him, but her mother said that Tithio had to work. Arancha looked as though she were about to throw a temper tantrum, but Planicio whispered a few words in her ear, nonsense words he'd invented on the spot, words that didn't mean anything but that calmed her down.

Outside, one of the Igueldo boys was waiting, wondering why he'd taken so long inside.

"Hey, your neighbor's here. Get a move on."

Planicio knew it sounded strange to have the marquis as his

neighbor, but that's the way houses were in those days. Once
again he told the messenger to go to hell but more angrily this
time because if the joke ever reached the marquis's ears, he
might think Planicio was the one who called him his neighbor.

That morning, Planicio outdid himself gathering balls on
the court. The marquis played two games, a singles game that
he won hands down and a mixed doubles with the French pro
as his opponent, each of them paired with a female partner,
elegant women but only middling players. They had fun with
the game, the two gentlemen yielding to the ladies, making it
easy for them to return the ball. Points were of little concern,
the service tending to get harder only when the other man was
on the receiving end. Planicio outdid himself because with six
balls in play, he managed to ensure, in a continual zigzagging
motion, that not a one was ever left lying on the court nor
even on the sidelines. He always gave the balls to the player
whose turn it was to serve without having to be told by anyone.
He knew that the marquis liked his ball boy to know whose
turn it was and to give the balls to that person. In a mixed
game it was more complicated because the women never knew
if it was their turn to serve or not, but Planicio made it clear,
"It's your serve, Señora." The women thanked him, and afterward, at the end of the game, they said a few words about how
gracious and nice he was and how he ran. The marquis smiled,
saying Planicio was his favorite ball boy and gave him a duro.
Planicio outshone himself not because he was expecting a duro
but because the day before he'd been just about the unhappiest
person on Earth—he assumed there had to be somebody
unhappier than he—and yet today he was the happiest of all.
He didn't do it for the money, but listening to the German
lady's peseta and the marquis's duro clinking together in his
right pocket, he thought that perhaps the time had come to
realize his cherished dream of putting aside an emergency
stock in the garret room, for example, a stock of the broken
cookies Francisca said they sold in Rentería at such a bargain

price, the ones he'd store in a tin box so they wouldn't go all soft from the humidity.

SILENCE SPOKE VOLUMES to Don Román. Sometimes Planicio and he sat without speaking, both of them reading. More precisely Planicio was reading, and he, to justify his silence, hid behind a newspaper that was of no interest to him and that, furthermore, was hard to hold. If the boy had a question about something he was reading, the don answered. Things of import only unveiled their mysteries to those who approached them with deep respect, silently and expectantly. And he seemed to see this aptitude in Planicio.

One afternoon Planicio told him as if it were the most wonderful thing in the world that the club groundskeeper's wife had given him cornbread with milk as a mid-morning snack. It meant something special to have the boy telling him such things. Moreso because Planicio always waited until he was alone with the don to tell him his news, as though no one else would understand or see the significance of what had happened.

ANOTHER AFTERNOON when the don least expected it—since he'd been waiting for two years already—the miller's wife from Salvatierra showed up. She was the second eldest in the family, one year younger than Don Román, and had seven children and four grandchildren. She was shocked upon her arrival in San Sebastian to see the condition her eldest brother was in, this same brother who was both the family's cross to bear as well as its pride. The Aldaiz's were a modest people from Alava. Their father had been an employee of the Delegation and that Román had had such a brilliant career, culminating in his appointment as Revenue delegate, exalted the family name.

"But just look at Román!" she said to her young sister. "He can't even move!"

Señorita Menchu sighed so that the rest of her family would know how she had had to suffer looking after the eldest. Rosa couldn't help feeling sad to see her brother looking so poorly, so changed, his chin lying on his chest, his tongue sticking out too far between his lips. And yet his eyes still had the same sparkle as he stammered out his thanks for her visit with a twisted smile that didn't conceal, in spite of its deformity, his desire to please even her, although she hadn't set foot in San Sebastian for two years. The remorse she felt to have such a brother and have neglected him so! It was her husband's fault because time and again she'd said to him, "We must go to San Sebastian to see Román," and he always said he couldn't. She reminded him that they were her brother and sister, and he said that was why he sent them a sack of flour every month. And that was that. All of which made her dread the effect her younger sister's pregnancy might have on Don Román.

"Heavens above, how could you not have been more careful!"

Her younger sister cried and sighed, but it seemed to Rosa that her sister needed comforting of a sort her older sister couldn't offer. Rosa only left Salvatierra very rarely, and in the country this kind of thing happened to girls more often but at a more reckless age, the perpetrator usually being a serious fiancé. In this case, however, the Revenue delegate's sister who was well into her thirties had been taken down by a man whose description only made the whole thing even more incomprehensible.

"What are you going to do?" she asked her young sister.

The latter kept quiet long enough for her older sister to begin making suggestions.

"Marry him?"

Señorita Menchu shrugged her shoulders with such hypocritical resignation that Rosa, who was still saddened by her brother's condition, felt her anger mounting and struck out, "He doesn't want to, is that it?"

This hurt and Señorita Menchu let a genuine sob escape her lips. Rosa reminded herself that Menchu was the youngest by a number of years, which is why she hadn't been brought up in the same way as the others, her older brother having already become an important man. Moreover, Menchu had been the one to look after Román, and who knows, maybe that explained why her time had run out and she'd made such a stupid mistake. Rosa put her arm around her sister's shoulders and told her not to cry. Actually she didn't have to stop crying, just explain a little further.

"What does he do?"

Señorita Menchu knew this would be the hardest part to explain. It wasn't the right time to remind Rosa that, after all, she'd only married a town miller, even though the war had turned him into an industrialist.

"Román has always said that Pachi is very intelligent."

So intelligent, thought her sister, that he set his sights on you. These were her thoughts as she listened in amazement to how her young sister had already worked everything out, even the dowry Román had been so painstakingly setting aside for her, which they could use to set up some kind of "small business" so Pachi could leave his current job. She'd even given thought to the kind of "small business" they should start up.

"Does he know about your dowry?"

Her sister's meaning was unmistakable, and Señorita Menchu took offense.

"No."

She was offended but not overly so because she needed her sister, who seemed to be willing to help her work toward a solution.

"Do you think he loves you?"

"Well, things would seem to point that way, wouldn't they?"

Her tone was such that Rosa started to laugh for the first time since she'd set foot in San Sebastian.

"Come on, tell me what happened."

Then they both started to laugh, and Señorita Menchu, highly embarrassed, told her it was the sort of thing one couldn't talk about.

DON ROMAN, for whom silence spoke volumes, sometimes held his peace because there was nothing to say—for instance, when his sister Rosa told him that little Menchu wanted to marry Pachi Lourido as though it were the best possible news, although her tone seemed to indicate the exact opposite. He couldn't get over how, after an absence of two years, his sister Rosa, with whom he got on splendidly because they were almost the same age, had disappeared moments after her arrival only to reappear two hours later to announce in a festive tone that sounded more like a lament that their little sister wanted to get married, without even specifying whether the other party was similarly disposed. But the miller's wife felt so guilty about her absences that she was ready to do whatever had to be done, and Menchu had insisted, "Tell Román before anyone else." Menchu seemed to have little doubt that the train station employee would see it her way, something the miller's wife was less sure of because at fifty-two years of age, and as a mother of seven and grandmother of four, she'd seen enough of life to know a thing or two.

"And if necessary," Menchu threatened, "we'll tell him I'm expecting a baby."

"Tell who? Pachi?"

"Heavens, of course we'll tell *him!* Why on earth not? This very afternoon in fact."

Menchu spoke fiercely, determined that Pachi should learn what his afternoon of fun had led to that day in late June during which she did agree to a repeat; but the man hadn't even shown respect for her Carmen robe.

"I mean," said Menchu with some urgency, "that if necessary we'll tell Román why I have to get married."

"No, let me look after it," pleaded Rosa who couldn't bear

the thought of adding the smallest burden to the one already imposed on her brother by his distressing physical condition.

"Well, you'll see what needs to be done," said Menchu defiantly, and her sister caught herself thinking that by virtue of being the youngest by a number of years, Menchu had been spoiled by them all. That is, this was not a girl feeling contrite because of a mistake she'd made, as would traditionally have been the case. Rather this was a woman who was demanding that her family help her marry a man Rosa could hardly wait to meet because of the unusual powers of attraction he must have.

"You have to understand," Rosa pleaded once more, "we can't upset Román like this. If everything goes as planned, there's no need for him to find out about the pregnancy. We'll just have to take things slowly."

"Slowly!" cried her young sister in fury. As slowly as Rosa? Who hadn't given a sign of life since Menchu's letter two weeks ago, and if Menchu hadn't telephoned her announcing they had to talk, nothing would have happened?

"Now," threatened Menchu, "you have to tell him now. If not, I will. It can't wait."

That's why Rosa, who was guilty of so many silences and absences, went about it all wrong. She broke the news with precipitation, telling Don Román how happy she was that Menchu had finally found a suitor and how relieved the whole family would be to see her married and what a help it would be for him, for Don Román, to have a man in the house.

In other words, the whole family—this was not what Rosa said but what Don Román understood—was so relieved because they were installing his aide-de-camp in his house via his young sister's bedroom. And suddenly for no reason whatsoever, he felt that this was the last failure of his life—it wasn't likely he'd have time for another one—and this realization made him hunch down farther in his invalid's chair, his eyes locked on the horizon with no interest at all in what might be behind the crimson line drawn by the setting sun, certain that in any case he wouldn't be transported there in a ridiculous steamboat because the boat would undoubtedly sink on the way.

"Say something, Román. Don't just sit there like that," his sister Rosa insisted, genuinely frightened by his silence.

"Pl–please, leave me alone," he said with the authority of an older brother, an authority he hadn't used in a long time, and Rosa complied.

To her younger sister, who'd been waiting in the refuge of her bedroom, Rosa at first reported that he hadn't taken the news all that well but that he'd get over it. But in short order, remembering her brother and the way he'd looked, Rosa dissolved into tears and what had once been laughter turned to reproaches. "But, Menchu, in God's name, how could you do this to Román?" And Señorita Menchu responded with tears and anger of her own. Had her brother and sister, selfish as they each were, living their own lives with their respective families, ever once thought about the fact that they'd left her alone to look after their paralyzed brother? Did they know what it was like to have to care for an invalid, seeing his condition deteriorate day by day, so much so that lately she'd even had to put his own trousers on for him in the morning? The same thing day in and day out for years, days spent with spinster friends like herself, she known in the city only as the sister of the Revenue delegate, an invalid whose infirmity for all one knew might be hereditary, and so no man had ever come near her.

"The only man who did come near me wasn't a man. He was an oaf who was only interested in me because he worked in the Delegation under Román! You hear?"

"Yes, but for God's sake please stop yelling."

"I am yelling, and if he hears me, all the better! Because at least Pachi likes me, you hear? He knew nothing about my dowry. It was me he was interested in, and he's been back several times since! Do you hear? But I didn't want to . . . not again. . . ." She couldn't speak she was crying so hard, and her fury dissolved into incoherent babbling. "Because it can't be. . . .

I just want to get married. . . . Understand that, Rosa, please. I know he'll want to too. . . . Rosa, please, I'm begging you. Once Pachi knows, he will get married. I know he loves me."

Locked in embrace, the two sisters wept, silently now, without reproaches.

"What's more . . . he brings me presents. The other day he brought me some sausage from Aranda. He'll change, Rosa. Truly he will."

"Of course he will," her older sister said. "Of course he'll change. Come now, don't cry anymore."

"If he marries me, I'll make him change. . . . Rosa . . . you'll see."

Of course he would change. She didn't have to keep on crying. They all changed.

"What's more . . . we'll start up a restaurant. . . . He knows a lot about cooking, and between the two of us we'll make it work."

Rosa had calmed down by then, and she looked at her sister tenderly.

"A restaurant?"

"Yes, it can't lose. Maybe you've seen a restaurant that's going out of business?"

Rosa was amused by her sister's commonsense approach, and she laughed lightly once again but very lightly because the picture of her brother hunched over in his invalid's chair, not saying a word, was imbedded in her mind.

IT WAS AN EVENTFUL afternoon at Ramón y Cajal. It was only natural for Señorita Menchu to stay in her room until everyone's position had been made clear.

Rosa entered the living room and asked her brother, "How do you feel, Román?"

"Fine," he said distractedly.

His sister returned to Menchu's side, and she in turn asked, "What did he say?"

"Nothing, just that he's fine."

"And what is he doing?"

"Nothing, just staring out at the horizon."

"He does that a lot."

In other words, the fact that he was staring out at the horizon wasn't worrisome in itself because even when nothing had happened, he did the same.

SEÑORITA MENCHU told Pachi that very night in the dining room, feeling only a relative amount of concern since the emotion-packed day had prepared her for the real thing.

Her sister Rosa timidly offered, "If you like, I'll speak to him first."

She spoke reluctantly with a note of resigned heroism, as though she were ready to pay for her sin of not having taken good enough care of her young sister from her home in Salvatierra, Alava.

"No, thank you."

No, thank you because her sister Rosa didn't know exactly what had happened on that afternoon in late June and would have acted like an older sister of the past, going down on her knees to plead for her virginal sister's honor, and Pachi, who was a good person but could only take so much, would undoubtedly break out laughing.

"No, thank you. I would rather do it myself."

And so they ushered him into the dining room for Señorita Menchu to tell him. At first Pachi kept very quiet, showing no reaction, with the ancestral caution of a doubting Thomas, amazed at the natural way the spinster told him she was expecting a baby. She didn't use the plural—we're expecting a baby—but it was understood.

"Are you sure?"

Absolutely sure with no qualms about calling him to account.

"It might just be a coincidence," the Galician said.

"What kind of coincidence?" she said, vexed. No, he hadn't meant anything by it. It was just something to say and he apologized.

"So now what do we do?" asked the Galician as though she might have thought of something.

"You'll know what to do."

Since he was the one who would know, he said what seemed to make the most sense. "Well then, we'll have to think about it."

She held her tongue, and the Galician, knowing what the situation called for, asked, "Should I speak to Don Román?"

He obviously didn't relish the thought, but if it had to be done, he would do it.

"No," said Señorita Menchu. "When you've thought it over, the person to speak to is me."

Pachi was amused by this decision and in view of her condition looked her over from head to toe quite impudently and said, "Well, it suits you, doesn't it?"

This comment, which could be taken as a compliment but to her ears sounded more like an expression of desire tinged with mockery, didn't offend her in the least. On the contrary, it emphasized the aura of complicity between them, which allowed her to say once more, "I want you to speak to me because only my sister Rosa knows about *our* little affair"—this time she stressed the *our*—"and I don't want anyone else to find out about it. Understood?"

The Galician nodded his head, amused.

"Especially not Don Román. Understood?"

"Yes, Señorita."

PACHI HAD NO intention of telling anyone, but he did need to consult someone, in this case the manservant from the count's household. Although it was just for the hell of it that people in Raimundo's bar called Jacinto a fairy, the *Cimarrón* knew Jacinto for what he was, even though he wasn't very adventurous about it. And history had shown that his kind understood what made women tick. Furthermore, Jacinto knew everyone in the neighborhood and could clue Pachi in.

The manservant was bowled over by the announcement.

"But how can that be?"

"Well, see here old friend. That's life for you."

"But . . . did you have intercourse often?"

"No, just one day."

"Talk about hitting the bull's-eye."

"I think it's more a coincidence myself," said the Galician modestly. "That's what I told her, but she didn't seem to appreciate it."

They had their conversation on a summer's evening, outside under the stars of a late August and out of earshot of the garret room so Planicio couldn't hear. Pachi sat in the late count's old chair, which spent the day indoors and was brought out at night, and Jacinto sat on a kitchen chair.

The manservant agreed that from the conversation they'd had in the dining room—short but to the point—it could be surmised that the señorita was looking for an offer of marriage, and he thought it the height of good fortune for Pachi.

"Do you like her?" asked Jacinto.

"Well, the woman does have a good foundation."

Jacinto already knew what Pachi meant by a woman's foundation, and he nodded his head in agreement.

"And being pregnant has brought out some of her natural attributes . . . not that she needed it"—he described with his hands what her bosom looked like now—"and totally changed her looks. Remember how she was always so pasty looking? Now she even has color in her face. She's quite beautiful."

His words conveyed his satisfaction with the role he'd played in this transformation.

"But," Jacinto told him, "she's known to be a pretty bad-tempered woman."

Pachi allowed that that was true, but what woman wasn't bad tempered?

"Listen, Jacinto," and this was the crux of the matter, "does she think that we're going to be able to live on what I earn as a porter?"

No, of course not. Jacinto already knew that Don Román had been saving money for his sister for years, but from the perspective of one familiar with the riches of the count's household, it didn't seem like the don's savings would be enough to live on.

"If it were only me, I'd go through with it and get married but . . . what then?"

They both remained silent because the unknown factor was a key one.

"I'm not talking about living off of his money, but how can I make ends meet with the son I already have, another one on the way and still others to come, plus a wife who's a lady?"

With respect to the last comment, Jacinto reserved judgment because he knew who the Aldaiz's from Alava were, a family of modest background, and Señorita Menchu would never have been a lady if it hadn't been for the position her brother had reached in his career. She didn't have a lady's class, which was why she couldn't get along with her help. To deal with servants one needed to be backed by tradition, and she had none.

"Listen," Jacinto asked, "you say that the sister from Salvatierra is the one she told, isn't that right?"

"Yes. She opened the door for me and said she was Menchu's sister. She looked to be a lot older."

They digressed for a while, talking about the family, their ages and activities, all of which Jacinto knew in minute detail because these were things he just naturally took an interest in. As they spoke it seemed to both of them that the older sister might have a part to play. At least they could try. It didn't make any sense to forge ahead blindly. They laid their plans carefully, and the next morning Jacinto, on his friend's behalf, rang her up to arrange for a meeting.

"When would it suit you, Señora?" asked the manservant with professional courtesy, in spite of his knowledge of her modest condition as a distinguished townsperson.

At the other end, he heard some quite unseemly whispering—she's consulting her sister, thought Jacinto—followed by her answer.

"Why not now?"

Her very precipitation showed her lack of class.

"Very well, Señora. He'll be right over." Then he turned to Pachi, who was following the conversation in the count's kitchen, and said, "That's it. You're on your way."

The older sister greeted him as though they were part of a conspiracy, speaking under her breath and ushering him directly into the dining-room-cum-meeting-room as though she were afraid the door to the living room would suddenly open.

"You had something to say."

Not much, just that the day before, Señorita Menchu had told him about her pregnancy and had more or less said, "You'll know what to do."

He didn't make himself clear, and Rosa exclaimed, "Who, me?"

"No, no, Señora, she was speaking to me. I was the one who would know what to do."

After a minute's silence he continued. "I assume she was referring to us getting married."

He paused a second time on purpose to see if she would object, and since she didn't, he concluded, "That's fine with me, but Señora, I'm a man who hasn't had much luck where work is concerned, especially since I came down with lumbago and had to give up going to sea."

Once he'd made his position clear, Rosa could get down to business. In Salvatierra, future alliances were the object of negotiations, not that it was a sign of bad faith, just simple common sense to see that the economic conditions of the alliance were clearly stated.

"It's getting hot in here. We should open the window a bit."

"Let me get it, Señora."

"Please, call me Rosa."

Pachi didn't drop the *don* he'd always used when addressing Don Román, but from that day on he called the sisters by their first names.

PACHI HAD ALWAYS said that the province of Guipúzcoa was more Catholic than the Pope. Perhaps to compensate for being on the wrong side during the civil war. He too was Catholic, as long as there was something in it for him. Still he had to admit that God did have a hand in some things—consider how depressed he'd been when he went to talk to Menchu's older sister. He'd been so sure that no solution would be perfect, and so when she felt him out about the restaurant he couldn't help but exclaim, "Hey, I'd be good at that!" In other words, when he played the Christmas lottery and imagined what he'd do with the big win, he never for an instant doubted that he'd open a restaurant-bar, not just a restaurant as Menchu's sister had said. A bar as well. Where he'd guarantee the quality and quantity of snacks served. Any leftovers were better thrown out than served stale the next day. Better to have too few than too many. If they ran out, they could always make light snacks of ham and cheese buns that didn't spoil. The cuisine wouldn't be too varied, but the ingredients would be chosen with care and the restaurant-bar would be renowned for its fish soup. When he made fish soup, people couldn't get enough of it. He didn't need a top-notch cook, just one who'd know enough to follow Pachi's instructions. The *Cimarrón* would be behind the bar directing operations and would look after buying the wine himself. This wasn't a job they were talking; it was a whole way of life. Furthermore, although he couldn't read and wasn't interested in learning how, he was extremely good at numbers. When bets were laid and all the others were still adding them up with pen and paper, he'd already figured it out in his head hours ago. To run a business you needed a good head for numbers.

THE MARQUIS followed the goings-on with friendly interest, being kept up to date by Jacinto, who was quite affected by what was happening to his friend. September was the month the elegant set spent in San Sebastian, and the count's household extended its stay to the end of the month. The marquis congratulated Pachi on his upcoming marriage and gave him advice on the restaurant-bar, mainly on how to decorate it in keeping with the regional style, with an accent on life at sea and a motif of regattas and pictures of rowing crews as a reminder of Pachi's feat as bowhand for Fuenterrabía.

Planicio was both happy and confused. *Aita* had told him he would have to work hard in the bar, which Planicio didn't object to in the least. But for the time being Planicio didn't know what to do, and so he kept going to the tennis club to gather balls. He didn't know where he'd be living either because *Aita* would be going with Señorita Menchu to the house on Ramón y Cajal where Pachi would be a great help with Don Román because Señorita Menchu clearly could no longer move her brother, whose condition was steadily deteriorating. But no one had mentioned Planicio, and he didn't ask either. Sometimes he thought he might be left alone in the garret room, which didn't seem such a bad thing.

When he went to Ramón y Cajal, there were always people around. The older sister was staying until the wedding, and her husband had come to spend a few days. Their brother from Bilbao was there as well, with his wife and children. Planicio didn't dare go further than the vestibule, but if Don Román happened to see him, he motioned him in, although they could hardly say a word to each other. The don spoke very little. Each time in the vestibule on their way out, all the relatives said, "Poor Román, he looks so ill!" Planicio couldn't see much of a difference. The don still smiled at him the way he always had and asked him questions, but then someone always came in and they had to stop talking. One day, Señorita Menchu—who had told him he could call her Menchu, something he couldn't bring himself to do—took him shopping for clothes. Money was no longer the issue it used to be either, and *Aita* gave him five-duro bills to buy food with. In any case, Planicio kept on going to the tennis club because he didn't know what else to do. He was confused because he didn't know where he was going to live, but the thought that *Aita* was going to own a bar was so wonderful it made up for that fact. He wasn't surprised to see them get married. He'd always noticed that Señorita Menchu treated his father differently than the others, even Don Román, whom she sometimes scolded.

Just a few days before the wedding, *Aita* told him, "Don Román wants to talk to you." The don must have really wanted to talk to him because when Planicio arrived everyone else left the room, leaving them alone for the first time.

Things weren't going well for Don Román because his reduced capacities meant that everyone wanted to be of assistance. Since they didn't know how to help, they ended up doing more harm than good. They pulled him this way and that instead of staying calm and following his instructions. No one knew better than he the evolution of his disease, and for every new difficulty he had moving his body, he tried to find a solution, but the others were convinced it was better this way or that way, and he ended up being martyred. He couldn't wait for the wedding to be over so he could be left alone with Menchu and his former aide-de-camp to figure out how they'd manage. Because Planicio was leaving. He had to go. The don didn't want the boy to live in this house, sharing the end that awaited him when he'd be nothing more than a grotesque excuse of a man who couldn't even lift a spoon to his mouth anymore. He didn't want Planicio to live with his stepmother for life. Or to get his education from behind a bar.

"So, Planicio, how would you like to go to school?"

It was strange, but whenever the don wanted to talk about something important, he hardly stuttered at all, especially if he was allowed to speak without interruption. But so the boy would understand how important this was, he had to tell him which school he meant. "I mean the monks' school, Ardaiz."

There were schools and then there were schools, and Don Román had always said that Planicio had to keep up with his studies, meaning, however, the evening classes given at Luises for instance. He had never before pronounced in front of him, Planicio, the magic word—Ardaiz, in the Urbasa mountain range, fifty kilometers away from Salvatierra on the edge of a forest of beech trees, a forest so huge that a student had once gotten lost there, and all the older boys, the monks and the local police had spent all night looking for him with torches and lanterns, and it so happened that Don Román had been the one to find him shortly before dawn, stiff with cold. At that time, Don Román was one year away from his baccalaureate, and Planicio assumed the don had none of his physical disabilities then, the proof being that he'd spent the whole night with the search party until they found the lost boy.

In the winter of 1942, which seemed so long ago now, when they used to push the invalid's wheelchair under sunny skies— the sun shining almost every day—up Mount Urgull, Planicio used to say to Don Román, "Tell me stories about Ardaiz." And Don Román could instantly recount stories that were every bit as interesting as the ones Planicio read in his books. What did you eat there? Mornings, they had a big cup of hot milk with bread; the cup didn't have a handle and was like a raised porcelain bowl. The boys were served out of huge coffee pots, metal ones, where the coffee and milk were already mixed together, and if they wanted, they could ask for more. In winter they all did because the milk was brought out steaming hot, and the cold was brutal. At lunch every day, they had red beans like the beans from Tolosa, except that the monks grew theirs in a garden that was out of bounds for the students. Of course they went in anyway, especially in September, to pick grapes. The monks also had fruit trees and all kinds of vegetables. That's why every evening they had vegetables followed by a potato omelet, more potato than eggs. It was said the omelet was made using half-fried, half-cooked potatoes with just a coating of egg smeared on the outside with a pastry brush as an afterthought.

Planicio thought it sounded like a great idea and asked whether the omelets were delicious. Don Román laughed and said yes, they were very good. But then Planicio remembered that the don hadn't finished telling him what they had after the beans at lunch, and the don tried to remember. "What else, Don Román? Tell me more about the school."

One winter it snowed so much that, mornings, they had to shovel a path through the snow from the school in order to get out. At night the wild boars came down and routed around in the garden. Hunters from Liárraga had to be called in to form hunting parties. During the day they saw wolves lurking around as well, and the monks didn't let the students leave the school grounds.

Planicio didn't know what to say because the Ardaiz school where Don Román had studied was a myth that had no connection with him. The connection was that Don Román had been the monks' tax consultant for over twenty years, not officially but because they always had one matter or another to consult him on. A year rarely went by but that he had to solve some problem or other with the Revenue Delegation for Vitoria, Pamplona or somewhere else in Spain because the Order had six boarding schools throughout the Peninsula. There was also a great deal of work with executors' meetings since, for the good of her soul, a lady from Ibarguren had bequeathed her property to the monastery and by so doing had become the bane of Don Román's existence because she, the testator, went about it so badly that Revenue ended up with more than half of the money in inheritance tax. The way the ecclesiastical administrator put it, it was like stealing money from God. Don

Román was able to settle the matter, and that time they gave him a watch which had been part of the estate. At other times they took their leave of him very warmly, assuring him that God would repay him. Don Román, therefore, felt he was entitled to ask them to accept Planicio as one of the students who, unlike those who paid tuition, helped with the gardening and kitchen chores in order to pay his way. The monks pointed out that they already had their quota of such students but that for a nephew of Don Román's space could always be found.

Planicio didn't know what to say, but Don Román knew what *he* had to say. "You'd have to leave as soon as possible, and they'll prepare you for the entrance exam in September. You won't have any trouble with it. All you need to know is how to read and copy down a dictation, as well as add, subtract, multiply and divide. Then, this same year they'll let you do your Levels One and Two of the baccalaureate together because of your age. Afterward . . . "

Afterward he described many of the things that would happen to Planicio as a result of the studies he was about to begin. It required a great deal of effort on Don Román's part since he could tell that the muscles of his diaphragm had ceased functioning, and he had the impression that his breathing was made possible only thanks to his auxiliary muscles—the supraclavicular ones. Breathing from the base of his clavicle while speaking at the same time was exhausting.

"Don Román, it makes me sad to leave."

Planicio spoke with his eyes wide open, staring straight ahead, yet accepting his fate as a given.

"Footraces were a big thing when I was there. You'll be able to show them what you're capable of."

"Long-distance or short?" Planicio asked because he'd already been told he was good in tests of endurance but not in short races because he didn't have the required velocity.

"All kinds. But the most important race of all is one that circles almost all the way round the forest."

In spite of the attraction, Planicio repeated, "Don Román, it makes me sad to leave." His eyes, so wide open, were shining brightly as though he were about to cry.

Don Román would have liked to comfort him, but he couldn't because he felt like he was suffocating from his clavicular breathing, and he knew that until he'd rested for a while, he wouldn't be able to talk. But he smiled at Planicio with his eyes, which were wet as well, with his mouth and with his heart, which he could feel straining from the effort.

He said, "You'll see how wonderful it will be."

TO PACHI, it seemed that everything was too good to be true, and then he started to think it wasn't true. At first he thought he could get along well with the family. He felt close to the miller from Salvatierra, who wasn't much different from the regulars at Raimundo's bar, although he obviously had more money. They went bar hopping together in the old quarter, and he noted that the miller held his wine well, like a man accustomed to drinking. The miller also liked to comment on the women passing by. The *Cimarrón* was prudent in this regard so his future brother-in-law would see he knew how to show respect for Señorita Menchu.

As they were leaning on the bar in one tavern, the miller said to him, "You'll be a great help since we all think that Román won't be able to do much of anything anymore. If this keeps up, pretty soon he won't be able to move at all, and the two of you will have to do everything for him."

Although the miller was not as chummy with Pachi as he could have been, it seemed to Pachi that they had a number of tastes and likes in common—a couple of days they went together to the Urumea fronton to see Salsamendi. They weren't that close though because the miller sometimes spoke as if he expected great things of Pachi. Or popped questions out of nowhere.

"Of course, Pachi, Rosa and I can't come to San Sebastian

that often since we can't leave our children alone. You do understand, don't you?"

This was the kind of question Pachi felt uncomfortable answering. The miller didn't mind his silence and continued.

"Moreover, I have to look after my business because times are tough."

Pachi already knew that times were tough, but he also knew from what Jacinto had told him that times had never been better for an industrialist in the flour milling business.

"But things are going well for you, aren't they?" the Galician asked.

"I can't complain," he admitted modestly, "but times are tough."

Furthermore, the miller made what was an unusual offer in 1942.

"When your restaurant is up and running, I'll send you flour. It will come in handy."

"Thanks," said Pachi, distrustfully.

"What's important," continued the miller, "is for Román to feel well-looked after. You'll be a great help because Menchu can't cope alone anymore. Poor man!"

The last straw was the brother from Bilbao—Justino—who arrived just three days before the wedding, acting like a typical Bilbaon entrepreneur of the post-war years, a man with little time to spare who went straight to the heart of any problem. He was the third eldest, seven years older than Menchu, and looked quite a bit like Don Román except that he was completely bald. He'd been an accountant for Altos Hornos, but in 1940 he started up his own iron warehouse. His first reaction on seeing his eldest brother was similar to that of the pair from Alava—remorse to see that poor Román was becoming a burden, which is why he told his sister Rosa, "Under the circumstances I understand why it is that Menchu can't cope alone anymore. It seems to me it's a good idea for her to get married to this fellow."

Rosa had put on such a good act for her husband and her brother Justino that she sometimes forgot they were marrying her sister because of a case of premature maternity. It felt to her like they were trying to convince Pachi to marry her sister so he would look after the invalid and let the two families—the one from Alava and the other from Bilbao—off the hook. It wasn't selfishness. It was just that times were complex and difficult while at the same time offering wonderful opportunities to warehouse owners, and it just so happened that the two heads of family were in the business, one in flour, the other in iron. The latter must have been in a better financial position since he said in no uncertain terms shortly after learning of the circumstances, "If necessary, I can help him set up the bar, but it has to be very clear that his obligation is to look after poor Román."

The brother-in-law from Alava wasn't prepared to make too much of a commitment.

"I already told him that I'd send him flour."

"Fine," condescended the Bilbaon. "I can give him money."

He drew the syllables out lovingly as he pronounced the magic word; Justino had not had it easy, what with having six children and working as a bookkeeper in San Sebastian's municipal exchange. Until, that is, Román managed to find him a job with Altos Hornos in Bilbao under what were, comparatively speaking, dream conditions, conditions upon which he was able to improve by taking advantage of the opportunity to start up his own warehouse. The upshot was that he'd only been in the business for slightly over two years and could now say quite easily, without it putting him out in the least, "I can give him money," because he was very grateful to his older brother for what he'd done and knew how to return the favor. He couldn't give of his time, his own time, because the opportunities were unique—with official and unofficial quotas—and too good to be passed up. All the operations were so delicate that he had to look after them personally.

Rosa was starting to get upset.

"Don't talk that way. If they want to get married . . . "

Then Justino corrected himself.

"I'm not saying I'll give him the money. I mean I'll give him an advance on what he needs. Listen, I just don't want to see Román saddled with this problem. He's got enough to deal with as it is."

Suddenly Rosa started to cry because it seemed to her that the violation consented to by her younger sister, Menchu, made more sense than this altruistic negotiation designed to leave Román's fortune untouched.

The two men commiserated with their sister. They were all nervous about the wedding, and everyone was sad to see how their eldest brother's condition had deteriorated so rapidly in such a short time.

"Not that short a time," pointed out Rosa in between sobs, "because we haven't been to see him for over two years, and for you," she accused her brother, "I think it's been even longer."

That wasn't true, pointed out Justino, who with some effort reconstructed his trip to San Sebastian. He couldn't remember the exact date, but surely it was less than two years ago. The miller didn't intervene in the discussion because when it came down to it, he was only related to the invalid by marriage, and furthermore, his brother-in-law hadn't found him a plum job like the one he'd found for Justino, a job that had been a springboard to his current position.

The brother from Bilbao was the last straw because he decided it was time to have a conversation with his future brother-in-law in the dining-room-cum-meeting-room in order to make his position clear. They—at least he, Justino Aldaiz— were prepared to help Pachi set up the restaurant-bar, but Don Román had to be well-looked after, which is why he needed a strong man like him, the *Cimarrón*, to help get him up, put him to bed, etc. Justino's manner was perhaps a bit brusque because he was short on time since he wanted to take advan-

tage of his two-day stay in San Sebastian to visit some facto-
ries in the Legazpi zone, some potential clients.

The Galician, faced with this type of approach, simply
answered, "Yes, Señor," but afterward in the street, he was
filled with foreboding at the thought that for his whole life
he'd have to carry poor Don Román around—Don Román the
trunk, he the porter. He didn't even go to Raimundo's bar
because the only thing people there could talk about was the
wedding, and Raimundo himself liked to give him, quite graciously, advice on the establishment he was going to open.
Although Raimundo knew Pachi would be his competitor, he
also knew that everyone was entitled to earn a living and that it
was a unique opportunity for the *Cimarrón*. Pachi didn't go to
Raimundo's bar, but he did go to other bars, drinking alone in
spite of it being against his principles because drinking with
one's cronies made sense, but drinking alone was something
drunks did and he was contemptuous of drunks. In any case,
this time he had to drink alone because the trunk was getting
heavier by the minute. At the train station, he hated it when
he had to load up trunks because they were so unwieldy. At
least where trunks were concerned you could stand them on
end, tilt the cart and push them into place with one good
shove, but that wasn't the case with Don Román. Worst of all,
he really cared for Don Román, a man who deserved the best.
Then in spite of his proverbial cynicism, a small sob escaped
his lips, sounding more like a drunk's hiccup because he realized he couldn't spend all day, every day, with Don Román in
his charge. And yet he loved him! But not as his charge, no.
That was the problem with drinking alone. He didn't talk,
didn't waste a second, just a quick dash in and out of each
drinking hole, and in less than an hour he'd downed a liter and
a half of wine. When he thought about it, it wasn't so much
having Don Román as his charge—poor man, he couldn't have
done more for Planicio!—but the idea of doing the same thing
day in and day out. The whole restaurant-bar thing, even

though he had a genuine vocation for it, shouldn't have to last forever. If he got tired of it, he'd like to be able to sell and with the money do something else or do nothing. Furthermore, when he thought about it, Don Román had made a fine mess of things with his obsession for sending Planicio away to school because the boy would have been a great help in the bar, and maybe even Pachi could have looked after the cooking himself, and Planicio could have done the till and the accounts since he was a whiz at anything to do with letters or numbers. What kind of mad idea was it to send him off with the wild boars in the Urbasa mountains! Why study so much? So he could end up paralyzed like the don? Sometimes the *Cimarrón* wondered if Don Román's paralysis hadn't started because he spent all his time sitting down, studying. God, the pain of it all!

The advantage of being a man accustomed to drinking is that such a man knows when to stop and how to imbibe a liter and a half with dignity, returning acquaintances' greetings without stopping since it was imperative he talk to that bloody fairy Jacinto, who'd gotten him into this whole mess. By the time Pachi arrived at 10-B Miracruz, the door was locked—it was past eleven—but he had his key. He climbed the stairs in the dark without any particular difficulty because he had the banister to help him. On the second floor he called at the service door, and the cook opened the door for him. She was very respectful of anyone who had dealings with Jacinto since she was well aware that he had banished her predecessor to the farm in Puente del Arzobispo, province of Toledo.

"Come in, come in," she said to Pachi, who was a favorite with the domestic head of the count's household as well as with everyone else lately because his marrying Señorita Menchu seemed like the Cinderella story all over again, except in reverse.

As soon as he saw Pachi, Jacinto knew something was up, and as soon as Pachi said, "Oh, Jacinto!" in an unnatural tone of voice, Jacinto took him out on the landing and whispered, "What on earth's wrong?"

"What a mess you've all got me into!"

This was the type of situation that galvanized Jacinto into action and gave him the strength to pull his friend out of the way as hard as he could, terrified at the thought that the marquis might come out and find him bracing a drunk in his arms. After ten-thirty the stairway was kept dark but could be lit from someone inside the two apartments, which each had their own timer switch. The marquis usually went out at night to a club that met in Café Xauen, and he could very well turn on the light at any minute. The marquis had a very poor opinion of Spanish drunks. Generally speaking, he didn't favor drinking for fitness reasons, but he respectfully recalled the drinking bouts after the Oxford-Cambridge regatta, truly exquisite displays that showed the levels of community spirit a people could reach. In this case, the British people. Spaniards weren't at all the same, although the Basques were a bit better. When they got drunk they sang beautiful folk songs that reminded him of Scottish folk music.

Once on the fifth floor, they were safe from the marquis, but while the *Cimarrón* kept whining, "Oh, Jacinto! Oh, Jacinto!" the manservant threatened, "Shush, we're going out onto the terrasse!"

The last stretch wasn't easy since it was narrow, without a banister. Pachi wanted to stop every minute or so to explain what a mess they'd gotten him into and to see why Jacinto, bloody fairy, hadn't been any help at all, just the opposite.

"Oh, Jacinto! What a sorry bunch of brothers-in-law I've got. They're going to be even worse than the lot from Alza!"

Finally on the last landing, in spite of Jacinto's earnest pleading, Pachi insisted on explaining that it was a sure thing that his brother-in-law, the one from Alza, was being cuckolded by his wife. This cheered Pachi up somewhat.

"Can you picture it, Jacinto? Two big horns, huge ones,

sticking out from each side of his red beret. Him, a Carlista? He's been nothing but a smuggler and a good-for-nothing from day one. Poor Bea. The way that bastard made her suffer!"

Having gotten this off his chest, Pachi let himself be led through the door out onto the roof, and there he finished explaining how on the day of his wife's funeral, on this very same terrasse, he told his brother-in-law—the one from Alza—how he'd kick his testicles up out through his teeth. In front of all the fellow villagers.

Jacinto was a born negotiator who also loved nothing better than hearing about the darker side of life. The story was one he didn't know in detail, the door to the terrasse was safely closed behind him, the weather that night was mild and Pachi's drunkenness was tolerable. For all those reasons, he could calmly listen to the whole story, from the day the *Cimarrón*, without their being officially engaged yet, took Bea by surprise in the apple orchard.

"In the apple orchard?" said the domestic head, feigning admiration.

Pachi suddenly became very animated.

"Just like I said, in the apple orchard! No better place for it!"

The *Cimarrón* had a habit of making these wild assertions—his claim to fame and the key to his acceptance by a large public, which for just that reason was willing to forgive him his weakness for gambling.

While they continued talking about apple orchards and their relative merits, Jacinto clung to the hope that Pachi's anger would blow over, be chalked up to a bad drunk; but once the night air had calmed him down, the *Cimarrón* stated categorically, "And so, I'm not getting married!"

"What are you saying?"

"You heard me. I'm not getting married."

"Please, don't yell. You'll wake up Francisquito."

"Don't call him Francisquito, you damn fool!"

"Fine, fine, don't get angry, but why on earth would you say you're not going to get married?"

Because the words spoken by the brother from Bilbao had cast a chill over him. What the other brother had had to say, the miller from Salvatierra, had been suspicious enough. Why should he be promising Pachi flour? Not to mention that flour was more a staple for bad cooks who used it to thicken their sauces, and Pachi didn't need that sort of thing. But the brother from Bilbao had been barefaced. He expected Pachi to look after their brother. Point-blank.

"But just this winter you loved working for Don Román, and you went on and on about your outings together and how well you got along. . . ."

Jacinto spoke to him as though he were a small boy who didn't want to take his medicine. Come on, be a big boy, it's good for you. Think about the bar. Think about Planicio. Didn't you say you got along splendidly with Señorita Menchu?

But suddenly the *Cimarrón*'s proverbial cynicism gave way to his sense of dignity.

"Fine, I'll marry Señorita Menchu but only when I've got enough money to."

Jacinto took Pachi's remark as a step in the right direction and said all right, to think it over but that he should go to bed. And Jacinto helped him into the garret room.

SEÑORITA MENCHU had to leave for Salvatierra with her sister Rosa so as to have her baby as discreetly as possible.

The day before the wedding, the *Cimarrón* disappeared, having signed up on a PISBE cod-fishing boat. That morning— the morning following the night he'd opted for his dignity—he woke Planicio up early.

"Listen, son . . ."

Planicio was half asleep but realized that something strange was going on because his father never said, "Listen, son." He always said, "Listen you," or just, "Planicio."

"Listen, son, we've postponed the wedding," or rather, *they* hadn't actually postponed it, but *he* thought they should postpone it. He was going to set sail, and with the money he earned over the season, they would get married. Did Planicio understand?

But, *Aita,* your lumbago. How could he get back on a boat with his lumbago that prevented him from doing so many things?

As a cook, he was signing on as a cook. They were in great demand on the cod-fishing boats that crossed the ocean.

Planicio was a boy resigned to not knowing. He'd been left without a mother and no one had explained to him what she'd died from. The following year his father forbade his going to Atocha, without an explanation, and hit him for having misunderstood. Señora Asun had said to him, "I'll call you when I need you for a delivery," and she'd never called him again. They'd made him run the race between the bridges and reamed him out for not winning, but shortly afterward his father had berated him for winning against the German lady who wore culottes. When things had started going his way and his future prospects were looking bright, he was told no, he had to go to Ardaiz. And now, *Aita* was explaining that it was better to postpone the wedding and that Jacinto already knew, but that in any case he, Planicio, should remind him so Jacinto in turn could tell Rosa, Señorita Menchu's older sister.

Although he was a boy resigned to not knowing, what he did know was that if he said, "No, *Aita,* you tell him," Pachi would hit him, not that it mattered, but he would rather have his father tell him, "Good-bye son. I'm leaving you twenty duros. You won't need any more because the day after tomorrow you're leaving for boarding school. Besides, on the shelf I've left you some potatoes and half a dozen eggs as well."

He didn't ever remember *Aita* kissing him because it wasn't something people did in Trincherpe. Pachi didn't kiss him this time either, but he did draw near the bed, and putting his arm around his son, he said, "Now that you're going to school, make the most of it, and when you play pelota don't let yourself be beaten!"

Pachi seemed to have trouble tearing himself away, and from the doorway he said, "Don't worry, we'll have our bar. *Alza Pilili!*"

At Pachi's cry, a knot formed in Planicio's throat because he knew his father hated the Alza lot, and if he deigned to use their battle cry it was to console him for something.

"Yes, *Aita.*"

Pachi still didn't leave. Instead, he walked back into the spartan room and pointed at the only wardrobe they had, the same one they'd had in Trincherpe and Fuenterrabía.

"If Señorita Menchu asks you, tell her I've left my wedding suit here so as not to ruin it."

Once he was sure *Aita* had left for good, Planicio put his head under his pillow for protection.

JACINTO WAS A BORN negotiator, and in spite of the enormity of what had happened, he felt the situation could still be turned around. He consulted the marquis, a man who loved giving advice. The reactions from the count's household were as dissimilar as could be. The countess sighed and repeated several times, "Goodness me!" and "Poor girl!" On the other hand, the marquis couldn't hide a certain pleasure because this sudden flight corresponded perfectly with the image he had of Pachi, and he prided himself on his knowledge of human nature. Once again his talent had been borne out. It was always reassuring to know one would be going through life with such a gift.

Of course the marquis dismissed outright the suggestion, made by Jacinto, that the supposed coercion of Pachi's future brothers-in-law had contributed to Pachi's case of cold feet.

The marquis could recall other well-known instances of a
fiancé leaving his betrothed at the very altar, not just meta-
phorically speaking but in actual fact, for no reason. There'd
even been an instance of it occurring during a ceremony in
which His Majesty the King was the best man. The incident
had not been taken lightly, naturally. The marquis gave him
some commonsense advice.

"In cases like these, Jacinto, one has to remain calm."

"Yes, Señor Marquis. Thank you very much, Señor Marquis."

In Raimundo's bar everyone looked on Pachi's absconding
as an absolute triumph. Without knowing why, all the regulars
gave each other big pats on the back, saying, "That Pachi! You
can't change a leopard's spots. What about his lumbago?"
Then someone said that his lumbago had located elsewhere.
The expression didn't mean anything, but everyone attributed
a meaning to it and they all broke into laughter. No one had
anything against the Aldaiz family and even less so against
Don Román, but it was too good an opportunity to pass up.
Jacinto begged them to show moderation and respect, but no
one bothered listening to him.

The news wended its way from Calle de Miracruz to Ramón
y Cajal, with a stopover at Raimundo's—Jacinto brought the
matter up in the bar in case anyone had had news of the *Cimarrón*—and the general impression was that Pachi was a lost
cause.

Francisca the concierge was relieved at the news because
Pachi had been a trying neighbor, always creating problems for
her with the elevator by arriving at the exact same time as
members of the count's household.

Jacinto knew to hold his tongue and keep quiet about the
pregnancy. Which is why people said Señorita Menchu got off
lucky.

The regulars from Raimundo's bar said that the *Cimarrón*
had his fun with her and now he's dropped her. But they

hadn't a clue about the pregnancy. They simply meant that he'd had his fun with the señorita, which they saw as a triumph because she belonged to a higher social class and was a church-going woman.

ON THE DAY before what was to be his last, Don Román met with an orderly who'd worked for him in the Revenue Delegation, a seventy-five-year-old, recently retired, tidy man with powerful hands. He'd always understood the don's difficulties with locomotion, handled him gently and waited for instructions without taking any of the initiatives the don hated so much. The man agreed to work for Don Román.

"You know, Don Román, I'd do anything I could for you."

They then talked wages, and the man thought it an even better deal. Don Román didn't want to tell him that he thought the job wouldn't last very long, among other reasons because what he wanted was one thing, but God's plans for him were another. In any case, Don Román assumed Menchu would be happy to know that she and her husband would be entirely free to do as they wished and would not be tied to managing the restaurant-bar. If they wanted to, they could even move out, although he wasn't sure it would be all that easy because apartments were hard to come by, and the apartment on Ramón y Cajal had bedrooms to spare. Even Planicio, on his summer break—maybe at Christmas too—could have a room to himself, a small room leading to an indoor patio. Suddenly, and despite how laborious breathing with his supraclavicular muscles had become, the don wanted to hold on to life until the following summer so he could spend it with the boy. Perhaps they could go for walks the way they used to— why not?—and finally realize his dream of eating wild berries in white wine and sugar. It would be harder for them to get him into his wheelchair, but that's what he'd hired an orderly for. Moreover, they would have so many things to tell each other, mostly about the Ardaiz school. They'd talk about whether the routine there had changed, not that there was any reason it should have.

Right after he said good-bye to the orderly and before he had a chance to give his little sister the good news, Jacinto arrived, asking to see him. He asked to see Don Román specifically because Jacinto was doing enough as it was, being the main news bearer, but he was not in the least bit interested in having to explain matters to the miller's wife, the only one in, the family who knew about the pregnancy. With Don Román, Jacinto could have a purely technical exchange of points of view on the necessity of postponing the wedding.

"Actually Don Román, I didn't speak to him directly, you know how Pachi is. In fact, Francisquito was the one who gave me the message. Anyway, last night we were talking and he mentioned something about postponing the wedding"—Jacinto had decided to refer to a postponement, nothing more—"but I didn't realize he'd already made his decision."

Don Román's silence could be daunting, not that he wanted it that way because he realized the countess's manservant might think he was keeping silent for another reason or might translate it as a show of animosity toward the messenger. On hearing the news, Don Román wasn't sure whether it was good or bad since he'd always found the whole matter of this marriage disconcerting. In any case, he resisted the temptation to let himself be distracted by the crepuscular triangle of the horizon, which would have meant making an abstraction of the circumstances of life itself, in this particular case, that his young sister would not be getting married right away. Of course, his hiring the retired orderly wasn't a waste even at that because Menchu couldn't cope alone anymore.

"Don Román, would you like me to give you my opinion?"

The don nodded his head.

"I think that Pachi was slightly offended because your brothers . . . you'll excuse me if I tell you what I think?"

"Yes."

Don Román would have liked to be more cordial with this man, but he couldn't, not just because talking was such an effort but because he felt the manservant was embroidering the facts. Moreover, he was thinking about Planicio and how he was being used by his father. He couldn't think about Menchu because he couldn't decide whether what had happened was good or bad for her. He decided to give Rosa the news first because it would be easier coming from another woman.

The manservant was reticent since he was unsure whether it was sufficiently clear that he would be forgiven for something he had to say anyway.

"Please go on, Jacinto."

Don Román might come from the same modest background as the Aldaiz's from Alava, but saints alive, the command gained from the many years he'd spent in important positions showed.

"Well, Pachi was slightly offended because your brothers, mainly your brother from Bilbao, offered him money to set up the restaurant in such a way that . . . "

Jacinto paused to let the don interpret for himself in what way they had offered the money to Pachi so as to offend him. The don had trouble interpreting his remarks because Pachi, who did have certain scruples—for example, he didn't like to take advantage of the don on their outings to the bars in the old quarter—did not have many qualms where someone else's money was concerned.

"I don't understand."

His remarks weren't meant to solicit an explanation from Jacinto, just to express what he felt. However, the manservant said quite reasonably, "You see, Don Román, Pachi has never put much stock in money. When he has money, he spends it; when he doesn't, he does without."

They sat without speaking for a minute, and Don Román's gaze turned to the setting sun, a risky proposition because then he tended to get lost in thought. The PISBE cod-fishing boats had to pass in front of him on their way to Newfoundland, Canada. From where Don Román sat, Newfoundland was on his left and Puerto de Pasajes on his right. In other words, the boats had to sail in front of his mirador. So the *Cimarrón* would be crossing that line drawn by the horizon, and there would be no surprises waiting for him because assuredly behind that crimson line was nothing but more sea. So heaven must be somewhere else. All Don Román knew with increasing certainty was that it did exist. This was a comforting thought, and furthermore, now he didn't have to wait until summer because he wouldn't be sharing his house with Planicio. What's more, under the circumstances the boy might be better off spending the summer at Ardaiz working in the garden as other poor students did for a daily wage paid by the monks.

"Listen, Jacinto . . . "

Jacinto knew how to bide his time respectfully during a prolonged silence when the silence was imposed by a gentleman and even more so in the present situation, which couldn't be turning out better. He congratulated himself once again on having dealt with this gentleman instead of with the miller's wife from Salvatierra, although in any case he would have pretended to know nothing about the pregnancy.

"Yes, Señor?"

That's exactly what Jacinto said—Señor—because the don was a gentleman in spite of his porcine air, which was no fault of his own, poor man, since it was a result of his obesity.

"How long will Pachi be gone?"

"The cod-fishing boats are usually out for six months at a time."

"Will he really earn money?"

"An experienced seaman such as Pachi, who is," here he allowed himself a smile, "a good cook as well, can come back with a few duros. I think that's his dream—to come back with something to contribute to the marriage. At least that's my opinion."

In his opinion the *Cimarrón* would spend his last centimo on wine and women in the first port they reached—if he had any left by then because he could just as well lose it all playing cards on the boat. The *Cimarrón* himself had admitted lately that luck wasn't on his side.

"Actually," he corrected himself as a point of honor, "it's more than my opinion. It's what Francisquito told me."

"Very well, Jacinto, thank you very much for everything. I do appreciate your dropping in."

A gentleman, no, a true gentleman was what Don Román was, and Jacinto regretted having brought up the matter—albeit with the best of intentions—in Raimundo's bar and that the gang of regulars had laughed at something they knew nothing about.

"I would also like to ask you a favor, Jacinto. . . ."

"Whatever you say, Don Román."

"Tell Planicio to be sure to come without fail to say good-bye tomorrow. Without fail, mind."

"Yes, Señor."

"What's more, tell him that I have something for him."

It wasn't true that he had something for him, but he would think of something; perhaps he would ask Planicio to do a big favor for him as soon as he got to the boarding school. Something to show him that nothing had changed, that all that had happened was that his father had left for Canada in order to put aside a bit of money.

WHEN ROSA told Señorita Menchu, the latter said, "Now we will have to tell Román."

Her eyes were still dry. All she said was, "That's a setback," as though postponing the marriage was just another complication. Rosa looked at her askance, surprised and frightened by such a reaction. Señorita Menchu had many grudges against Justino and his wife—who went for months at a time without giving a sign of life—against the miller himself, an increasingly coarse man who never dreamed of excusing himself, and so she had no desire to receive the least bit of sympathy from them. From Rosa, yes, because she'd done everything she could to help her in this matter, but right now Menchu didn't want sympathy. The only thing that concerned her was that Román had to be told about her pregnancy because she was about to miss her third period in a row, and she could see that with every passing day her waist was losing its shape. Which is why she said, "Now we will have to tell him."

"Wait a bit," said Rosa. Based on how poorly her brother seemed to be doing, she thought that if they put it off, he just might never have to find out.

The next morning, on what would have been the morning of the wedding, Planicio showed up at Ramón y Cajal. Señorita Menchu opened the door to him quite naturally, and the boy blushed, not daring to set foot inside.

"Come in, come in," she said. "Don Román is waiting for you."

Planicio was wearing his new clothes, the ones she herself had bought for him a few days earlier. They were a bit big on him, actually quite a bit too big, but anyone could see Planicio was going through a growth spurt and would end up being even taller than his father. So he had two new outfits, the one his father had bought on credit and this one that Señorita Menchu had already told him would have to last until he was of age. It just might last that long since the fabric looked to be of good quality. It was sturdy—that's why it scratched so much—and he'd decided he would only wear it on holidays and for traveling. He was wearing it that day because his departure was scheduled for that evening.

"Tell me," said Señorita Menchu, drawing him over to a corner of the vestibule, "what did *Aita* say before he left?"

Señorita Menchu never called his father *Aita,* and that she had pulled him over to a half-lit corner to do so, her eyes swollen and red, had to mean something. At least Planicio felt closer to her than when she'd been pretending to be nice and giving him bread and chocolate.

"He told me to tell you he left his wedding suit in the wardrobe so it wouldn't get ruined."

"That's all?"

"He also said for me not to worry, that we'd start up a bar."

He didn't explain that his father had then let out the war cry *"Alza Pilili!"* because the señorita wouldn't have understood.

KNOWING PACHI, as the señorita thought she knew him, his saying that he'd left the wedding suit behind so as not to ruin it was more encouraging than all the explanations her sister Rosa had given her the night before, as she'd insisted heavily, "Don't worry, dear, it happens to a lot of men. When the time comes they take fright, but then they think it over and come back." And Rosa recounted a number of similar cases, especially in the province of Alava, in such a way that she gave the impression that it was customary for Alava men to make two or three stabs at getting married, the bride all dressed up with nowhere to go, before the final "I do."

"But when will he be back?" insisted Señorita Menchu when it was well nigh on to morning because the two sisters had spent the night comforting each other and crying. Theoretically Rosa didn't need comforting. However, deep down she was terrified by the idea of appearing in Salvatierra with her little sister in the family way and no known husband. She was amazed to see that since telling Menchu not to worry about Román, and that she Rosa would look after it, her little sister had been totally calm, thinking only of her loved one en route to Canada without considering that in 1942 having a baby out of wedlock violated officially established morals and was looked on as an act of opposition to the Regime. In spite of her desire and obvious obligation to comfort the little one, from time to time—worn out from the fatigue brought on by their sleepless night—a lament escaped her lips.

"Worst of all is what will we do with the baby! . . ."

Señorita Menchu looked at her in surprise.

"You don't want me to throw it out with the garbage, do you?"

"No, heaven forbid dear, I was just thinking."

She was thinking that in Salvatierra her sister couldn't give birth under these circumstances and that she would have to consider sending her to a farmhouse after making an arrangement with a midwife she could trust, as had been done by others before her.

"Furthermore," Señorita Menchu rebuked her sister, "didn't you say he'd be back? I don't see what the problem is."

Even if he did come back, which was asking a lot, he would have been gone long enough for her sister's waistline, which was gradually losing its shape, to have turned into a huge belly because the Aldaiz women traditionally piled on the weight during their pregnancies—five months into their pregnancy they already looked like they were ready to give birth at any minute. They had a cousin who lived in Salvatierra as well, who had swollen up so much that everyone kept saying, "This time it's got to be twins," and then she ended up giving birth to a rather scrawny son who did, however, have a big head. Apparently it was his head—all the Aldaiz men had big heads— that had made his mother look so big.

Looking at things in the best possible light—by now the news would have got around in Salvatierra that the delegate's sister had been left standing at the altar—the fact that she was pregnant as well would be an aggravating circumstance in an unfortunate situation but nevertheless more dignified than a pregnancy caused by an unknown father. A simple case of human frailty. Precipitation might be another way of putting it. The deception of a poor girl. The only jarring note being that the poor girl was well into her thirties even though they all still called her the little one.

Consequently not much reciprocal comforting went on that

night. Instead, Rosa spent most of her time worrying and
Señorita Menchu crying, with from time to time a glimmer of
hope. At times Rosa's concern turned to admiration and even
envy to see her sister's desperate belief that her young, strong
and likable man would be coming back to her.

"Do you really think he signed on to save money for the
wedding?"

Menchu had asked herself the same question, with slight
variations, more than a hundred times. "And why not, dear?"
answered Rosa. Sometimes she added, "He has to come back.
Remember he's left his son, Planicio, here."

"Tomorrow, as soon as Planicio gets here, I have to talk to
him," said Menchu excitedly. Which is why she opened the
door herself for Planicio and set such store by the wedding suit
kept in the wardrobe so as not to ruin it and the bar they'd set
up. She thought it best to stop there, and said to Planicio,
"Go on in to see Don Román."

Don Román had several matters of concern to discuss with
Planicio, and that was why he'd asked to see him. First, how
would Planicio be taking his clothes to school?

"I packed them in a bag from home because *Aita* took the
wooden suitcase."

What a relief for Don Román to see that Planicio, thirteen
going on fourteen, had taken it all in stride and was still prepared to go away to school as though nothing had happened.

"But listen, how can you show up there with your clothes in
a bag? What will they think of us?"

Didn't Planicio realize that the don had told the monks
that Planicio was his own nephew? No, Señor, he hadn't
thought of that.

Don Román called Rosa to bring in a suitcase, and she gave
him the oldest one she could find.

"Isn't there anything better?" asked Don Román.

Of course there was, but Rosa thought this one would do.

"It's the only one I could find."

It was old, made of fine leather, and although one of the locks didn't work, a rope could be used to hold it together.

Rosa brought a dust rag and cleaned the case inside and out, leaving it shining. Then Don Román exclaimed, "Look, it's the suitcase I took to Madrid when I went to prepare for the Revenue competition."

If they had been alone, the boy would have asked him all about his trip because he never tired of asking Don Román questions. If Rosa hadn't been there, he would have said once more, "Don Román, it makes me sad to leave."

But he said nothing, just kept looking straight ahead, and Don Román told him that he would have liked to accompany him to the station but that he didn't dare because he had a bit of a cold. Rosa was surprised to see that he didn't even make a gesture. That morning it had been a real struggle just to get him out of bed. His face was pallid, but his eyes shone as always, and his hair was black and unruffled. When Planicio took his leave, the don stretched his right hand out to him without lifting his elbow off the armrest so as not to lose his balance, and the boy held the don's hand in his two hands.

"You'll see how wonderful it will be," Don Román said once more.

Rosa turned her back, unable to watch.

"Good-bye, Don Román."

ONLY JACINTO WENT with him to the station.

The marquis gave him five duros and said, "I'm glad to see you're going to school, but I want to see you back here next summer."

"Yes, Señor Marquis," answered Planicio.

Julio the groundskeeper looked at him with not a trace of distrust and asked, "When will you be back?" Planicio wasn't sure. Perhaps next summer. "Then be sure to come here," he said.

And his wife—"Come over here and let me give you a kiss."

She kissed him twice as did Arancha who said, "Tithio, good-bye."

He had to take a mail train that left at eleven at night and would take him as far as Alsasua. There, in the same station, he'd have to wait until seven in the morning to catch the bus but—mind!—it had to be the bus to Olazagutia, Zudaire and finally Barindano. He had to get off in Barindano; Ardaiz was two kilometers away. He couldn't get lost as long as he didn't get on the bus for Larraona, by mistake of course. In that case, it was hard to say what would happen. Another awful thing that could happen was that he might not wake up when they arrived in Alsasua and might end up going to Madrid. If this should happen, Jacinto explained what he had to do in the station because in Madrid, if he used Jacinto's name in certain places—there were a number of them—he'd find the help he needed. In any case, Planicio decided he wouldn't go to sleep; in fact he didn't see how he could sleep.

The manservant bought him some comic books at the news stand and a box of madeleines in the cafeteria. Then he took him personally to car number three. All of its wooden seats were occupied and people in the aisles were seated on suitcases, but luckily Planicio had a reservation. His seat was occupied by a soldier, but Jacinto said firmly, "This is the boy's seat."

Planicio found it strange to see the man stand up without a word and felt embarrassed to be taking his seat away from him. But he didn't want Jacinto to think he didn't appreciate everything he was doing for him. They then had a hard time putting the suitcase up in the bag net because in those days people traveled with lots of parcels. Finally Jacinto spoke to some ladies in the car.

"This boy is getting off in Alsasua."

The women nodded their understanding. Jacinto took his leave, patting Planicio's head and wishing him a safe trip. He didn't kiss Planicio because of his reputation. Once alone, Planicio felt that everyone in the compartment was looking at

him and that it was taking the train forever to leave. When it
finally did start up, he concentrated on looking out the nearest
window, sure they'd be going over the Hierro Bridge. The part
he could see best was the street opposite—Paseo de los
Fueros—where he'd run on the day of the race between the
bridges when the Raimundo bar regulars had called out to him,
"Alza Pilili!" He remembered it perfectly, some of them standing on the wall, others on a bench, waving their berets and
their arms and yelling out the Alza war cry. That's why he'd
waved back gratefully even though *Aita* said, "Quit fooling
around and run."

Anyway, those were the things Planicio liked to do, and he
didn't see why he had to study to become an important man,
but Don Román knew best, *Aita* had said so, and Planicio had
to do what he was told because it was for his own good. His
father had also said, "You're not going to spend your life running after tennis balls." Actually he wouldn't have minded.
He'd had fun playing tennis with the two brothers from Igueldo who, used to win all the time at first but not anymore.
Besides, with *Aita* gone he couldn't stay alone in the garret
room.

It turned out that he couldn't see when they went over the
Hierro Bridge because it was pitch dark out, but he assumed it
was when the train's wheels clanged louder. Then he began to
worry because he could feel himself nodding off, although every
time they arrived at a station—Villabona, Irura, Tolosa . . . —
the train stopped for a good while, and he woke up but with a
start. One of the ladies Jacinto had talked to said, "Don't
worry, sleep tight. In Alsasua the train changes locomotives
and stays put for almost an hour. We'll wake you up."

Planicio thanked her just like *Amá* had taught him to ever
since he was a little boy. He wondered if *Amá* had stayed
behind in the stretch of sky directly above the garret room at
10-B Miracruz, thinking how he'd miss her. He'd been so nervous that he'd forgotten to tell her he was going away to board-

ing school. And so while dozing off again, he said "*Amá,* I'm over here." He'd tell her again once he was in Ardaiz.

San Sebastian, October 2, 1942

Dear Planicio:

We received the letter you sent to my brother, may he rest in peace, and were happy to learn that you've arrived safely at school. I hope you are doing well. I am writing to give you the sad news of the death of my brother, Román, may he rest in peace, a week ago today, the same night you left for boarding school. The next morning we found him dead. Rosa and I were alone, and you can imagine how we felt. The doctor told us he didn't suffer at all because his heart just stopped, and he probably wouldn't have felt a thing in his sleep. It's a comfort for us to know he didn't suffer because the poor man suffered enough while he was alive, and now he's certainly in Heaven. The funeral was very moving because all of San Sebastian was there. The whole Revenue delegation was there and all the neighbors as well. You know how much they loved him. He loved you very much as well, and the night he died, he told us he hoped you wouldn't get on the wrong bus in Alsasua.

Tell the monks so they'll celebrate masses for him. He did them many a good turn. I am going with Rosa to Salvatierra for a while. If you have news of your father, please write. My address in Salvatierra will be 5 Calle de Correos. If we can, we'll come to see you.

Rosa sends her best.

Yours affectionately,

Menchu

PRINTED IN CANADA